FLIRTING WITH DISASTER

FLIRTING WITH DISASTER

Deborah Nicholson

This first world edition published in Great Britain 2005 by
SEVERN HOUSE PUBLISHERS LTD of
9–15 High Street, Sutton, Surrey SM1 1DF.
This first world edition published in the USA 2006 by
SEVERN HOUSE PUBLISHERS INC of
595 Madison Avenue, New York, N.Y. 10022.

British Library Cataloguing in Publication Data

Nicholson, Deborah, 1961-
   Flirting with disaster
   1.   Carpenter, Kate (Fictitious character) - Fiction
   2.   Women theatrical managers - Alberta - Calgary - Fiction
   3.   Murder - Investigation - Alberta - Calgary - Fiction
   4.   Detective and mystery stories
   I.   Title
   813.6 [F]

   ISBN-10 : 0-7278-6281-2

Typeset by Palimpsest Book Production Ltd.,
Polmont, Stirlingshire, Scotland.
Printed and bound in Great Britain by
MPG Books Ltd., Bodmin, Cornwall.

I am surrounded by a group of cheerleaders. I would like to dedicate this novel to them, as a thank you for their unending belief and support.

Best friend ever Carol Whyte; super-agent Anne Dewe, super supporter Leslie Horton, everyone at Firehall # 4, Leighton and Rebecca and Samantha Stockton, Mom and Dad and Elizabeth, Wendy Stewart and the Calgary Public Library.

As always, Sandy Stockton, it wouldn't happen without you.

A charitable donation in the name of this novel has been made to the Calgary International Children's Festival.

Prologue

The girl moved a little on the car seat beside him, pulling at her bound hands, in a semiconscious state as the drug slowly wore off. He wasn't worried. She was bound and gagged and he had more drugs if necessary. But it was always a little more exciting when they struggled. He felt a little rush of adrenalin as he thought about that, and a stirring in his loins. He looked at her bare throat and remembered how it had felt, his head buried in the hollow, listening to her pulse race in terror, as he had thrust himself inside her. He remembered the scent of her sweat, the taste of her mouth, the sweetness of her blood and the terror in her eyes as he had bound her to the bed and then slowly, very slowly, undressed her. That was the best part. The anticipation. The game. The sex was gratifying but the game was the real turn on.

He shook his head, banishing these thoughts. The game may be the turn on but she was no longer the game. A new game was about to begin and she was only one of the pawns. If he stopped now, all would be lost. He would never get this time again. He got out of the car and pulled her out after him. He put her bound hands over his head; they looked like a drunken couple headed home after last call, desperate to get to a bed before the mood passed. He stopped a couple of times, on the way to his destination, to kiss her, or feel her breast or drop his hand down the back of her pants, just in case anyone was watching.

When he was where he wanted to be, he unhooked her arms and set her gently down on the pavement. He kneeled beside her, pulling up the cover to the drainage system and setting it aside as quietly as he could. He took one last look at the girl; sad that she wasn't yet conscious enough to realize what was happening to her. Her eyes turned the most beautiful shade of

1

green when she was terrified. He pulled a capped syringe out of his jacket and quickly slid it into her arm. Just enough to relax her for another twenty-four hours or so, maybe a little dangerous, but nothing more dangerous than what he had planned for her. He slid her feet into the opening where the metal cover had been, and then grabbed her by the shoulders and pushed her in. He had measured correctly; there was enough room for her with a couple of feet to spare. The water was cold but not too cold and there were only a couple of inches. Enough to drown in if she managed to turn over, but then he couldn't be expected to control everything, could he? He pushed her back as far as he could, not wanting the game to end too early, and then reached for the metal cover.

'Excuse me?'

Shit! The voice was far too close. Someone had seen him.

'Hey, what are you doing, man?' the voice said, as the arm came down on his shoulder.

Fuck. He had almost been free and clear. He turned his head to see who had found him out. It was a volunteer security guard, barely out of his teens.

'Oh, sorry, sir,' the boy started. 'Do you need some help with . . .'

He shook his head at his stupidity for being caught. Oh well, he had wanted a little more excitement tonight and now he was going to get it. He grabbed the hand on his shoulder and pulled hard, flipping the young man expertly over his shoulder. His hand was on the young man's mouth, muffling the surprised scream before it even came out. It wasn't the first time he had done this and it wouldn't be the last. He knew what to expect. He stared down into the boy's eyes, seeing the recognition mixed now with a small spark of confusion and a huge burst of fear, lighting them up so they almost glowed in the night. He smiled and felt a rush of excitement racing up and down his spine.

'Boy, you need to learn to mind your own business,' he taunted the young man, repositioning himself so his knee was painfully pushing into his breastbone. 'Now, I'm going to take my hand off your mouth, and you are not going to scream. If you scream, you will die. Do you understand?'

The young man nodded fearfully, eyes wide with terror.

2

The man removed his hand slowly and the hostage remained silent. He pulled out his roll of duct tape, and had the lad gagged and bound quickly.

'Now, I just need to finish what I was doing here. I'll be right back.'

He stood up and replaced the metal grate, looking around to ensure nothing was out of place. Then he pulled the security guard up and walked him over to his car, without further intrusion. Once he had him settled and secure in the car, he ripped the tape off his mouth.

'What's your name?' he asked.

'Danny.' It came out as a whimper. His eyes were blinking mightily, fear producing tears that threatened to overflow the lids.

'And Danny, how old are you?'

'I'm nineteen.'

The man leaned very close, smelling the fear emanating off his hostage. He noticed a tear escape Danny's eye and he stretched his tongue out to lick it gently from his cheek, and he felt Danny shudder and felt himself start to respond.

'Tell me, Danny,' he whispered into the young man's ear. 'Have you ever had sex with a man?'

Danny's eyes opened wide and tears flowed unbridled now. The man looked closely at him, savouring the sight and the smell, knowing he would have a lovely evening of games ahead of him.

'You have such beautiful blue eyes when you're scared,' he laughed, finally pulling himself away from his conquest. He put the car in drive and pulled out of his parking spot. 'What say we go to my place for a while.'

Friday

My name is Kate Carpenter. I am thirty-four years old, blonde, or so I say, with blue eyes and my first set of wrinkles, which I used to think were cute and now are just annoying me. I work for Calgary's largest theatre company, Foothills Stage Network, as the front-of-house manager. I know it sounds exciting but it really just means I work almost every night and weekend. In reality I spend most of my time counting cash floats for the sales tables and adding up how many T-shirts we have sold. The smell of the grease paint, the roar of the crowds, that's what the actors get. I get liquor inventories and audience complaints. But I love it. Working nights and weekends suits me, as I am not known as a morning person. I get to drink all the coffee I want and I supervise smart-ass staff that to an outsider would seem to have little respect for me. It's all an act. We are a bunch of misfits who have found each other.

Now I was stuck in the middle of a little misunderstanding with my boyfriend, Cam. We live together in a tiny loft apartment in downtown Calgary. The living together kind of happened by accident but we were working hard at trying to make it work. We had been through a rough time this winter, but the end was in sight, or so I thought. This little misunderstanding had started innocently enough. My friend Sam had called me and asked for a favour a few weeks ago. Well, she had already said I would do the favour, but she was my friend and she thought it would be good for me. But since she was my friend, she should have known that I have a brilliant aptitude for screwing up the best-laid plans. This big favour turned out to be me taking a contract for the Dandelion Festival. And she talked me into going to the orientation just to check it out before making any commitment, because I was still fighting the inevitability of this train wreck. Being late for this stupid meeting didn't help that sense of dread, I thought, as I put my hand on the doorknob to the meeting room and opened the door as quietly as I could.

I snuck in to the back of the room, late for the start of the meeting as I had suspected, and not pleased with myself. They were willing to pay me a lot of money for a week's work and I didn't intend to be late or make a bad impression, it just happened. I stood just inside the door, looking around to see if there was an empty chair. Someone tapped me on the shoulder and I turned to see him pulling a chair from the pile and quietly setting it down beside where he was sitting, in the last row. I gratefully slid quietly into the empty seat; glad not to be standing out, where everyone who had been there on time could glare at me.

'Doug,' he whispered, leaning in towards my ear and holding out his hand.

'Kate,' I answered on autopilot, trying to ignore those amazing blue eyes and trying to pay attention to the producer who was speaking at the front of the room. That was until I took his hand and felt the spark from it. I pulled my hand away and tried really hard to concentrate on the current speaker again.

I sat ever so quietly and listened to the producer, the associate producer, the technical director, the transportation manager, the volunteer coordinator, the box office coordinator, the fund raising coordinator, and the Chairman of the Board of Directors, before the producer finally returned to the podium. He introduced me and I had a quiet moment of panic, thinking I was going to have to address the audience as well. However, he just explained why I had joined their team so late in the game and closed the meeting. We then adjourned for coffee or milk and Oreo cookies. Nothing but the best for the festival staff. I nodded a quick thank-you to the lovely gentleman who had provided me with a seat and then hurried off to the table. Time for a quick coffee and hello to a couple of the volunteers that were helping with my department and then I was out of there.

The first time I saw Doug was at this orientation meeting. But after I had thanked him and got up, I didn't really spend a lot of time thinking about those eyes or that spark, because I wasn't single. What a difference a week can make.

I was happily chatting with a couple that I knew from my theatre, when I felt a hand on my shoulder, squeezing in a highly intimate manner, a finger brushing across my neck. I turned, my automatic House Manager smile on my face, which quickly vanished when I realized who it was.

'Jeff?'

'Kate.' He smiled, pulling me into a very inappropriate and untimely embrace. One of his hands settled way too close to my bottom for comfort. 'I'm so happy to see you. When I heard you might be managing the festival market, I decided I would volunteer this year.'

I pulled away from him, trying not to spill the coffee I still held in my hand.

'That's nice,' I said, the fake smile back on my face, matching the fake enthusiasm I was forcing from my lips.

'I just thought it would give us a chance to get caught up. I mean, we've hardly seen each other since I left the Plex to work at the Jubilee Auditorium.'

'Yeah, that will be great. Look, I'm sorry to cut you short, but I have another appointment I have to get to. Really nice to see you again.'

'No, that's OK, I'm here with someone else anyway,' Jeff told me. 'Maybe you'd like to meet him?'

I put my empty coffee cup back on the table and hurried past Jeff, towards the door. I exited the room hastily, pushing through one of the employee-only exits, knowing he couldn't follow me beyond that locked door.

'That's the one,' I heard Jeff say to someone, as I started down the stairs.

That guy always gave me the creeps, I thought, good thing the festival is only a week long.

But the one other thing I hadn't noticed at that meeting was that there was one person in the room that wasn't watching the producer, or any of the other speakers, but instead he was watching me. I could have probably avoided a whole lot of trouble if I'd noticed that sooner.

Saturday

Yet another night I lie in bed, not sleeping. It is dark, the room quiet, my body tired but it is one of those nights where I can't get my brain to shut off. I feel guilty for not talking to Cam about the Dandelion Festival and that guilt sends my mind wandering back and forth, touching on all those images that I had been trying to bury for weeks. Images that kept haunting me on nights like this, nights where Cam was snoring quietly beside me, innocent to my suffering, and he was no help in taking my mind off my troubles. Not that I wanted to bother him. I didn't need to bring it all up again, not when we had found an uneasy peace after all these months.

Lying on a surgical bed, my feet up in the cold metal stirrups, a nurse holding my hand while I tried not to notice the instruments set up all around the room, just waiting for the doctor to clean out the detritus of my uterus. D&C they called it. Nice name so you didn't think about what they were actually doing to you. About what you had actually lost.

'How are you doing, Kate?' the doctor asked, looking down at me, one of those caring smiles on his lips, slightly wrinkled brow.

'Fine.' I smiled, putting on the brave face that everyone was expecting from me.

'Everything's going to be OK,' he assured me. 'Everything looks really good, Kate. I don't think you're going to have any problems. Now close your eyes and you're just going to go to sleep for a little while.'

'Good,' I muttered, wondering what I was supposed to say.

I stifle a sob and feel Cam stir beside me. I desperately turn my mind from that image, try to remember lying on Long

Beach, soaking up the sun, Cam lying beside me, holding my hand despite the heat. Our happy times. But instead . . .

It was a week after I had left the hospital the first time. I had been brought back in because my ultrasound said there were still retained products of conception within me. I hadn't had a complete miscarriage and the doctors had needed to complete the process. I lie on the hospital bed, my hand on my stomach, trying to fathom why I felt this strangely empty feeling. I hadn't wanted to be pregnant; I had barely carried the baby for a couple of months, I had only known about it for a couple of weeks before I lost it. And yet here I lie, pondering this emptiness, tears running down my cheeks. I was surprised by the whole maternal feeling that had come over me. How quickly I had accepted this baby that I hadn't planned for, thought I hadn't even wanted, and I was crying over it, wishing I was still carrying it.

'Katie,' a sleepy voice reached through the night. 'You OK?'

'I had a bad dream,' I whispered. 'Go back to sleep.'

'What did you dream about?' he asked, trying to wrap an arm around my waist and pull me closer to him.

That was a good question, I thought. I wasn't up for the real answer at three o'clock in the morning.

'I dreamed I was playing chess with the Bishop,' I lied, my stomach churning, as I remembered promising myself I wouldn't lie to Cam anymore.

'The Bishop?' he asked, sounding more awake.

'It's nothing.'

'Katie, you don't know anything about the Bishop do you?' he asked.

'No, no. It's just that it's in all the papers and on the news.'

'Well, we need to stop watching the news before we go to bed.'

'I guess so,' I sighed.

'You want a cup of tea or anything?' he asked, but his voice was already growing heavy with sleep again.

I smiled at the offer of tea, his thinking that tea would erase some of the images from my mind. He was a man, and he didn't know what it felt like to be violated, either by a rapist or by a doctor's curette scraping your uterus.

'No, I don't want tea or anything,' I assured him, rolling over and separating myself from him a little more. But he was already asleep and didn't notice.

He is such a sweet man, I thought, and I have treated him so badly recently. Maybe he was right; maybe we should go for some counselling or join a support group. It seemed I thought I was OK in the brightness of day; but as I lay here at night, these images replaying over and over, I am beginning to doubt my ability to recover from this. I can't stand these thoughts wandering around in my mind, unresolved feelings rolling around my gut as I toss and turn and pray for the release of sleep to come upon me.

I opened the door to the apartment and heard my Kalan Porter CD playing softly on the stereo. I shut the door behind me and walked further into the apartment, finding candles burning on the coffee table and wonderful-smelling aromas coming from the kitchen.

'Hey, you're home early.' Cam smiled, putting the lid back on the pot he had been stirring. He wiped his hands on the towel he had tucked into his belt, took my bag and tossed it into the corner and turned me toward the living room and sat me on the couch. He kissed me on the cheek and then sat down beside me.

'Wine?' he asked, holding up a bottle for my inspection.

'I'd love some.' I smiled back. 'What's this all about?'

'I just thought we should have a special night together. We used to do this a lot, remember?' he asked, pulling the cork from the bottle and filling my glass for me.

'Yes, I remember.' I smiled. 'And it wasn't all that long ago.'

'Seems like forever,' he said, taking a sip from his glass.

'I thought I was the melodramatic one,' I laughed at him.

'Katie, I've missed you.'

'I've been right here.'

'Things haven't been normal between us. I'd like for us to try to get back to normal again,' he said, taking my glass and setting it on the coffee table, then kissing me.

'Cam, I can't,' I said, pulling away from him.

'Katie, you saw the doctor, he said everything was fine. It's been over six weeks since the accident.'

'I'm sorry, Cam. Maybe I'm fine physically, but the doctor doesn't know how I feel inside. I'm just not ready yet.'

'Ready for what?' he asked. *'To kiss me? To let me hold you? I don't care if we make love or not tonight, but I'd like to be able to kiss you again. To put my arms around you without you finding some excuse to pull away from me. We need to find some way to start working this out.'*

'I know,' I admitted, picking up my wine and taking a big gulp.

'I don't mind taking it slow, at your speed, but we're not moving anywhere now. Can't we go forward, just a little?' he asked.

'I'm sorry, Cam, I don't know what I'm so scared of.'

'I think you're scared of getting pregnant again,' he said quietly.

'I think you're right,' I agreed.

'I'm not insisting that you have sex with me tonight.'

'I know. And I know this has been hard on you.'

'It's been hard on both of us,' he said.

'You're right, it's time to carry on with our lives.'

'Where should we start?' he asked.

'How about dinner in front of the TV and a good movie?' I asked. *'I think I can promise some serious cuddling if you ply me with enough wine.'*

'That sounds like a good start to me.' He smiled, picking up the bottle and offering it to me. *'More wine?'*

I laughed, and for the first time in a couple of months, it felt really good.

I had thought that would be the beginning and that I would be able to start back on track again. But it hadn't been. Instead, I had worked harder than I normally worked, staying late, coming home after Cam was already asleep, pretending I was asleep when he got up. Curled up alone, on my side of the bed. I was scared. I wanted things to be normal and I don't know why I wouldn't let them be. I pretended it was other things. I pretended work was busy, or I didn't feel good. And most of the time he pretended to believe whatever I was pretending at the time.

* * *

10

As winter had turned into spring, Cam worked a lot and so did I. We got very good at pretending that everything was normal in front of our friends and co-workers. And I hardly ever talked to my best friend, Sam. Talking to her always led to a confrontation about how I was leading my life and dealing with things. And if I couldn't talk about that with Cam I certainly wasn't going to with her. And then spring finally came.

I stood on the street, outside the stage door, waiting for Cam. I was so tired I didn't even know where to begin. Obviously, so was he.

'Katie, I know things have been rough,' he said.

Oh God, I thought, here it comes.

'Katie, I want us to get over this,' he said. 'I want us to go away. Maybe if we can get away from everything and everyone for a while, we can get beyond this. Don't you think a little holiday would make you feel better? Well, maybe we can go to the travel agent together tomorrow,' he suggested. 'Just to have a look at some brochures or something.'

'I have to work.'

Cam pulled the car over to the curb, right under the no parking sign across from City Hall, and put it in park.

'I think I have been the supportive boyfriend, holding your hand and trying to get you through this loss. But no matter what I do to try and help, all I get is scorn and sarcasm.'

'Cam, please let's just go home.'

'We don't have a home anymore, Katie. We have an apartment. But if you want to go and spend another frigid night there, pretending everything is normal while you cringe every time I accidentally touch you, then that's what we'll do. Because we all know that my life right now is about nothing more than trying to please you.'

'Fuck you. If you're so unhappy, why don't you just leave?'

'You want me to leave?' he asked.

'No,' I screamed. 'I don't want you to leave. But you're going to anyway so why don't you just quit dragging out this agony and get it over with.'

'You think I'm going to leave you?'

'Yes.'

'Katie, I will never leave you,' he said. 'I don't care how

11

hard things are, I am going to work to make our relationship last.'

He got out of the car and came around to my side. He opened the door and pulled me out on to the street. He held both my hands in his, and his face close to mine, forcing me to look him in the eyes.

'Katie, do you know what I learned this year?' he asked.

'No,' I sobbed.

'I learned that I didn't want a baby. What I wanted was a family. And with you, that's what I have. We are a family now.'

And then I really thought it would be better. I thought I could just forget it and move on. And I did, I actually started to move on and have good times again. But every once in a while I had nights like this, nights where I couldn't get to sleep because these visions kept dancing in my brain and then when I did get to sleep, the nightmares took over. I don't know where they came from or why.

'No!' I screamed, waking myself from the restless sleep I had finally fallen into.

'Katie?' Cam asked, sitting up beside me, reaching for the light.

'Leave the light off,' I told him.

'What's wrong, did you have another bad dream?' he asked.

He didn't reach out to hold me when he was awake, not like he used to. Sometimes, when he was half asleep, he would reach out for me, but then he would wake up and move away. He was scared too. He never knew what I would do, how I would react. I'd pulled away from him so many times in the past that he had stopped reaching out to me. This was not how I wanted to live any longer.

'I had a horrible dream,' I said. 'It's been going on day and night ever since we lost the baby. And I want it to end.'

'It'll be fine,' he said, trying to comfort me.

'No it won't, Cam,' I said. 'Not like this.'

'Let me get you a cup of tea, OK?' he asked. Beverages were safe. To make tea would involve us being in separate rooms.

'I want to make love with you,' I whispered.

'What did you say?' he asked.

12

I moved closer to him, ran my hand over his stomach, feeling his muscles tighten as I lightly traced the waistline of his pyjama bottoms with my fingernails.

'I need you, Cam,' I whispered, moving closer to him and finally kissing him. It had been a long time since I had touched Cam and I revelled in the feel of his taut muscles, his soft skin.

'Katie, not like this,' he whispered in my ear.

'How else?' I asked, my fingers running down the inside of his thigh, producing that gasp of breath that it always did.

'Are you sure you're ready?' he asked, and I could hear the tension in his voice.

'I'm ready,' I assured him.

He pulled my hands away and flipped me over, holding my hands above my head and looking into my eyes, trying to see the truth within them.

'I'm ready,' I whispered.

It had been a long time for both of us and it didn't take any more convincing than that.

Now, I thought, things really would start getting better. And they would, I promised myself. Until I thought about the festival again.

Sunday

Itrudged on to the elevator and checked my watch. It was official; I was fifteen minutes into my vacation. Last night had been closing night, today had been paperwork hell day, but payroll and banking were done, schedules were posted and I didn't have to see the theatre for the next thirty days, barring flood or earthquakes. I had even snuck into the festival storage lockers and done up the inventory, getting that done before I had to explain anything to my boyfriend. I had taken the LRT home because it was still broad daylight and would be for the next several hours. Calgary was becoming a ghost town at night because of the Bishop, with no one walking the streets, opting instead for the safety of a taxi or private car.

I was planning one night of rest and relaxation in the safety of my own home tonight and then tomorrow I started the festival. I had signed the contract. They were paying me a ridiculous amount of money to look after their concessions for a week and then I still had almost three weeks off. That was assuming I survived telling Cam I had taken the job. He hadn't reacted very well when he'd first heard about it.

'I've missed this,' Cam whispered in my ear.

We were lying on the couch together, trying to watch Casablanca, *but somehow the romantic nature of the movie seemed to overtake us. He had kissed me during the first strains of* As Time Goes By *and now Bogart was already at the airport watching Ingrid Bergman board the airplane, buttons were undone and belts askew. Then the phone rang.*

'Let the machine get it,' Cam said, wrapping his arms around me, holding me tight so I couldn't get up.

'Come on, it might be something important,' I whined at him.

14

'Katie, I refuse to let you go right now. I have other things in mind for you.'

I slid out from under his arm and grabbed for the phone.

'I promise I'll keep it short.' I smiled at him and then turned to the phone. 'Hello?'

'Kate, it's Sam.'

'Hey Sam, can I call you back later? Cam and I are right in the middle of something.'

'You can make out anytime. Remember that great opportunity I told you about? Do you remember that opportunity only knocks once and you have to answer the door before it goes away?' she asked.

'OK, but now is not a great time. Cam's looking a little impatient.'

'Kate, the festival needs an answer. Come on, you've checked out the orientation, you've talked to them about it, what else is there? And it's great money for not very much work,' she reminded me.

'Yes, but I don't think I can do it. And you know I don't want to spend a week helping you do dishes or cook.'

'I know, I wouldn't even bother asking you that. But the market manager has quit and they need someone to fill in quickly. If you take this job it is going to look really good for me,' she said triumphantly.

Cam gave me one last dirty look and when he saw I wasn't about to get off the phone, he decided to head into the kitchen for a beer.

'No way,' I whispered into the phone. 'I've got a whole month off. I haven't taken a whole month off in years. And Cam is really looking forward to us doing something together.'

'Kate, they're willing to pay an amazing amount of money and they're kind of desperate.'

'Tell me how much again?' I asked, thinking of summer coming up and two months of slow season in the theatre business. Since I was paid per show, I always worried over summer about paying bills. My weak spot was my independence.

'No!' Cam hollered from the kitchen. 'Whatever it is, just say no!'

'Fifteen hundred for the week plus you have to do inventory the day before and hand in a final report after it's over.

15

Plus whatever preparation is left to do. Most of the volunteers and paid staff are scheduled, though, so I don't think you'll have to put much effort into the preparation.'

'That's not bad for a week,' I said and she knew she was winning. 'Tell me what's all involved during the week?'

'Standard market stuff. Inventory, cashing out and bank deposits. Just like you do at the theatre. Except you get to do it outside and I'll feed you very well all week.'

'It sounds interesting,' I said. 'But, Sam, I just don't think I can.'

'Look, Kate, they need an answer. Do you want to talk directly to them, do you want me to call them? What do you want to do?' she asked. 'Because they need an answer.'

'Call them,' I said.

'And say what?' she asked, hope rising in her voice.

'Tell them I'll take it,' I whispered, but Cam had heard me.

'No,' Cam said again as he walked back to the couch. He turned the movie off and switched the TV to a football game, turning the volume just a little too loud.

'For sure?' she asked.

'For sure,' I said, trying to talk over the TV. 'I have to go, I'll talk to you tomorrow.'

I hung up the phone and turned to Cam.

'What's up?' I asked.

'What do you mean?' he asked, a little too innocently.

'Why did you suddenly decide to turn up the game so loud while I was talking to Sam?' I asked.

'I'm sorry, was I bothering you? You should have said something.' He sounded way too sarcastic and I sensed a fight in our near future.

'Cam, I was talking to Sam about a job,' I began to try to explain.

'I'm aware of that. And it's during our vacation, am I right?' he asked.

'Yes, but it's only a week and we'll still have three weeks off.'

'I thought we could go away somewhere,' he said.

'I know you were thinking about going away but you hadn't said anything about that for sure. I thought maybe we were just going to hang around here.'

'Not for an entire month,' he said, turning the TV up another notch.

'The money's really good,' I explained. 'We could have lots of fun for the three weeks after the festival.'

'This isn't about money,' he said. 'This is about us being together.'

I cuddled up to him on the couch, pulling his arm up over my shoulder. It was the coldest hug I had ever received from him but at least he didn't pull his arm away.

'Can we please just talk about this and see if we can work it out?' I suggested. 'A compromise maybe, like grown-ups do?'

'You mean the Kate compromise?'

'What do you mean by that?'

'I mean we do it your way and life is happy. We don't do it your way and you make my life hell for the next month?'

'That is totally unfair.'

'Is it?' he asked.

I pulled myself out from his embrace, which had not warmed up anyway.

'Yes it is,' I insisted. 'I try to make this work just as hard as you do.'

'It's totally up to you. You make the decision. You just have to decide whether the money is more important than us spending the time together.' He leaned forward, grabbed his beer and turned the TV up even louder.

'Cam, that's not what this is about at all,' I said, raising my voice to be heard over the television.

'Katie, I really want to watch the game.'

I ripped the remote from his hand, used it to turn off the TV and then tossed it over the edge of our balcony. It took several seconds before I heard it break up as it hit the paved alley.

'I'd really like to talk about this,' I insisted.

He got up, crossed the room and turned the TV on manually.

'I really want to watch this game. Can we do this later?' he asked.

'Fine!' I said huffily, getting up off the couch and storming upstairs to the bedroom.

17

I threw myself on to the bed, curled up facing the wall and tried to read. I was having problems concentrating between my anger and the football announcers screaming away downstairs. But, a few minutes later, I heard the TV shut off and Cam come up the stairs. He lay down beside me on the bed and wrapped his arms around me.

'I'm sorry,' he whispered into my ear. 'I'm so sorry.'

I put my book down and rolled over to face him.

'I'm sorry too,' I said back, tears stinging my cheeks.

And that was the last time Cam and I spoke about the job . . .

I smiled to myself, thinking about those glorious three weeks we were going to have after the festival was over, as the elevator released me and I hurried down the hall to my apartment. I slipped my key into the lock and opened the door to the apartment. Cam was supposed to be home, but the place was dark. I locked the door behind me, dropped my coat at the door and tiptoed quietly toward the living room, just in case he was napping.

'Cam,' I whispered.

'I'm in here,' he called back. 'Just follow the sound of my voice.'

'Why is it dark in here? Did I forget to pay the utility bill?' I asked.

'No, I just wanted a nice romantic night with my girl.'

I saw his face silhouetted as he struck a match and lit a couple of candles sitting on the coffee table. Looked like my rest and relaxation was going to happen sooner than I thought.

'What's the occasion?' I asked, dropping my bag and joining him on the couch.

He gave me one of his great kisses, as if we'd been apart for months instead of a few hours, and then popped the cork on the wine bottle and poured us both a glass.

'You're on vacation, I'm on vacation, and we don't have any company,' he explained as he handed me a glass. 'I think that deserves a little celebration.'

'I think there's something I should tell you,' I said, suddenly feeling a little guilty. I hadn't exactly discussed the festival contract with Cam since that night.

18

'I don't want to discuss anything more serious than pouring you another glass of wine.'

'Cam, there's something I need to tell you.'

'And I have a surprise for you,' he said, smiling as he kissed me again.

'What?'

'I did it.'

'Did what?'

'I did what we were talking about. You know, when we were talking about what we should do while we were on vacation.'

'I didn't realize we had been talking about anything?'

'Katie, you've been working too hard. You mentioned the festival contract you had been offered and I suggested we take a trip. Remember? And we talked about it in the car. That's when I first suggested it.'

'And I asked you what you had done and you said you hadn't done anything.'

'Well, I might have lied just a little about that,' he admitted. 'We were in the middle of a heated moment.'

'I didn't think we had actually made any decisions . . .' I stammered, trying to get out of this but not really finding a way to accomplish that.

'Well, we didn't exactly. But you haven't mentioned the festival again so I went out and bought cruise tickets.'

'I didn't mention it again because we were fighting about it,' I tried to explain. 'I can't believe you actually went ahead and bought the tickets. We didn't even discuss where we should go.'

'I thought I'd surprise you,' he said. 'I've got it all planned out. I hand picked the islands we'd stop at. I've got a great cabin for us. With a balcony.'

'Cam, how could you do this?'

'I did it because I thought you'd be pleased,' he said. 'Most women would be thrilled that their boyfriend was taking them on a Caribbean cruise.'

'I am thrilled that you thought to do that, Cam, but I might have had some plans of my own and wanted a say in it.'

'What plans?' he asked.

'I might have wanted to do something else. Maybe I bought

us tickets to Europe. Or even Vancouver Island. We had such a good time when we went to Long Beach.'

'You took that contract with the festival, didn't you?' he demanded.

'Yes, I did,' I admitted quietly, waiting for the explosion that was sure to follow.

'Katie, I thought we were going to talk about things like this. What happened?'

'I think that goes both ways, Cam. You didn't exactly discuss this cruise with me.'

'I wanted to surprise you.'

'You've had these for a while, haven't you? You had them when we were in the car fighting. You were going to tell me and you chickened out.'

'I was just waiting for a good time to surprise you,' he told me. 'A time when you might be happy about it and not psychotic like you've been recently.'

'Psychotic?' I screeched, not even liking the tone of my own voice.

'You're a little unpredictable these days.'

'Well I just want to earn a living. I am off work for most of the summer, without pay. And summer's here.'

'You don't have to worry about money. We're a two-income family now.'

'We're nothing right now, Cam. We're living together; we have no commitment of any sort. We split some bills. I'm not exactly going to risk my security and future on this relationship yet.'

'Now you're complaining that I haven't asked you to marry me?' he asked. 'Not too long ago you were begging me not to ask you that. God, what am I supposed to do to make you happy?'

'Just let me be a part of the decisions. Ask me if I want to go on a cruise or not.'

'Where is all this coming from?' he asked. 'You seem to have a lot more on your mind than this stupid cruise.'

'No, no. It's about the cruise and how we make decisions together.'

'If you'll recall, one of the big reasons our relationship is like this is because you refuse to make it anything more right

20

now. Every time we discuss our future you go running in the opposite direction.'

I took a big gulp of wine and a deep breath and tried to attack this from a new direction.

'Cam, I think we're getting off track,' I started. 'I'm just a little insecure about relying on you financially yet. Besides, the contract is only for a week, we still have almost three weeks together after that. Can't we do something then?'

Cam leaned over and blew out the candles and then flopped back on to the couch. We sat there in the dark, not saying anything. One of the things I had liked so much about my relationship with Cam was the fact that we could be very comfortable in our silences. This wasn't one of those times.

'Cam, I'm sorry. But we need to . . .'

He slammed his wine glass on the table and stood up. 'I'm going to take a bath.'

I watched him storm to the bathroom and slam the door after him. I poured myself another glass of wine and chugged it back, but it didn't make me feel any better. I finally worked up the motivation to do something, and took the plates of hors d'oeuvres into the kitchen and put them away. I corked the wine, rinsed the glasses and headed upstairs to the bedroom.

I turned the bed down and undressed. Cam had been in the bathtub for a long time and I decided to go check on him and see if we might have a better chance of talking calmly yet. I pulled a T-shirt on and went back downstairs. I turned the knob on the bathroom door and found it was locked. He'd never locked the door before.

'Cam, are you all right?' I called through the door.

'I'll be out in a couple of minutes,' he called back. Nothing more.

I brushed a tear out of the corner of my eye and went back upstairs. I climbed into bed and propped some pillows up behind my back. I opened my book and read, waiting for Cam to come upstairs. I was almost asleep when I heard him open the bathroom door and tiptoe upstairs, obviously hoping not to wake me. I set my book down and watched him come into the bedroom. He dropped his towel and quickly pulled on a pair of sweatpants before climbing into bed beside me. He turned his back to me and pulled the covers up around him.

'Are you going to read for a while or can I turn off the light?' he asked.

'Cam, I don't want to go to sleep with us being so angry.'

'I'd rather talk in the morning. I don't want to say something I might regret later,' he said. 'Light on or off?'

'Cam, please, we both made a mistake here. Let's just talk about it.'

He reached over and turned off the light, pulling at the covers angrily. I put my book away and closed my eyes, but sleep was a long way off. I decided to push my luck.

'I don't care if you don't want to talk or not, I do. Tell me why you're so angry about this stupid cruise?' I asked.

'I told you I wanted to surprise you. Obviously work is more important to you than I am.'

'You know that's not true. You are the most important thing in the world to me.'

'Then why didn't you talk about this contract with me?'

'Why didn't you talk about the cruise with me?' I countered.

'I asked first.'

'Cam, I'm still not used to talking about things. I've been making decisions on my own a lot longer than we've been together. It's hard to become dependent.'

'I don't want you to be dependent, Katie; I want you to share my life. And you seem very reluctant to do that. I really believed we were actually starting to do that and then you pull this. That's why I'm so angry.'

'Cam, I'd love to go on a cruise with you. Let's just do it a week later.'

'It's too late, the tickets are booked.'

'I'll pay for new ones. I am making great money next week.'

'So you've said.'

'It's not like we haven't taken a vacation together before,' I tried.

'This was supposed to be different.'

'What was so special about it? Just tell me so I can understand.'

'What's so special is that I love you. I really thought we needed this time together, after everything we've been through.

And then I find out that you would rather work. I just didn't realize I had such a different agenda in this relationship than you did. But now I'm finally beginning to understand.'

'Cam, that's not what this is about. Taking the contract with the festival has nothing to do with the way I feel about you.'

'Then tell them you can't do it. Break the contract,' he said. 'Take the cruise with me.'

'I can't do that,' I said. 'I've signed it.'

'And what if I said it's the festival or me?' he asked.

'That's not fair.'

'Life's not fair, Katie.'

'Why can you make me choose but you don't have to? I could say it's the cruise or me?'

'Are you going to make a decision or not?' he asked.

'I have never broken a contract in my life,' I tried to explain.

'Fine,' he said, a cold calmness in his voice.

He threw back the blankets and stormed across the bedroom to the closet. He pulled a pillow and blanket out and turned back to me.

'I'm going to sleep on the couch tonight,' he said.

'If this cruise is so fucking important to you, maybe you should take it . . . alone!' I shouted at him.

'Maybe I will,' he said as he threw the pillow to the floor. He grabbed a sweater out of the closet and pulled it on over his head.

'Where are you going?' I asked.

'On the cruise. I'll see you when I get back.'

'Cam, it's dark out, it's not safe. Please don't go out there,' I begged him. 'Please . . .'

But he ignored me, storming down the stairs and out the door without another word.

It was too soon. He knew that. Part of the reason he was so successful was because he was able to stay in control. But she was on his mind now. Now that he'd seen her and he knew what he was going to do to her, he was excited. And he was having problems controlling that excitement this time. So the best way to deal with it was to find somebody to play with. And that's why he was here. Out in the dark. It was dangerous to be out here in the dark. All the newspapers said so. Dangerous because the Bishop might get you. Even more dangerous for him, because everyone was looking for him. But he was an expert at fitting in. At looking like one of them. That was all part of the game. He stood outside the bar, dressed in jeans, a black T-shirt and leather jacket, and looked like any other bouncer at any other bar. The only thing was that this bar didn't have a bouncer. But the people going in and out the door didn't know that. And then she came out the door; cute, blonde, young, looking a bit like the one he'd spent so much time thinking about; and when she stopped and smiled at him, he smiled back at her.

'Hi there,' she said, showing her straight white teeth.

'Hi,' he said.

'Slow night in there tonight,' she said, nodding back into the bar.

'Slow night all over the city,' he said. 'But I do know a place where it's a little bit more lively than this.'

'Really?' she asked.

She wore a backless halter-top, held together by a few strings and a prayer, with a short, red leather miniskirt and some very high heels. He wondered what she was going to think when he started cutting the laces on that halter-top. Would she scream then or would she just think that he was interested in her? What would it take to get that fear he so craved to show in her eyes? He felt a shiver run up and down his back and took a deep breath, trying to maintain his control.

'Wanna go?' he asked.

'Aren't you working?'

'I just got off,' he explained. 'I was just hanging around to see if anything was going on.'

'Do you have a car?' she asked. 'It's almost impossible to get a taxi.'

'I have a car,' he said, holding his hand out for her to take.

She rewarded him with another warm smile as she took his hand and he led her to the end of the block and around the corner, where his car was parked under a broken street light. He opened the door for her and helped her in, noticing she was a little unsteady on those high heels. He closed the door and got in the car himself, engaging the locks from his door.

24

'What are you doing?' she asked, startled at the sound of the locks closing.

'I just want to make sure you don't get away from me now that I've finally got you,' he said, turning the car on. The radio was playing loudly.

'That's funny,' she said sarcastically. 'Can you turn the radio down?'

'If I turn it down, someone might hear you scream.'

'What are you talking about?' she asked, her smile beginning to fade.

'So, what kind of things do you like to do?'

'I like to dance. I thought we were going to dance?' she said.

'Do you know what I like to do?' he asked, checking the mirrors, making sure they were alone on the street.

'What?' she asked.

He reached under the seat and pulled out a roll of duct tape. 'I like to play games.'

And as he grabbed her hands and tried to wrap the duct tape around them, he saw the first spark of fear lighting up her eyes and he knew it was going to be a good night.

Monday

I woke up the next morning to find myself alone. I didn't want to get up and face the day, but dragged myself out of bed anyway. I was so disappointed and worried that Cam hadn't come home. I missed the smell of the morning coffee perking, his warm musky smell after his morning run, even his obnoxious goofy morning grin. I climbed out of bed, missing the warm spot in the bed next to me, a spot that I always rolled over and curled up on in the last few moments before I dragged myself out of bed and headed for the shower. When I got out of the shower, I heard some noise upstairs. I went running up to the bedroom, a smile on my face, hoping to find Cam contrite and ready to make up. Instead I found him packing a suitcase.

'What are you doing?' I asked, my heart in my throat, slumping down into the armchair.

'I'm packing. I've got a plane to catch.'

'Are you really going?' I asked, not believing he would actually leave me.

'That's what you suggested last night, if you recall.'

'Cam, we were angry, we were fighting, it's not like we haven't done that before. Let's not get too carried away.'

'Too late for that,' he said, closing his suitcase. 'I'll send you a postcard.'

'Cam, you said I wouldn't lose you. You told me that we could get through anything together.'

'Katie, I love you,' he said. 'But I can't have a relationship with just me in it. You have proven time and time again that you want to be independent. You don't want to work as a team. I feel like I'm a roommate, not a soul mate. I just can't live that way anymore.'

'Why does this cruise mean so much to you?' I asked.

26

'It's not the cruise itself, Katie,' he said wearily. 'This is just the final straw. I just can't keep torturing myself like this. If you really don't want to be with me, I'm not going to stay here and try to force it.'

'But I do want you here,' I sobbed. 'It's just so hard for me. I've never lived with anyone before . . .'

'It's hard for me too, Katie. It's too hard and I just can't put myself through it anymore. I'm sorry.'

'Cam, don't do this,' I said, standing up and blocking the stairway. 'I'm not going to just let you walk out of here.'

'I'm really sorry,' he said, his hand caressed my cheek and then he picked up his suitcase, and pushed past me. I heard the door slam downstairs a moment later. Cam was gone.

I moved slowly around the apartment, wondering what had happened. I caught my reflection in the mirror and for a moment I didn't recognize myself. I suddenly didn't know how to define myself all of a sudden. My name is Kate Carpenter. I am in my mid-thirties but feel older right now, my hair is mostly grey and I have wrinkles. I used to be able to say that I had a wonderful boyfriend named Cam who works at the Plex too, in the maintenance department. He is incredibly good looking and a fitness nut, which is fine because when he used to go out running, he didn't mind if I slept in. Cam was my knight in shining armour, moving in to protect me. I don't have a great track record with relationships and Cam was divorced, but we had been struggling through so far. I have always said that Cam's greatest attribute was that no matter how hard I pushed him away, he kept coming back. Until now. God, what had I done?

I stood there for a very long time, dripping on the carpet and wondering how I was going to get through the day. There was only one way I could do it, I finally decided, and that was to pretend nothing had happened. I took a deep breath and decided in that moment that Cam was just visiting his parents.

'I'm not going to cry,' I said out loud.

I dropped my towel, picked out some clean blue jeans and a sweater and got dressed. I stared at the neatly pressed clothes in my closet, knowing that Cam had ironed them all for me. What would my life look like in a week without him?

'I said I wasn't going to cry,' I repeated out loud, blinking my eyes rapidly to dry up the tears that insisted on forming again.

I finished my outfit with some Birkenstocks and headed back to the bathroom and dried my hair. I would deal with this relationship thing next week. This week I had a job to do and I was going to do it. By the time I had my makeup on and my bag packed, I had almost convinced myself that nothing was wrong. Avoidance was one of my strong suits and I had years of practice at it.

I walked the few blocks to the Plex and stood on the corner, watching the activity going on all around the Plaza. It was almost seven thirty now, and the last of the set-up still had to be done for the lunchtime opening ceremony. I spotted Sam directing a couple of volunteers setting up some tables. I had some relationship mending to do with my friend Sam too, as we had had our share of harsh words over the past few months, starting with when I was still in the hospital.

'Kate?' I heard a voice call from the doorway.

I hurriedly wiped my eyes and turned to see who was there.

'Hi Sam.' I tried a weak smile in her direction.

She pushed her way in through the door and sat on the side of the bed.

'Wow, you look rough.'

'It looks worse than it actually is,' I said. 'No permanent damage.'

'That's not what I hear,' she said. 'You want to talk?'

'No, I'm fine.'

'Kate, you've had a big shock. Hell, you've had a month of big shocks. I think we should talk.'

'I'm not up to it right now,' I said, more harshly than I meant to.

'Where's Cam?' she asked. 'He called me to tell me you were here, I assumed he was here with you.'

'I sent him home. I needed to be alone for a while.'

'Not a good move,' she scolded me.

'Look, I'm not exactly at my best now. I didn't need him

here, fawning over me and holding my hand. I just want to be alone and sleep for a while.'

'Kate, you're not the only one who lost a baby. He did too.'

'I told you it's no big deal. I barely even knew I was pregnant.'

'I don't believe you,' Sam said. 'Kate, you need to reach out to your friends right now. We're here for you. You and Cam especially need each other right now.'

'No, what I need right now is to be alone. I'm very tired.'

'Kate, please don't push me away,'

'Do I have to call the nurse or are you going to leave on your own?' I asked.

'I'll go for now, but you're not getting rid of me that easily. I'm not going to leave you alone, Kate, no matter what you say or do,' she said standing up.

I turned over and pulled the blanket up over my ears, pretending to sleep until I finally heard the door gently close behind her.

Sam had come to visit every day too, no matter what I said to her. And I don't think I had really apologized to her yet either. And she never held it against me. Sam really was the greatest friend I have ever had. I shook my head to try and clear the memories and crossed the Plaza and made my way over to her.

'Hey, Kate, it's nice to see you up at this time of day,' Sam joked.

'Enjoy it now, because after this week you're never going to see me at this time of day again.' I smiled weakly at her.

'So, I'm guessing that since you're here, everything went well with Cam? You managed to smooth things over?' she asked.

'Yeah, something like that. You know, sometimes I think this whole relationship thing is over-rated.'

'You didn't smooth things over.'

'That's not what I said,' I tried, but I knew that trying to fool Sam was almost impossible.

'Is he coming down later?'

'No.'

'Should I have Ryan drop by and have a coffee with him?'

Sam asked, referring to her husband, who had become good friends with Cam.

'He's in Saskatchewan visiting his parents.'

'Look at me,' she commanded.

'What?' I asked, turning to face her directly.

'You're lying.'

'And just what makes you think I'm lying?'

'Because you do that thing with your face.'

'What thing?' I asked.

'Kate, if I told you what that thing was, you would stop doing it and I would never be able to tell if you were lying or not.'

'I don't want to talk about Cam right now, OK?'

'Not really,' she said. 'But I'll give you a temporary time out on the subject. It is morning and I realize this is not your best time of day.'

'Now where's the coffee?' I asked.

'I don't have any yet. I'm still waiting for some deliveries. And for my assistant to show up. I hate using volunteers in catering, you just can't count on them.'

'I thought you were happy with the guy you got this year?' I asked.

'Well, he was a cook at Joey Tomato's for a year, so the guy knows his way around a kitchen.'

'But?'

'But, Kate, I've been here for a couple of hours and do you see him anywhere? There's a whole lot of prep work to do, you know, this stuff just doesn't happen by magic.'

'It doesn't?' I asked, a sly smile on my face as I tried to lighten the moment.

'OK, it is all magic,' she laughed. 'Either way, I need to find this guy and talk to him about his commitment level to me and the festival.'

'I'm sure it will all be fine,' I said, checking my watch.

'Kate, your volunteers sell T-shirts, mine work gas stoves and make lunch for 500 people. Do you see the difference here?'

'I'm sure I will when I finally get a little caffeine in me.'

'I hear rumours the boys in the security trailer have some coffee. That's where they've left all your stuff too,' she said, pointing across the Plaza. 'It's over in the north corner.'

'Well that's where I'm headed then. I'll see you later, after I get organized.'

'Kate, are you really all right?' she asked.

'I'm fine,' I lied to her. 'Why?'

'You just seem off. Did you guys have a big fight?'

'It's morning, Sam. You know how I am in the morning.'

'OK, go get your coffee then.' She smiled at me, not really believing a single word of what I had told her.

Sam pulled out her cell phone and called the volunteer co-ordinator while I meandered across the Plaza towards the security trailer. When the Calgary Arts Complex was originally built, this part of town was a little on the unsavoury side, hosting the prostitutes and drug addicts who frequented this part of downtown. There was a large contingent of folks that believed the patrons of the Symphony or Theatres would prefer not to be dropped off in the middle of the 'stroll', and rightfully so. Funds were raised, land was purchased and the police drove the problem from one area of the city to another. The end result was our beautiful Performing Arts Plaza; there was an amphitheatre built into one end, with soft grass seats, a reflecting pool, which became a skating rink in the winter, fountains, statues and monuments all befitting the performing arts and the people who had raised money to make all this happen. The Plaza also became a great site for outdoor festivals and concerts during the summer. And this is where my festival was taking place. Just a few hundred feet from the comfort of my theatre.

I was checking out the various tents and stages going up as I passed by. There were already some clowns wandering around – I mean that literally, of course – and a sound check blasting off the music stage. I hurried as I got closer to the trailer and smelled the unmistakable scent of coffee brewing. I knocked but when I didn't get an answer, I opened the door and climbed the step up inside. No one was there, so I helped myself to a cup of coffee and sat on the banquette, the kind that was the dining table during the day and folded down for extra bed space at night. I was quite enjoying my first coffee of the day in peace and quiet. I saw a box sitting beside me with my name on it and flipped open the top. There was a festival T-shirt and nametag sitting on top, with lots of paper-work underneath. I decided to deal with the T-shirt first and the paperwork later, being that it was still morning and I was not functioning at optimum level yet. The curtains were already closed, so I locked the door and pulled off my sweater. I was shaking the festival T-shirt, trying to loosen some of the fold marks, not really paying attention to anything, so I almost jumped through the roof when I heard a door open behind me. I turned around and saw a great-looking guy coming out of the bathroom, just pulling up his blue jeans. He looked up and saw me wearing nothing more than my jeans, bra and the blush that was growing on my cheeks. He stared for a moment longer than I felt comfortable with, but it didn't seem to matter because I was staring just as intently back at him. Until I suddenly remembered I didn't have a shirt on. I grabbed the sweater that had fallen to the floor and held it in front of me, suddenly feeling very modest. He quickly finished pulling up his pants and zipped them.

'Hi.' He smiled at me. 'I'll just go back in here and let you finish changing. We can exchange pleasantries and introduc-tions after we're both fully clothed, if that's OK with you?'

He turned to go into the bathroom.

'It's OK. It's not like you haven't already had an eyeful,' I said, quickly turning around and pulling the T-shirt on over my head, thanking God I had put on one of my sexy bras this morning, not one of the ugly but functional ones. 'But just so you know, this isn't how I normally would introduce myself. I like to leave getting naked for when I've actually gotten to know you better.'

He laughed and I felt immensely relieved. I recognized him from the orientation meeting, but I couldn't remember his name or what he did. I was just hoping that he wouldn't have me thrown off the festival site the first day I was on the job for lewd or lascivious behaviour.

'I'm Kate Carpenter,' I said, extending my hand to him.

'I remember you from orientation. I'm Doug Walsh.' He smiled back, shaking my hand. 'And I'm sorry too. I've been here alone for the last two days while they've been setting up. I guess I kind of forgot there'd be more people around today.'

'Not a problem.' I smiled back. 'I did knock, just so you know.'

'I was in the shower, just so you know. I see you found the box of stuff they left for you,' he said, as he poured himself a coffee.

I wished he would put on a shirt. I was finding it all a little distracting so early in the day.

'More coffee?' he asked.

'Thanks,' I said, holding out my cup and letting him fill it.

He put the pot back, took a big gulp of coffee, set his mug down and finally pulled on a T-shirt, all events I watched as closely as I could out of the corner of my eye, without being obvious. I turned my attention back to the box I had sitting beside me, while Doug opened the curtains in the trailer. Daylight streamed in and I felt a little more in control of myself. He hooked a walkie-talkie to his belt and sat at the table across from me.

'Do you mind if I open the window?' he asked.

'Not at all,' I said. 'It looks like it's going to be nice out there today.'

'It's a beautiful day out there already,' he commented.

'Great way to start the festival.'

'Yeah, I hope it holds. I sure like working in the sunshine more than I do spending a week outside in the rain.'

'Well, I think you're in luck. It's supposed to be like this all week. I intend to finish up with a great tan.'

'You do know that sun exposure is bad for you, don't you?' he asked.

I pulled the sunscreen out of my bag and plopped it on the table.

'Feel free to help yourself.'

'Isn't that going to crimp those tanning plans?' he asked.

'No, I'm hoping to get some colour and avoid sun damage. Think it can be done?'

'Doubtful,' he said. 'But it's good to have goals, right? That is if you're not run off your feet first.'

'Not going to happen, I have it all planned. I'm going to spend an exhausting morning training my volunteers to run everything and think on their feet. And then once they're ready, all I'll have to do is rounds every couple of hours and, in between, I'll be on a lawn chair outside this trailer with a trashy novel and a cold drink in my hand.'

'Have you ever worked one of these festivals before?' he asked me.

'Not exactly, but I manage the Centenary Theatre. It's like a festival every night up there.'

'Well, I think you may be in for a few surprises.' He smiled at me.

I kept pulling things out of the box; copies of schedules, extra nametags, keys to the safe, memos. My eyes drifted away from the box of work and to the window again and the sunny day beyond it. Suddenly, a big clown head popped up in front of us.

'Boo!' the clown hollered in the open window.

I jumped back as the painted face appeared right at the window, and then I got angry. I understood why some people were scared of clowns and this guy wasn't helping that reputation. He had a bright red slash across his face, the typical painted eyes and rainbow coloured wig, but he also had a big star on his cheek.

'Not funny,' I yelled at him through the window.

'If the trailer's rocking don't come . . .' the clown started.

I reached over and slammed the window shut. 'I hate clowns.'

'I've always wondered if they were meant to entertain children or scare them into submission,' Doug said. But he watched to make sure the clown wasn't bothering anyone else as he made his way down the Plaza.

I laughed and turned my attention back to my box of goodies.

'There's a note here that one of the first things I'm supposed to do is meet with head of security,' I said. 'Do you know where I can find him?'

'I'm him.' Doug smiled at me.

'All right then, did I make a good first impression?' I asked, the blood rushing back to my cheeks.

'You made a great first impression. So far, based on your initial greeting alone, I would highly recommend you for every festival I'm working this summer.'

'I'm sorry,' I said, trying to get serious but still feeling slightly embarrassed. 'I've had a bad month and I was late arriving for orientation night and I missed the introductions. Besides, you're not wearing a nametag yet. And I believe the festival manual says that all staff are to wear their nametags at all times while on the site.'

'I know. I'll get it on eventually. But since I actually wrote that part of the manual, I feel free to take a little liberty with it. So should we have our meeting then?' he asked.

'About what? I certainly feel like I know everything there is to know about you. Except whether you're circumcised or not.'

'We have to leave something for tomorrow.'

'Right. Then what's left?'

'We need to talk about your cash pick-ups and bank deposits. We're supposed to accompany you whenever you're doing cash runs this week. And there's a whole lot of other rules and regulations about handling the money and bank deposits, safe drops, things like that.'

'They afraid I'm going to skim some for myself?' I asked.

'No, they're afraid someone else might see you as an easy target. See, there are only three of us that are actually paid professional strong guys. The rest of the security staff are volunteers. They are very enthusiastic but not very well trained. We let them handle crowd control and parking and stuff, but you need to be working just with us regular guys. I'll introduce you to the others this morning. We just want to make sure that if there's a problem, it's one of us that you come to, OK? Some of the security volunteers are a little over-zealous and they might try and help you out, but you should probably just find something else for them to do.'

'Trust me, I know about dealing with volunteers.'

'Plus, it's for your own protection too. You don't want your reputation besmirched because someone saw you doing something not according to the rules and regulations.'

'Besmirched?'

'Give me a break. It was on my word-a-day calendar, OK?'

'Indubitably.'

'So I guess we'll get to know each other really well this week?' he asked, ignoring the last of my smart-ass comments.

'I think we've already covered that,' I laughed. 'But do I get to see the other guys with their pants down too?'

'Is that important to you?' he asked.

'Well, a little comparison-shopping never hurt. I need to see who can protect me the best this week.'

'They're all younger than I am, so I'm sure you'll be much more impressed with their attributes than you were with mine.'

'Well, experience counts for a lot.' I smiled back, much more suggestively than I meant to.

'Experience I have.' He smiled back.

I was beginning to feel very uncomfortable, until his radio broke the mood.

'Tommy to Doug, over.'

'Looks like I'm on duty.' He smiled, pulling the microphone to his mouth. 'Go for Doug, over.'

'Do you want to head over to the food stands, we've got some people who want to set up a stand but I don't have them on the list, over?'

'I'll be right there, over,' he answered. 'You want to come along and meet the other guys?'

'Sure, there's nothing here I can't deal with later,' I said, as I stood up and pulled my nametag on over my head.

He held the door open for me. 'After you then.'

'Thanks,' I said, brushing his chest as I passed by him. It was a good thing I was getting out of that trailer and into the fresh air. I pulled my sunglasses down over my eyes, hoping they would cover the slight blush I felt rising in my cheeks again, and followed him out across the Plaza. I couldn't remember the last time someone had made me blush three times in an hour except for the night I met Cam.

You see, I've learned a lot about security guards while working at the Plex. I've learned that some are incredibly dedicated to their jobs, I've learned that some just enjoy the sense of power that comes with wearing an orange vest and walkie-talkie, and just today I've learned that some have the most incredible blue eyes. Eyes that can pull you in and almost make you forget who you are for a moment. And in that moment, you can totally destroy everything you've built up in your life.

And then I felt my eyes start to sting again. I trailed slightly behind Doug, blinking rapidly, and wondering why I was having a physical reaction to him, especially when I was still upset over Cam. I'm sure it was some strange psychological protective defence that had to do with Cam walking out on me, but shouldn't I at least have some sort of a mourning period first? Although it was certainly making me feel better to have a handsome younger man flirting with me. I wondered how much younger he was? He had to be close to thirty, but I'd be surprised if he was thirty yet.

'Stop it,' I chided myself.

'Stop what?' Doug asked, turning around to look at me.

Had I said that out loud?

'Sorry, I was just thinking out loud,' I stammered, feeling that blush come back.

'There are the guys.' He pointed over to a row of tents being set up, and we caught up with them in another couple of steps.

'Tommy, Bruce, this is Kate Carpenter. She's the market coordinator.'

I shook hands with both the other young men.

'So who is it that wants to set up?' Doug asked.

'They're just over here,' Bruce said.

'Doug, you guys go deal with this, I'll catch you later,' I said. I smelled Sam's cooking and decided it was time for breakfast now that I had some coffee in me.

Sam looked up when she saw me approaching and smiled.

'I knew as soon as you smelled breakfast cooking I'd be seeing you,' she laughed at me.

'What are you making?' I asked.

'I see you've had your coffee, but you're still a little short on manners. So let me help you out here . . . I'm doing fine, Kate, how is your day going?'

'It's still morning, Sam, don't press your luck with too much conversation,' I warned her.

'OK, OK,' she gave up. 'What do you want to eat?'

'What have you got?' I asked.

'I've got some Danish fresh out of the oven.'

'I'll take two.' I smiled as she put them on a plate for me. 'I don't suppose you have any cappuccino back there?'

'Sorry, Kate. Though I do I have an assistant now,' she said, nodding over her shoulder.

He was a nice-looking man in his early thirties, I guessed,

already in the spirit of the festival, instructing some volunteers in the finer art of using the grill.

'I was going to ask about that,' I said, feeling slightly bad that I had forgotten Sam's set of troubles in favour of mine.

'Yes, I'm sure you were,' she laughed at me. 'But I still don't have any coffee. You're going to have to find someone else to supply your mood altering drugs for you right now.'

'I was just going to walk around the corner to Grounds Zero and get one, would you like to come with me?'

I turned around to see Doug had come up behind me.

'I'd love to.' I smiled at him. But I must have smiled a little too warmly because I noticed Sam's eyebrow rise in a question mark.

'Sam, this is Doug Walsh, he's in charge of security. Doug, this is my friend Sam and she's in charge of keeping me well fed this week.'

They smiled at each other but I didn't trust the look on Sam's face. I picked up the plate of Danish and decided to beat a hasty retreat before she could get any digs in but I was too late.

'Does Cam know you're eating all this junk food?' she asked, a laugh on her lips but a harsher look in her eyes as they bore into me.

'Who's Cam?' Doug asked.

'Come on, Doug, let's get going, I have a ton of stuff to get done this morning,' I said, ignoring them all.

We stopped at Grounds Zero and got our coffee, stopped upstairs at the office to pick up the floats for the markets and then headed back to the security trailer so I could load up the cash boxes and get the volunteers started for the day. I already had several of the young strong volunteers bringing the stock up from the storage rooms in the basement. I was hoping another enterprising volunteer might start setting up the displays and not wait for me to direct them. Graham, my assistant at the theatre, usually handled that kind of stuff for me. I had thought about calling him, but I knew he was happily ensconced in a new romance and I had heard him mutter something about camping and I just didn't have the heart to interrupt his vacation.

I had everything ready to go in under an hour, happily, as

I found it was starting to get hot in the trailer and realized it must be warming up outside. I decided to change into my shorts before I headed out, only this time I did it in the bathroom with the door locked. I rolled up the sleeves on my T-shirt to minimize the tan lines, pulled my hair into a ponytail and put on my baseball cap. Now I felt like I was energized and ready for the festival. I don't think it was the outfit, so much, as the four or five cups of coffee I'd consumed.

I picked up my walkie-talkie and tucked it into my belt like I'd seen Doug do, feeling really silly having to wear it, and called security to let them know I was ready to venture out into the cold cruel world.

'Kate to security,' I said, hoping I was doing it right.

'This is Bruce, Kate, go ahead, over.'

'I'm ready for my code five,' I said, feeling really silly. It brought back the old days of listening to my dad talk on his CB radio. But we weren't supposed to talk about money on an open line and I had to use our secret super agent codes and I suddenly felt like a spy with my new vocabulary.

'I'll be there in a minute, over,' Bruce replied.

'Doug to Bruce, I'm already at the trailer, I'll go with Kate, over,' Doug cut in.

'I copy Doug, Bruce out . . . literally, over and out.'

I felt a blush growing on my cheeks again, along with a little spot of guilt beginning to form in a corner of my mind. I squashed that down quickly, grabbed the cash boxes and put them inside the cloth grocery bags I had and opened the door to find Doug waiting for me. I was partly relieved but still a little disappointed to see that he was suddenly all business, as we headed over toward the first market tent.

The volunteers at tent one were my new favourites, as they had already unpacked all the stock I had arranged to have moved to their tent and had everything set up and ready to go. There was a nice girl named Janice who seemed to have everyone under control and organized and I had to remember to talk to Graham next week and see if he knew anything about her. This was the kind of person I would like to have working for me at the theatre. I answered a few questions they had about pricing and then I dropped off the cash box, having counted the float with both the volunteer cashier and

Doug watching. I chatted with the volunteers for a few minutes, making sure they were ready to go and didn't have any other questions, before we headed off to the other market tents.

'Anyone have any questions?' I asked, standing by the door ready to leave for the next tent.

'Where do we go if we want to have a cigarette?' one of them asked. 'If we're not supposed to be caught smoking while on shift.'

'There's a great festival lounge on Banquet Terrace,' I explained. 'That's where lunch is served too. Even if you don't smoke, make sure you spend some time up there. It's a great place to meet other volunteers and the performers.'

'You mean we could meet Billy Klippert?' one of the young girls asked.

'It's possible. But I have to warn you that affairs that start during a festival usually end around the same time a festival ends,' I joked.

'What about the closing night party?' another one asked.

'I see you guys have your priorities straight here. I'll go find a volunteer package and bring it down. All that stuff is covered there. I was hoping you'd be more interested in questions about selling techniques, things like that.'

They all laughed appropriately at my joke, as I was their supervisor, after all, and I headed out for the next tent.

Tent two was Jeff's tent; he had been made the volunteer team leader and was a former volunteer at my theatre. Jeff had started out as a nice guy. Kind of harmless but a reliable volunteer. He never went out of his way to do anything independently but he always did what you asked of him. Until one day when he asked me out on a date. I gave him a polite no and my little speech about not dating people who worked for me and I thought everything was going to be forgotten. But then he had made me crazy, asking me out for several months until, thankfully, Cam and I started going out officially. That got him off my back and he got a job as an usher at the Jubilee Auditorium shortly after that, leaving me and my theatre. I had let him leave with dignity, as he told me I could always call him if I was ever short staffed and he would be happy to help me out, but after he was gone, Cam and I had raised a beer in celebration, I have to admit. I hadn't been all that fond of him back then, but I decided I would approach him this week with a fresh attitude and hoped he would do the same to me. He already had tent two looking good, everything was set up, priced, counted and ready to go. And the volunteers all looked happy, chatting and getting to know each other. I noticed he even had a tray of coffee and muffins in the back for them, along with a case of bottled water. Maybe things were going to be different this time around.

'Hi Jeff.' I smiled at him, as Doug and I entered the tent. Doug stood back by the entrance, looking very official, while I went up and checked everything out.

'Hi Kate.' Jeff smiled, pulling away from a conversation he was having with another volunteer.

'I've brought your float,' I said, handing him the cash box. 'There's lots of small change, but if you need any more during the day, just call me.'

'No problem.' He smiled. 'Come see what we've done with our displays.'

He put his arm around my shoulder and pulled me over to one of the tables. I felt really uncomfortable, as he kept his arm around me while pointing out various items in his tent.

'It's nice, Jeff,' I said, slipping out from his grasp to straighten a couple of items.

'Great, we've been working really hard to get everything ready. I've got a great team of people here. You know, Kate, I thought maybe we could have a contest with the other tents for best sales. I've found that things like that can be very motivating for volunteers. It really gets them motivated to work with the customers.'

'OK, I'll ask the others and see what they think. Is there anything else you think you'll need?' I asked.

'How about lunch with you today?' he asked.

'Sorry Jeff, I don't really have a lunch break scheduled today.' I felt myself stammering as I tried to come up with an excuse.

'Aw, come on, you have to eat sometime. They make great hotdogs just down the block from here.'

'Jeff, I just don't think it's a good idea.' I smiled weakly at him. 'Why don't we just drop the subject for now, OK? Maybe we'll get some time to have a coffee later in the week?'

'I'll drop it for now, but I'm not letting you off the hook that easily,' he said, smiling at me. 'Besides, I want to hear all about the murder in the theatre. I'm sorry I missed all the excitement.'

'Sure,' I lied to him, having no intention of spending a minute more with him than I had to.

'So, are you going to the concert tomorrow night? Maybe I could go with you to that?' he tried again.

'I think the lady said no already,' Doug said, stepping forward and trying to be helpful.

'Doug, hold this,' I said, handing him the last remaining cash box. 'Jeff, I'd like to see you outside for a minute.'

I stormed out of the tent and turned on Jeff as soon as we were out of earshot of the other volunteers.

'What is with you?' I asked him. 'We went through this at the theatre. I have explained to you that I am dating someone else and I am not interested in seeing you.'

'I just thought a simple lunch . . . I mean I haven't seen you for ages . . .'

'Jeff, I am your supervisor and I am not interested in seeing you socially. Now we can work together and stay off this subject or we can't work together at all. It's your choice.'

'I'm sorry, I didn't know this was so upsetting for you,' he said. 'I was only trying to be friendly. I'm really sorry and I promise I won't mention it again.'

'Thank you. Now, you better get ready to open up the market,' I said. 'I've got to get to the other tents, OK?'

'OK. I'll see you later,' he said, quickly heading back inside.

'Doug?' I called.

'Yes, ma'am?' he responded quickly, jogging to catch up with me as I headed for the next tent.

'Boy, you're suddenly in a hurry,' he commented.

'I'm mad,' I commented, trying to cool down.

'I know, that guy was a bit of a jerk.'

'I'm over that. It's you I'm mad at now.'

'Me?' he asked.

I stopped and turned on him, barely giving him time to stop and avoid crashing into me.

'Look, I appreciate what you were trying to do in there.'

'What do you mean?'

'You were trying to rescue me from Jeff. But please, don't ever undermine me in front of one of my staff again.'

I started walking again and he had to race to catch up once again.

'I'm sorry. I didn't realize . . .' he tried.

'If I need help I'll ask for it. I can take care of myself.'

'I'm sorry. I'll wait for you to ask from now on,' he promised.

'Thank you.'

We dropped the cash box off at the last market tent. In tent three they weren't very organized and didn't have much set up yet. I didn't know any of these volunteers from my time at the Plex, so I quickly introduced myself, picked a tent leader out of the bunch and told them what we were going to be up against, long hot days and huge crowds. Then I gave them some directions for stocking and set-up to get them started. Once I was sure they were comfortable with what they were doing, I promised I'd be back and then Doug and I headed back for the security trailer. I no longer had cash on me but Doug was still following closely at my heels. I knew there was something he wanted but I wasn't in the mood to ask. He wasn't as reticent as I was, though.

'So are you going to be mad at me for long?' he asked, noticing I was not going to talk to him.

'No,' I promised, trying to put a bit of a smile back into my voice. 'Another coffee and a cigarette and I should be over it.'

'Thank God. I like the happy you much better than I like the angry you.'

'You and most of my friends,' I said, opening the door to the trailer and climbing in.

'So what was that about a murder?' Doug asked.

'Do you live in Calgary?' I asked him.

'Yeah.'

'Do you remember when they found the dead body in the washroom at a theatre last fall?'

'Uh huh?'

'That was my theatre. I kind of helped the police find out who did it.'

43

'Didn't you help them find the killer while being dropped off a forty-foot catwalk or something?'

'Yeah, something like that.'

'That would mean you were the one who got shot by that crazy French woman too, right?'

'Boy, those newspapers just have to print everything, don't they?'

'Well, is it true?' he asked.

'Yes, it's true,' I admitted, a little sick of these stories after already telling them several hundred times. 'You want a coffee?'

'No, I'm going to head back out and see how everything's going. I do work here, you know, not just entertain wayward theatre people,' he said.

'Funny – don't let the door hit you on your way out.'

'You'll be OK?' he asked.

'I'll be fine.'

'Well, just whistle if you need anything. You do know how to whistle, don't you?'

'Yes, just put your lips together and blow. You like old movies too?' I asked.

'We can talk about that on our next cash run. Give you something to look forward to.' He smiled as he headed off.

I hated it when someone else got the last word.

My plan for an easy-going day had gone downhill quickly. I went back to tent three and it took about an hour to get everything set up and the volunteers confident enough to run it. We had about ten thousand people turn out for the opening ceremony and free cake that came along with it. At least another fifteen thousand came down to join them before the afternoon was over. There were marching bands, dignitaries, and people from all walks of life. The markets had been insanely busy, several volunteers had forgotten all about their shifts, and the ones that did show up worked like crazy with me, for what I hoped would turn out to be a record breaking sales day. The temperature in the market tents went up to well past thirty degrees Celsius and I thanked the heavens above that the festival had a water sponsor. We had one volunteer doing nothing but running cases of bottled water to all the tents and the poor volunteers baking away inside of them. I especially pitied poor Sam with her grills and ovens. I had made what seemed like thousands of runs. Graham would have been inspired to see me working this hard, as he always thought he did all the work at the theatre and was pretty sure I didn't remember how to work hard. I had been bringing up more stock, doing deposits when the cash registers got too full, and carting more rolls of change from the bank than I cared to see in one lifetime.

The festival site closed at six o'clock, with no evening activities planned for the first night, but the crowds didn't start to clear until close to seven, as a lot of people stayed and had picnics, being entertained by the street buskers that slowly moved in as the festival closed down. I was supposed to get the tents closed at four o'clock every day, but between the late crowds and the inexperienced staff, myself included, I didn't actually get the markets cleaned up and closed until well after eight o'clock. As predicted, tent three was a bit of a disaster, but Janice in the first tent had stayed all day and everything ran really well. Jeff's tent was organized and his volunteers were all happy, but I had problems getting his cash-out to balance, and I finally gave up, locking it away for the night and deciding I'd tackle it with fresh eyes tomorrow morning.

I made my way around the Plaza, double checking the three market tents, making sure nothing had been overlooked and no street people had managed to sneak in and find a covered place to spend the night. By the time I had made my rounds, the volunteers were gone and there were only a few strag-glers left on the Plaza, lying on the grass trying to enjoy the evening breeze. A lone busker remained, sitting in the far off corner of the Plaza, playing a guitar and singing Bob Dylan songs.

It was close to nine when I finally made my way back to the security trailer and sat on a lawn chair the boys had set up, at least three hours later than I had planned to be sitting here. The sun was becoming a distant memory in the sky as it made its final appearance behind the mountains in the west and the sky began to turn pink. I pulled my baseball cap down over my eyes to block out the last rays of the setting sun. My feet were so sore they felt like they were going to fall off, my arms were sunburned and I was sweaty and sticky from the long hot day. I swore if I had to make change for one more dollar or fold one more T-shirt I would break down in tears. I heard a lawn chair scrape the concrete as it was set up beside me, but I didn't have the energy to open my eyes and see who was there. I felt something cold settle on my leg and that did motivate me to look up and see Doug holding out a can of beer for me.

'You are a life saver.' I smiled at him as I took the beer and popped the tab, even that small bit of effort being almost beyond me right now.

'So, you still think you're going to spend the week working on that tan?' he asked.

'I stand corrected. I don't think I've walked this many miles in one day – ever.'

'Are your feet sore?' he asked.

'No, they were sore a couple of hours ago. Now they're just numb.'

'A hot bath will do you wonders,' he said.

'I'm sunburned,' I whined, showing him my arms. 'I'm not getting anywhere near a hot bath.'

'You didn't use that sunscreen?' he asked. 'I thought you were all prepared, just like a Girl Scout.'

'Things didn't exactly go as planned and I didn't have time to put any on,' I sighed, taking another long drink of my beer and finding it was empty already.

'You need another?' Doug asked.

'Yes please.'

He got up and went into the trailer but was back in no time with another couple of beers.

'There you go,' he said as he handed one to me.

'Thanks.' I smiled, taking another drink. I already felt a little buzz and realized that I hadn't eaten since breakfast. Beer was probably not the best choice to try to quench my thirst right now. But getting drunk didn't sound too bad either. 'I'll stop at a liquor store tomorrow and refill your fridge for you.'

'No need, Tommy has already gone to the Cecil Hotel, I think the off-sales counter there is still open. You can get it next time.'

'Doesn't he ever run out of energy?' I asked.

'He's twenty, Kate, surely you remember what twenty was like?'

'I have a nineteen-year-old assistant at the theatre. I know exactly what they're like. Most of the time it exhausts me just to watch him.'

'Well don't worry about Tommy. It was his idea to go.'

'Hey Kate, I thought you'd be home by now,' a voice called out to me from the other side of the trailer.

I looked up and saw Sam striding over to me.

'I did too. But I thought a lot of things this morning that just have not come to be.'

'Well, I'm just heading out. Are you going home?' she asked.

'Thought I'd have a beer with the boys first.' I smiled at her.

'I can drive you,' she offered.

'Bruce to Doug, over,' the radio interrupted us.

'Go for Bruce, over,' he answered.

'Can you meet me at the Concert Hall entrance, over?'

'I'm on my way, out,' Doug said, as he stood up. 'You going to be here for a bit, Kate, or should I lock up the trailer?'

'I'll be here,' I decided, wondering what Sam was thinking and afraid I was about to find out.

'All right, I'll be back as quick as I can.'

Doug walked off across the Plaza and Sam took his seat.

'It's amazing how you always get along so well with the guys,' she said. 'At the theatre, you're always hanging out with the technicians, and here it's the security guards.'

'They're nice guys,' I said.

'So, did you want a ride home or is Cam coming to get you?'

'I told you, he's in Saskatchewan visiting his family.'

'Yeah, but I just assumed you were lying to me,' Sam said. Good point.

'I'll take a cab later,' I said.

'Kate, what's going on? I know Cam was pissed off about this festival thing, but did you have some sort of major blow-out?' she asked.

'What makes you think that?'

47

'Well, to start with, there's the fact that you two are normally inseparable, I haven't seen him once today. And then you haven't even mentioned him once today. And let's not forget Mr Good-Looking Security Guy. My final clue is that you are avoiding a direct answer to every question I ask you.'

'What do you mean, Mr Good-Looking Security Guy?'

'OK, that was catty,' Sam admitted. 'But since you brought it up, I have seen you two together a lot today. And he seems to be happy about that.'

'OK, Sam, you win.' I decided to tell her, rather than playing this game all week long. 'Cam and I had a fight and it appears we've broken up. But I don't want to talk about it right now. Please?'

'Kate, I'm your friend and I have this need to help you with things. But how can I help if you won't talk about it?' Her voice grew soft as her suspicions were confirmed.

'I don't need help. I need to forget about it for now. I've got to get through the festival this week and I'm not going to do that by being all weepy and whiny now, am I?'

'I don't think diving into another relationship is exactly the answer either,' Sam said.

'I'm not diving into another relationship. It's harmless flirting and it's making me feel better. Wouldn't it make you feel good to have a handsome young man flirting with you?' I asked her.

'Yes, it would. But I haven't just broken up with my husband nor do I find myself in an emotionally vulnerable position.'

'And neither am I,' I said angrily. 'I'm just fine with all this. It's actually a relief. No more fighting, no more stress, no more trying to balance a relationship with everything else in my life. This is for the best, Sam, and that's all I want to say about it for tonight.'

'Kate . . .'

'I swear, next Monday, after we've finished here, you can come over and do whatever it is girlfriends do for each other after a break-up.'

'I think it's Ben and Jerry's ice cream and possibly some wine.'

'OK, Monday I'm all yours. Hell, I have three weeks off, you can go at me for several days if you want.'

'All right, all right, don't get smart. I know when to back off. Are you sure I can't give you a ride home though?' she asked. 'I don't want you wandering the streets. It's not safe.'

'No, I'm going to finish my beer first,' I said. 'And I'm not going to do anything foolish, OK?'

'Promise me?' she asked.

'I promise you.' I smiled, with my fingers crossed behind my back. I know it was childish but it made me feel better.

'OK. Call me if you need anything,' she said, pulling her keys from her pocket.

'I will,' I promised and watched her walk down the Plaza and turn the corner to the parking lot.

Doug returned and sat back down beside me just as Sam rounded the corner.

'That looked like a pretty heavy conversation,' he commented as he picked up his beer. 'Not that I was listening in or anything.'

'It's OK. You know how friends are, they always think they know what's best for you and they get great pleasure in spending hours telling you what that might be.'

'And what do your friends think is best for you, Kate Carpenter?' he asked.

'I don't care what they think. I think another beer would be best,' I said, holding up my empty can. 'I'll get it this time. Do you want another one?'

'You're not driving anywhere tonight are you?' he asked.

'No officer, I'll be taking a taxi home tonight. May I proceed?'

'You may, but only if you come back with two beers.'

'And you're not on duty tonight, are you?'

'No ma'am, my shift ended at 2030 hours this evening and I have assigned one of the young lads to take my night shift. I am not on duty again until 0800 hours.'

'Ten-four good buddy.' I saluted, standing back up on my aching feet. I hobbled into the trailer and grabbed two beers from the fridge. I managed to make it back to my lawn chair and groaned as I sat back down and handed him his beer.

'I grabbed a newspaper on the way back,' Doug said, pulling off the first section of today's paper.

49

'Anything good happen today?'

'They found another one.'

'Another what?' I asked.

'Another dead girl.'

'Oh God. Is it him?'

'She was found in Scarborough, near the tennis courts. Her clothes were put on backwards, she was missing her right kidney. And she had a Yahtzee score card in her pants pocket.'

'The Bishop?' I confirmed.

'They don't come right out and say it here, but who else could it be?'

The Bishop had gotten his name when his first victim was found, clinging to a bishop chess piece. Since then, three other bodies had been found, all had clothes rearranged strangely, various parts of their body missing and some sort of game piece with them, a Monopoly boot, a pair of dice, a Trivial Pursuit game card. This would be the fourth. The city was starting to get scared. And not just women. Two of the Bishop's victims had been men. Street people were flocking to shelters at night, despite the warm weather, parents were enforcing tight curfews, and taxis were doing a great business as everyone was afraid to walk anywhere after dark.

'You know, this sort of thing isn't supposed to happen in Calgary. Serial killers are supposed to live in the really big cities and leave us alone.'

'Calgary's getting up there, though.'

'Yeah, but maybe we could move into the big leagues in other ways, with a hugely successful symphony, head offices flocking to move here – not getting our first serial killer.'

'Well, I hope you're being careful at night.'

'I have been getting lots of rides,' I promised him. 'But I miss walking. I've lived here long enough that I remember when mom and dad didn't lock the front door at night.'

'You know those days are gone, right?'

'Yeah, I discovered that when my boyfriend . . . I mean my ex-boyfriend put two extra locks on my apartment door.' I felt my throat catch at saying 'ex' out loud.

'Because this Bishop guy is serious stuff.'

'And I am very motivated to keep all my internal organs,'

I laughed. 'What is that about anyway? What do these guys do with that stuff?'

'Do you really want to know?' he asked.

'Oh, I forgot who I was talking to. And no, I don't really want to know, I was making polite conversation.'

'I have a theory though.'

'What's that?' I asked.

'I think this Bishop guy is doing a lot of things just to keep the police looking in all the wrong directions.'

'Really?'

'Yeah, it's just a personal theory though. But he's not taking things in the order I would have taken them.'

'There's an expected order for evisceration?' I asked. 'And you've thought about it?'

'Well, there is a type of logic involved. Even insane people seem to have certain patterns that you can track and predict. And the way the clothing is always rearranged; it doesn't seem to have to do with anything else either. Like what organ is missing or what game clue is left.'

'And the game pieces?' I asked.

'Well, I think that might be his one true clue. I think he's trying to tell the police that he's playing games with them. And he's winning.'

'Have you told the police about this?'

'No. Kate, there are always lots of details that the police leave out of the news conferences. I'm sure they're way ahead of me on this. I'm only making guesses from what I've seen in the newspapers and on the news.'

'Well I think you're being falsely modest,' I told him. I kicked off my sandals and wriggled my toes, trying to get some blood flowing back into my feet. 'I'm getting too old for these long days,' I said, changing the subject. Serial killers were not what I wanted to talk about before I headed home to my empty apartment. I sank deeply into the chair and pulled my baseball cap back down over my eyes.

'Give me your feet,' he said, sliding his lawn chair around so he faced me.

'Why?' I asked, not really trusting him.

'Because I know how to make them feel better.'

'I don't know if I know you well enough,' I protested.

He leaned over and picked my feet up off the ground, setting them on his knees, and then started massaging them. I thought I had died and gone to heaven. He had strong hands and he was working his way up my foot, moving all the joints, digging deeply into the aching muscles, not missing a single spot, just like Cam used to. And then I felt a twinge of guilt and I pulled my feet down and slipped them back into my sandals.

'Thank you,' I said, smiling weakly.

'Sorry, did I hurt you?'

'Oh, no. It's just that it's getting late and I better get going,' I said, finishing my beer and picking up the empties.

'Are you OK to get home?' he asked, seeming to ignore my sudden change of mood.

'Oh sure, I just live at the other end of downtown. I'll just hop on a C-train or take a cab and be home in five minutes.' I smiled. 'Are you OK here? Do you need me to help you into the trailer or anything?'

'I've been living here for the last three days, I think I can find my way. And I've got everything I need right here to get me through the night. Well, almost everything.'

I ignored him and continued tidying our mess.

'All right, give me your empties and I'll take them back inside for you,' I said, waiting for him to pass his last empty can to me.

He gave me the empty cans and I rinsed them out in the sink in the trailer and then packed them up in a bag. At least it wouldn't stink like stale beer in here tomorrow morning. I didn't think I could handle that while I was getting my floats ready. I packed all my stuff back up into the box that had been waiting for me and set it on a corner of the banquette. I did a final check and was happy that everything was clean, tidy and in its place. I turned around and stepped out the door just as Doug was coming in. He stood on the first step and I was on the second, nose to nose with him.

'Well, I guess that's my stuff taken care of then, I'll see you tomorrow.'

'Maybe tomorrow I can buy you a real drink in a real bar, if you're not too tired?' he asked, finally stepping back out of the trailer and helping me down.

'That's if either of us can still walk by the end of the day,' I laughed.

'No, I really mean it,' he said, waiting for an answer. 'I'm asking you out.'

'Oh. Well, then, I guess that would be all right.' I smiled at him, feeling my knees grow weak at the thought of it.

'Great.' He smiled, still holding on to my hand.

'Goodnight, then,' I said and impulsively kissed him lightly on the cheek before I pulled out of his grasp and ran down the Plaza and around the corner. I found a cab at the stage door. Impulsively, I had him stop at the grocery store on the way home. I filled my cart with brownie mixes, canned icing, chocolate chips, cookie mix and ice cream. I looked up as I put the second quart of ice cream in my cart and thought I noticed a face I recognized. I looked down at my cart and quickly wondered how I was going to explain this weird inventory, but when I looked up again the face was gone and I realized I must have been mistaken. I hurried to the check-out and guiltily unloaded everything in front of the cashier, a sixteen-year-old lad trying to look more experienced than he was.

'Oh, doing some baking tonight?' he asked.

This boy has never been dumped by a girl, I thought, but just smiled weakly and nodded to him, handing him my cash and hurrying out to find another cab. I waited a nerve-wracking fifteen minutes before one finally showed up and drove me the four blocks back to the loft. I was just as scared of walking at night as everyone else in the city.

As I put the key in the door, I hoped beyond hope that the apartment wouldn't be empty. But as I opened the door to darkness and silence, I knew I was still alone. I dropped my grocery bag on the kitchen counter and looked at the contents for a few moments. I decided the brownies and cookies were just too much trouble. I put the ice cream in the freezer and popped the top on the canned icing, grabbing a spoon and moving to the couch. I sat in the dark living room for a few minutes eating spoonfuls of icing until I started to feel ill. I actually picked up the phone to call Sam at one point and then hung it up before I worked up the courage to dial. I even toyed with the idea of heading back down to the Plaza and seeing just how interested Doug was in getting to know me better. But that wasn't fair to him and it probably wasn't really an appropriate way for me to handle things either, so instead, I headed upstairs and undressed, wrapping Cam's robe around me. I set the icing on the bedside table and lay down on the bed, but after tossing and turning for an hour, I realized I couldn't sleep here alone, at least not tonight. The bed just suddenly seemed way too big for just one person. I took my pillow and headed down for the couch, turned the TV on and fell asleep much later, after I finally wore myself out crying.

The streets were deserted and it wasn't safe for him to be out here, so noticeable on the empty street. But that made it more exciting. A car drove by and he pulled up the collar of his leather jacket to avoid being seen. He wandered around the building twice, checking out exits and entrances, fire escapes, and the parkade access. He had to know where everything was, how to get in and out quickly without being noticed, how to get to her. It was all part of the game and, if nothing else, he was excellent at playing games.

Tuesday

I had awoken early from my restless night. My eyes were puffy and I had a great red slash across my face from a night of crying. I gathered my empties from the apartment and threw them in the garbage. One pint of ice cream and one can of chocolate icing – it wasn't such a bad night after all. I hid the other junk food in the cupboard and put the coffee on. I had a quick shower and then soaked a face cloth in some ice water and held it over my eyes while I had my first cup of coffee. It took me about a half an hour to finish getting ready and get enough coffee in me to face the day. I looked better outwardly but I sure didn't feel much better inside. Feeling safe in the daylight, I chose a good, sturdy pair of shoes and walked down to the Plex. I headed for the catering tent, but didn't see Sam anywhere. I turned to leave but suddenly there was a hand on my shoulder.

'Kate?'

I turned to see who it was, not recognizing the voice.

'I'm sorry, do I know you?'

'You are Kate, right?' he asked again.

'Yes. And you are . . .?'

'I'm Sam's assistant.'

'Do we know each other?' I asked again.

'Sam told me about you,' he laughed. 'She likes to talk while she works.'

'Well I hope she had good things to say about me,' I joked, feeling a little uncomfortable. 'Do you know where Sam is?'

'She's up at the festival office. She shouldn't be much longer.'

'OK, well tell her I came by,' I said, turning to leave again. But that hand was back on my shoulder, stopping me again.

'Wait.'

'What?'

'Don't you want something to eat?' he asked. 'I couldn't help but notice you like chocolate. Sam's always talking about bringing you chocolate goodies. Well, I'm a pretty decent pastry chef and chocolate is my specialty, so why don't you let me put a plate together for you?'

'No, no, I'm fine. I'll see Sam later.'

'Come on, you can be the judge on whether I can cook as well as she can or not.'

'I've got some stuff I have to do right now.' I tried to get away again.

'Really, it's my pleasure to do it,' he insisted.

'No,' I said, a little more firmly than I had meant to. I needed to have a cigarette and drink my coffee and this guy was getting on my nerves. 'I'll get something later. But thank you very much.'

He smiled a funny smile and I was worried that he was going to continue to argue with me. I didn't need to have both him and Jeff annoying me this week. But this time he let me go and I wandered across the grass. I sat on the edge of the reflecting pool and despite the early hour and the fact that the water was freezing, I had my feet in the pool. They were still sore from last night and the cool water felt so good. Hopefully it would help until the Advil kicked in. I had a steaming cappuccino sitting beside me and I was searching my pockets for a light, regardless of the fact that I kept insisting I was going to quit smoking.

'I thought you were really going to try to quit this time?' a voice beside me asked.

I looked up and saw Sam standing over me with a cappuccino in one hand and a paper bag in the other.

'Oh look, it's my conscience,' I said sarcastically.

'Nope, not today,' she said as she sat down beside me. 'If you're not in the mood to talk, I know better than to try to force anything out of you. I brought food instead.'

'So I can't smoke but I can overdose on sweets?' I asked.

'At least you won't die of lung cancer.'

'No, I'll just die fat and alone.'

'I don't think you'll have to worry about the alone part,' Sam laughed and then quickly tried to cover herself. 'And that wasn't any sort of comment on anything. I swear.'

'You sure?' I asked, pretending to be angry.

'Yes, my resolution for the day is to be less of a nag.'

'It's OK, I'm working on being a little less sensitive today.' I smiled, letting her off the hook. 'But you don't happen to have a match do you?'

'Sorry. So are you doing OK, Kate?' Sam asked.

'I'm sort of OK. I think I'm in shock.'

'You want to tell me what happened?'

'Nope. Not right now.'

But then she gave me that look, the one that all mothers seemed to possess. It must be a hormonal thing, something you developed after successfully pushing that baby out when the big hormone surge took over your body to make you forget all that pain you had just suffered, and I caved in.

'It was just a stupid fight, Sam. He wanted to go away this week and I wanted to work the festival and then go away. And then we both said some stupid things and he packed his bag and left.'

'He walked out on you?' she asked, astounded.

'Yes.'

'I can't believe Cam would do that.'

'Well, it was sort of about the same time I told him to leave,' I admitted. 'Besides, I think if I had to live with me for the last couple of months, I would have left too.'

'Oh, Kate,' she said, putting her arm around my shoulder.

'Please don't do that,' I said, shrugging her off.

'What?'

'I am trying really hard to hold myself together right now.'

'I understand,' she sighed, letting me go and sipping her coffee.

'It's for the best. You know that Cam and I were not very good at the whole living-together arrangement. We both wanted totally different things and we couldn't seem to find middle ground.'

'Welcome to marriage,' Sam laughed. 'Or even life, for that matter.'

'Don't tell me that, I still have this wonderful romantic idea of marriage.'

'That could be half your problem.'

'No, I just think I was meant to be single,' I said. 'And I'm going to enjoy it.'

'Just don't do anything you may regret,' she warned me. 'You know you can't undo a thing once you've done it.'

'No regrets, I promise.'

Sam checked her watch.

'I better get going,'

'You have an assistant who is here on time today. You can sit and visit with me.'

'How do you know that?' she asked.

'Because when I got here I was looking for you. He was very solicitous and tried to set me up with breakfast. He said he had some great chocolate stuff for me.'

'Well, at least we should have a better start to the day then,' Sam said.

'And he said you told him all sorts of things about me.'

'I told him that if you came by, you got your food comped. That's all I told him.'

'Really?'

'Kate, I spent most of the day trying to keep him in the tent and feed those thousands of people. Don't take it personally, my dear, but I didn't exactly have hours of free time to talk about you.'

'Well, I think I'm insulted,' I laughed at her. 'But since you have that assistant, can't you stay and chat for just a few minutes?'

'I do have an assistant, but kitchens are not like festival markets. Things burn in kitchens.'

'Delegate, Sam, that's the key to good management.'

'You delegate, I'm already busy. I've got to make six dozen more of these things for the morning rush,' she said, handing me the paper bag she had been carrying.

'More Danish?' I asked as I opened the bag.

'Nope, double fudge muffins.' She smiled.

'Coffee and chocolate, it would be a perfect morning if I could only find a match.'

'I'll see you later, Kate.' She waved as she trotted off across the Plaza.

I opened the paper bag and pulled out a muffin, setting my cigarette aside in favour of chocolate. I took a big bite, followed

58

by a sip of coffee and thanked the heavens that Sam was my best friend.

'I think I can arrange for a light if you're willing to share that muffin.'

I turned and saw Doug standing beside me.

'You're lucky she gave me two muffins. I'm not very good at sharing,' I said, patting the concrete beside me.

He joined me, took the muffin I offered him and pulled his lighter out from his pocket.

'See, we make a great team,' he said. 'You've got the food connections and I'm like the Boy Scout, always prepared.'

'Oh, now I see, you just like me for my Danish and muffins?'

'I like you for Sam's Danish and muffins. I just don't think she likes me enough to give them to me directly. Otherwise I'd be lighting her fire for her,' he joked.

'Oh, she's OK. She's just a little overprotective of me.'

'Either way,' he said, taking a big bite of muffin. 'This is delicious. Your friend is a great cook.'

'Yes, she definitely comes in handy sometimes.'

'We don't usually get fed this well at festivals. It is a nice change.'

'Do you do this all summer?' I asked. 'Going from festival to festival?'

'Pretty much.'

'Just the three of you?'

'Well, I have a bunch of guys I can call in, depending on the size of the job or if we have trouble.'

'And you work days and nights?'

'Well, most festivals only last for five days at the most. It's not as bad as it sounds. We each patrol for three hours a night and sleep the rest of it,' he said. 'Besides, it's like I said, they're all in their twenties. And you remember how you could go for days and days when you were young.'

'We're hardly old,' I laughed.

'OK, younger then.'

'I'll accept that.'

I finished my cigarette and he finished his muffin in peaceful silence, watching as the Plaza slowly came to life. I wished this moment right here and right now would last forever. But they never do.

'Well, I suppose we should get to work,' he finally said.

'Sure. Feel like running upstairs with me and picking up the floats?'

'I'm at your disposal,' he said, standing up and holding out his hand to help me up.

I accepted his hand, pulled myself up and slipped back into my shoes. We hurried upstairs, got the money out of the safe, and Doug deposited me safely back in the trailer, where I poured myself another coffee and got down to work.

It was the second day and the work became repetitive, which was good. Everyone started to realize what was going to happen, what was expected of them, and most of them had all their questions answered the day before. After I dropped the floats off and got the tents opened for business, I brought up extra stock from the basement and then decided to spend some time with my volunteers. I liked to bond and make them feel like part of a team. I started off in tent one, selling T-shirts, puppets and face paints. They didn't really need me there, as several of the volunteers were stepping up and taking charge here. Janice wasn't scheduled until later, but she had trained these volunteers well and we weren't going to suffer for her lack of attendance this morning. So I stayed and worked, mostly to bond with the volunteers. The temperatures soared but we found we could get a bit of air blowing through if we opened the tent flap in the back and got a cross-breeze blowing through. Business picked up at lunch hour, as I moved to tent three. They definitely needed me more here, but they were slowly getting the hang of things. And it wasn't that I was avoiding Jeff's tent so much as I knew it was going to be more time consuming for me to visit there, so I decided to get my duty at tents one and three done first. Tent three was close to the live music stage and there was a Rolling Stones cover band performing. We sang along to all the oldies but goodies while people meandered through the tent. Unfortunately, I was one of the few this morning who actually knew all the words to most of the songs, but then I was surrounded by high school and university students at my theatre job too, just like here, so I was used to feeling like the oldest person in the room.

I left tent three just after one o'clock and took a bottle of

60

water out to the grass to cool down before I headed to tent two. The clown who had been so obnoxious at the trailer yesterday was sitting peacefully on the grass, blowing up balloons and folding them into flowers for the kids who had gathered around him. I watched, fascinated by how good he was with the kids, even the ones who seemed scared of him at first. Now, at this point some might say I was avoiding tent two and I wouldn't argue. But then I suddenly became amazed by the progress of a woman on stilts, leading a parade around the edge of the Plaza. All of this to the tune of *Jumping Jack Flash* blasting over the sound system. It all seemed a little surreal. I finished my water, realized there was nothing left to distract me, took a deep breath and headed for tent two.

Jeff had seen me coming from halfway across the Plaza. I know because he smiled and waved. But he was busy with customers at the cash register so he couldn't rush out to greet me. I made my way into the tent and helped the group that was unpacking yet another carton of T-shirts for the sales table.

'So, how's it going in here?' I asked.

'It's a little warm,' one volunteer offered.

'And busy.'

'Busy is good. Is this your second box of T-shirts today?' I asked.

'It sure is,' Jeff said, having found someone to cover the cash register for him. He let his arm drape around my waist and squeezed me in greeting. 'Good you could finally come and join us.'

'Well, there's only so much of me to go around,' I joked, pulling away and grabbing another pile of T-shirts that suddenly looked like they needed refolding.

'So, how are we doing against the other tents?' he asked, moving around to help me.

'Well, we won't be able to tell until I cash out tonight. But I'll let you know first thing in the morning,' I promised. 'So it's pretty hot in here, huh?'

'A little but we're managing.'

I took one last shot at getting away from him and headed for the back of the tent. 'The guys at tent one figured out that if you open this flap up back here you can get a bit of a breeze blowing through the tent.'

'That's a good idea,' he said, following me.

I started to untie some of the flaps, while Jeff leaned over me reaching for the top ones. I was never going to be rid of him this week. As much as I wanted to slap his face as he leaned over me, his warm breath blowing across the top of my forehead, I knew I couldn't do that here in front of everyone. I took another deep breath, finished the tent flaps and ducked out from under him.

'There, that should help.' I smiled at all of them.

'Kate?'

I looked up and saw Doug at the front of the tent.

'Tent one asked me to come and find you. They've got too much cash and they'd like you to take some of it off their hands, if you have a few minutes.'

Thank God, I thought. 'Of course I have time. You guys are doing just fine here without me. I'll be back on my normal rounds in a couple of hours,' I told them, leaving the tent quickly and racing across the Plaza to keep up with Doug.

'Everything OK?' he asked.

'Of course it is,' I assured him. 'Your timing is impeccable, however.'

'Should I ask to what you're referring?'

'It's probably one of those things that you really don't need to know.'

'You sure?' he asked.

'You'll sleep better,' I assured him.

I picked up cash from the tent and as we were walking up to the festival office, I was surprised to see my favourite clown sitting on the steps at the main entrance of the Plex, smoking a cigarette.

'Hey, there,' I said, stopping in front of him. 'Long day?'

'Fucking long day filled with fucking spoiled little brats,' he laughed, taking a drag of his cigarette.

'Um, I'm not sure if you've read all the rules regarding how we're supposed to behave while we're in costume on the site,' I began.

'Are you going to bust my balls for smoking a cigarette while I'm dressed up like a clown?' he asked. 'Because if you are . . .'

'Actually, I was going to add that you probably shouldn't

say things liking fucking spoiled brats or busting your balls, as well, if you want to get really specific.'

'There's no kids within earshot,' he said. 'Besides, I'm a clown, not the Pope.'

'Look, there is a festival lounge on Banquet Terrace,' Doug said. 'I think it's important that since you're in such an obvious costume that you should probably try and watch your behaviour while you're on the site, don't you?'

He stood up, tossed his half-smoked cigarette on the ground, and stamped it out with his ridiculously over-sized clown shoes. I tried really hard not to laugh at that visual, because I agreed with what Doug had said. But I couldn't stifle a giggle as the pouting clown stomped away down the Plaza. Doug and I turned and continue up to the festival office.

'Should we report him?' he asked.

'I always like to think that we should give people a second chance,' I said. 'Though I'm not always great at living up to that motto.'

'OK, but I'm going to keep an eye on that clown.'

And I giggled again, despite the dirty look he was giving me.

The afternoon got busier and busier; as we approached evening my time passed in a blur of cash pick-ups, inventory runs and successful avoidance of Jeff. I was surprised when suddenly it was after six and I realized we were late closing up again. But you couldn't just turn away paying customers now, could you? As was becoming my usual pattern, I closed up tents one and three first – leaving two for the last. When I made my way over there, the flaps were closed, so I was hoping this would be quick and I could get out of there without any sort of confrontation.

'Have you even asked her yet?' I heard an angry voice come from inside the tent.

'No.'

'What are you waiting for?'

'These things take time. I'm working on it.'

I wasn't sure what was going on, both voices sounded like Jeff, the only difference being that one was angry and one quite timid in the face of that anger. Was he talking with himself now? I decided that if he were actually crazy, that

63

would be as good an excuse as any to cancel the rest of his shifts this week. I came as close to the tent flap as I dared without being discovered and put my ear to the canvas.

'Well I'm tired of waiting,' the angry voice said.

'Another day or two at most, I promise. It'll give you more time to come up with a good idea.'

'I already have plenty of good ideas. Aren't you anxious for this to happen?' The angry voice had now become almost seductive. 'This was your idea. I would think you could hardly wait to be alone in a room with her.'

'Yes. I can hardly wait. It's all I've been thinking about. You of all people should know that.'

Enough of this, I thought, I wanted to know who Jeff was talking to. I pushed through the tent flap, my eyes taking a moment to adjust to the dimness of the light inside.

'Jeff?' I asked, startled to see him standing alone.

'Hi Kate.' He smiled, blinking at the bright light I had let in.

'Who's in here with you?' I asked. 'We're supposed to be closed.'

'No one,' he laughed nervously. 'I must have been talking to myself. You know how it is after a long day.'

'It sounded like a pretty heated argument to have with yourself,' I joked.

'You must have heard me singing or something. After hearing the Rolling Stones all day I was probably channelling a little Mick Jagger or something.'

I noticed the tent flaps in the back of the tent blowing in the breeze but I decided to drop the subject, as I wasn't getting anywhere this way.

'Anything to report for the day? Any problems?' I asked.

'No, it was smooth sailing around here.'

'OK, well don't forget to secure the flap in the back there before you leave. And I'll see you tomorrow.'

I hurried from the tent before he could try and ask me out for a coffee or anything else, and bumped into a clown in my haste. Just what I needed.

'Sorry,' I said.

'No, I'm sorry,' he said.

'It was my fault. I wasn't watching where I was going.'

'No, I was apologizing for scaring you the other day,' the clown said. 'I didn't think you'd be scared of clowns but you looked a little frightened when you first saw me.'

'Oh, that. Already forgotten,' I told him, surprised at his change in attitude. 'Frankly, it was today I was a little more worried about.'

'Oh, that's not going to happen again. I know how important the kids are to the festival.'

'Good, I'm really glad to hear that.'

He smiled back at me, the red paint on his face splitting into a huge gash on his face.

'Thanks for that, Ms Carpenter. It's my first time at this festival and I don't want to make a bad impression.'

'No worries.' I smiled again, and then turned for the trailer.

When I got to the trailer, I saw he was still watching me as I climbed up the steps. I ignored the bad feeling I was suddenly getting, realizing that Jeff was making me downright paranoid. I shook it off and turned to the job at hand. I poured a coffee and sat at the table, money spread out in front of me, trying to make the numbers add up. I heard the door to the trailer open and I looked up from the adding machine tape I was studying. Shit, I forgot to lock the door and it was Doug. He was going to yell at me.

'Kate, you know you're supposed to lock the door when you're in here doing the bank deposit,' were the first words out of his mouth.

'I know,' I agreed, no point making excuses.

He shut the door and locked it behind him before crossing over to the table where I sat.

'And you are supposed to close this curtain,' he said, leaning across the table and closing the curtain. 'People walking by can see right in here.'

'Sorry, I was distracted. And I figured if I couldn't be out in the sunshine myself, I could at least enjoy it vicariously.'

'You can tell that to the police after somebody robs you,' he said, and then he softened slightly. 'You want more coffee?'

'Please.'

He filled my cup and poured one for himself before joining me at the table.

'So what's wrong?' he asked.

65

'What do you mean?'

'You look stressed.'

'Well, I seem to be a little out on cash here. I can't make it balance.'

'You're using volunteers as cashiers. There's bound to be some mistakes made.'

'Not two hundred dollars in a couple of hours.'

'Are you over or short by two hundred?'

'Short,' I said, pushing the adding machine aside and picking up my coffee.

'Which tent?' he asked.

'Number two.'

'We'll have to keep an eye on that. You might have to change cashiers.'

'Don't make me do that,' I sighed, 'That's Jeff's tent and I have no desire to get into a fight with him.'

'Well, we can keep an eye on things, see if anything unseemly is happening there.'

'I'd appreciate it.'

'It's all part of the service, ma'am.' He smiled. 'Now if that's not going to balance, how about if you finish the deposit so we can get that money up to the safe?'

'OK, give me another fifteen minutes?' I asked. 'I'd just like to have one more go at it and then I'm giving up.'

'OK,' he agreed, finishing his coffee and rinsing his cup in the sink. 'I'll go do a tour of the site and come back for you. And lock the door behind me, or I'll report you this time.'

I stood up and walked over to the door.

'I got it,' I said, closing the door behind him.

'And keep the curtains closed,' he called through the door.

'Yeah, yeah, yeah,' I muttered, returning to my seat at the table. I started to go through the cash tape one more time, trying to make it balance. But it didn't and I had other things to do, so I did up the deposit, sealed it in an envelope and called Doug on the radio to let him know I was ready. What I was really ready for was this day to end. It was just after seven o'clock and I was tired and stressed and longing for the comfort of my air-conditioned theatre.

*   *   *

66

We put the money in the safe and then the day was finally finished. I had a few more minor tasks, like realizing we had run out of kids' sized T-shirts. And just to end the day on a really fine note, I found we were short on inventory in tent two as well. I went over the list but could not find eleven missing T-shirts and a few assorted performers' CDs.

I gave up on balancing anything tonight and went to help the last of the crew move the merchandise back into the storage area inside the Plex. When we were finally done, I closed and locked the door to the caged-in area and made my way back upstairs to the slowly emptying Plaza and headed for the security trailer. I could hardly wait to get my nametag and T-shirt off and feel like a civilian again. Trooper was playing tonight at an outdoor concert and I intended to dance and drink beer until I couldn't stand up, then go home and get a couple hours sleep before I had to get back here for work in the morning.

'One of you boys better get your butt off those chairs before I finish changing,' I warned Bruce and Tommy, as I climbed into the trailer.

'Sorry Kate, these are security chairs. And you're not even on duty right now,' Bruce yelled after me.

I ignored him as I shut the door. I had brought a change of clothes and grabbed them as I headed to the washroom to change. I pulled off my shorts and T-shirt and pulled on a pair of jeans that I had spent hours working on, so I could get the knees ripped just right. I pulled on a little cable knit cropped sweater. I was admiring myself in the mirror and suddenly decided I should get my navel pierced. Maybe next week I'd talk Sam into going with me. I pulled off my baseball cap and freed my hair from the ponytail it had been forced into all day. I brushed it out and decided it would do, but maybe I would get it cut after I got my navel pierced, and maybe coloured too. Go for a whole new look. I added a fresh coat of lipstick, some earrings, wiped some mascara smudges away from my eyes and did a last check in the mirror. Luckily, Sam's morning treats hadn't started to show on my waistline yet. Yep, I looked like a girl who was going to dance the night away! I dumped my dirty clothes in the corner of the couch, added a spritz of perfume, kicked off

67

my clunky shoes and slid into a little pair of strappy sandals.

I grabbed a beer and exited the trailer to a couple of appreciative wolf whistles, which didn't bother me in the least this evening.

'You got a hot date or something tonight, Kate?' Bruce asked.

'Why sir, I don't know what you're talking about. This is just how I throw myself together when I'm hanging around the house,' I said, fluttering my lashes at him. 'Now, are you going to get your butt off that chair or am I going to have to wrestle you for it?'

'If those are my choices, I pick wrestling,' he replied.

'Fine, I give up.' I smiled, and plunked myself down on top of Tommy. 'These feet need to sit down until they stop hurting or I ingest enough beer to anesthetize them.'

'So who are you planning on dancing with tonight?' Tommy asked.

'Well, I seem to recall that Doug said something about accompanying me somewhere,' I began.

'I guess that means we won't be attending the party,' Bruce said.

'Well, if he's not available, I'll just troll through the Plaza until I find me someone ready to dance the night away.'

'You better be careful,' Tommy warned me. 'There's some unsavoury characters downtown at this time of night. You might pick yourself up some sort of a loony-toon.'

'Or something worse,' Bruce added.

'But I know my friendly neighbourhood security guards will protect me.' I smiled sweetly at them. 'And make sure I get home safe and sound . . . and alone.'

'So if all my staff is sitting here entertaining the market coordinator, who's securing the Plaza?' Doug asked as he came up behind us.

'We got the volunteers out patrolling,' Tommy explained. 'They can handle things until the crowd starts gathering for the band.'

Doug leaned under the trailer and pulled out two more lawn chairs.

'One of you guys couldn't manage to get Kate a lawn chair?' he asked.

'You never told me there were more chairs,' I said, swatting Tommy across the head before climbing off him and settling into my own chair.

'I was kind of enjoying this,' he teased.

'You two want to do a quick walk around and see how the volunteers are doing?' he asked.

'Oh, he wants to be alone with Kate,' Tommy joked.

'No, I was actually hoping the festival wouldn't notice that they're paying a fortune for us to sit here and drink beer.'

'Iced tea,' Bruce protested, holding up his can. 'I am still on duty after all.'

Tommy and Bruce got up and meandered across the Plaza.

'So you wanted to be alone with me?' I asked Doug, raising my eyebrows suggestively.

'No, I didn't want to be paying them for sitting here, just like I said.' He smiled back.

'I guess I'm losing my touch,' I commented, flipping my hair back over the chair and laying my head back. I looked up to the sky and saw the moon had started rising in the east, followed by a couple of stars just starting to peek through the barely darkening sky.

'No, you're not losing your touch, I'm just trying to retain my professional distance.'

'Well I'm relieved,' I said. 'But I'm off duty and I thought you had offered to be my escort tonight?'

'You may be off duty but I'm not yet.'

'Well you better be off duty soon or I'll have to find myself somebody else.'

'Trust me, you won't have to do that.' He smiled.

'Good,' I said, as I reluctantly pulled myself up into a standing position.

'Where you going?' he asked.

'I'm going to see if Sam has anything to eat. If I have dinner with her, do you think you'll be off duty by the time I'm done?'

'I think I can manage that.'

'All right.' I smiled. 'I'll be back for you.'

'And I'll be waiting.'

I set my empty beer can down beside the lawn chair, and walked slowly toward the food tents. I put a little extra sway into my walk, but didn't look back once to check if he was watching. I was very proud of my self-control.

I saw Sam arguing with her assistant over the top of a deep fat fryer and I was tempted to head in the opposite direction and let her finish her argument. But the smell of hamburgers grilling pulled me in her direction.

'Can't a person get a little service around here?' I yelled, banging my fist on the table, hoping to distract her from her disagreement.

Sam turned in my direction, ready to yell back, until she saw it was me. Reluctantly, she withdrew herself from her argument; a smile breaking through once her back was turned on the volunteer.

'Things not going well back there?' I asked.

'He's a great worker but disappears a lot,' she admitted. 'And he's a little stubborn.'

'Right, because you would know all about being stubborn,' I teased.

'Because it's my catering company and it's my way or the highway when my reputation is at stake,' she insisted.

'OK, OK, I was just teasing. Sorry.'

Sam took a deep breath and forced a smile back on her face. 'Well, you look dressed for trouble.'

'That's good, 'cause trouble is exactly what I'm looking for tonight.'

'Kate, worrying about you is making my hair grey.'

'Your hair was grey years ago.'

'Right around the time I met you,' she pointed out.

'Then don't worry about me,' I told her. 'Or I can recommend a good home colour for you.'

'Worrying about you is part of being your friend. Someone has to look out for you.'

'I'm a big girl . . .'

'Yeah right, I've heard that all before.' She rolled her eyes. 'Let's not go there again. You here for food or company?'

'Both. Food first, though. I think you should have something too. I think your blood sugar might be a little low.'

'What do you want?'

'One of those great-smelling hamburgers.' I smiled, looking toward the grill and feeling my mouth begin to water.

Sam crossed back over to the grill, pulled out a bun and toasted it to golden perfection before putting the fattest burger from the grill on it.

'What do you want on it?' she asked me.

'Double everything.'

She obediently loaded it up with fried onions, pickles, tomato, lettuce and a huge serving of her secret recipe barbeque sauce before wrapping it up in a napkin.

'I don't think I can get anything else on it,' she said as she handed it to me.

'Why don't you grab one for yourself and join me?' I asked. 'Take a break from the fight.'

'Kate, trust me that I would love nothing more. But we're expecting several thousand people down here in the next two hours. I've got a ton of work to do.'

'Please, just take five minutes,' I whined. 'Let that assistant of yours prove himself.'

Sam loaded up a plate with some onion rings and handed them to me.

'Here, this will make up for the lack of my company.' She smiled. 'But I promise we'll hook up tomorrow, no matter what. OK?'

'OK,' I said, greedily accepting the onion rings. 'If I can't have you, the next best thing is your barbeque sauce.'

'You're too easy,' she teased.

'Thanks babe.' I smiled, making my way over to one of the picnic tables.

I sat myself down, stuffed an onion ring into my mouth and bit into the hamburger. It was crunchy on the outside from the grill, and full of messy juices that ran down my chin as I bit into it. I grabbed a handful of napkins and staunched the flow of barbeque sauce down my chin as the tomatoes and lettuce shot out the back of the bun. I was just trying to put it all back together as Jeff sat down across from me.

'Hey Kate, how's it going?' He smiled broadly.

'Jeff. You guys had a great day in the market today,' I replied, trying to keep the subject on business.

'You look great,' he said, changing the subject back to the place where I didn't want it to go.

'Jeff, I appreciate the thought but . . .'

71

'You going to the dance tonight?' he interrupted.

'Yes.'

'Great, me too. Will you promise me a dance?'

'Jeff, I've tried to explain to you that I really want to keep our relationship on a business level.' I reluctantly put my burger down and wiped the grease off my face, trying to look very serious and businesslike. 'It's really making me uncomfortable that you seem unable to do that.'

'Kate, just a harmless dance. There'll be thousands of people around.'

'Jeff, I don't think that would be appropriate. Look, we've all worked really hard today and I just need some time away from volunteers and festival stuff, OK? So would you like to find another spot or should I?'

'Kate, I'm really hurt that you're taking such offence at something that I meant to be totally harmless,' he said, his voice growing cold. 'So don't worry yourself, I'll find someplace else to sit. There's lots of people around here who appreciate my company.'

He stood up and stormed off before I could say another word, muttering away to himself. He finally settled down at a table several hundred feet away. Sam's assistant wandered over with a couple of burgers and joined him. Oh great, I thought, Sam's irresponsible assistant and my greatest nemesis of the week were going to become best friends and gang up against us. All I needed now was the clown to join them for a beer and a cigarette.

I decided not to let it ruin my appetite and enjoyed the rest of my burger, after draping myself with napkins. Dancing the night away with big barbeque sauce stains on my top was not going to make me the belle of the ball. After I was finished, I contemplated my bloated stomach and wondered whether I should put on a longer sweater. Oh well, a little dancing would wear the hamburger off, and maybe tomorrow I'd actually have to take Cam's advice and go jogging to burn off those onion rings. This was the downside to being single again, getting self-conscious and worrying about every ounce. But I noticed it wasn't stopping me from enjoying Sam's cooking.

The Plaza was filling up again, as the people who had come and picnicked on the lawn were now being joined by the after-dinner crowd, and it sounded like the band was starting to do a sound check up on the stage. I found a big empty table in the group that had been set up around the dance floor, and claimed it as my own, with a reserved sign I had swiped from the catering tent. Graham and his girlfriend Mandi were standing in a corner across the dance floor from where I sat. He had his arms draped around her and was nuzzling her neck. I waved across at him and motioned him to come and join me. He waved back but I saw his lips form a distinct 'no thank you' before they returned to work on Mandi's neck. I saw Doug starting across the Plaza and strolled over to meet him halfway.

'It looks like I'm just about on time,' Doug said, taking my hand and kissing my cheek in greeting.

'You're wearing your radio,' I noticed, disappointed.

'Sorry, Kate, I have to keep it on just in case the guys need me.'

'All right, but I hope you're planning on spending more time with me than on the radio.'

'If everything goes well I am.'

'Good, let's get over there and see what's going on,' I said, pulling him back towards the dance floor.

'They're just doing sound checks,' he said.

'I know, but I don't want to miss the first dance. I said I was going to dance every dance tonight and I meant it.'

'I never pictured you to be a party girl,' he said.

'I'm not usually. I think I have some sort of festival fever or something. Come on, let's go,' I said, pulling him after me towards the table. 'Leave your jean jacket on the table so we don't lose our seats. It's too easy for someone to take the reserved sign off if it gets crowded.'

'What's the hurry?' he asked.

'The bar is open and there's no line-up,' I said, pulling him over to the bar. We started out with two pitchers of beer and a tray full of beer mugs for whoever would wind up joining us at the table. The band just started playing their first song as we dropped off the drinks, and we then worked our way through the gathering crowds and finally reached the front of the dance floor. I pulled Doug through the crowd and he finally gave in and pulled me close to him, taking my hand

73

in his and then twirling me around. I was impressed . . . and a little breathless.

'So Doug, is that a radio in your pocket or are you just happy to see me?' I asked, as he held me close to him and led me across the dance floor.

'Sorry,' he said, sliding his radio around to the back of his belt. 'But I get the feeling you've been waiting a while to use that line.'

'Shut up and dance.' I smiled at him.

We finished our first dance before Doug got called away, the first of several times, mostly to help deal with people who had a little too much to drink and wanted to have a little too much fun. I made my way back to our table and managed to keep myself busy with filling it up with people I knew from the Plex. A group of technicians from the theatre were the first to join me, Trevor, Scott and Dwayne. Dwayne had his wife with him, Trevor had his Golden Retriever and Scott joined me on the dance floor, so he could better scope the area and find his girl of the night. A few local actors that I knew showed up too, and soon we had three tables full of friends and I was enjoying myself immensely. I'd already had too much to drink, but it was hot and I convinced myself that I was dancing most of the alcohol off and I certainly wasn't planning on driving anywhere. Besides, my techies wouldn't let me do anything too embarrassing; they were very good at protecting me, especially from myself. I came back from the dance floor, hot and tired but frustrated that I couldn't get anyone else to dance with me at the moment. I consoled myself with another mug of beer and sat down beside Trevor.

Trevor is the technical director and the oldest of the technicians, which is why, I guess, he always fell into the fatherly role. He's a California boy, but talks with a trace of a southern accent. He had the cutest little stomach that peeked out of his shirt like Winnie the Pooh's, but he had been doing Atkins, hoping to slim down a bit and find himself the woman of his dreams, and he was losing that, no matter how much of Sam's baking I had tried to ply him with over the last few months. Trevor leaned over close to me, so I could hear him over the band.

'Where's Cam tonight?' he asked.

74

'He's away.'

'Without you?'

'I'm working.'

'Oh, is that what they call this,' Trevor laughed. He sat up and had a drink of his beer. I thought I was home free until he leaned back toward me. 'You know, Dwayne and his wife had a miscarriage last year. I don't know if you knew that or not.'

I turned to look at him, shock showing on my face before I could bring my emotions back under control.

'It's a hard thing to work through, I've heard. I bet they would be happy to talk to you about it, don't you think?' he asked.

'Cam and I are fine.'

'Dwayne told me that they ended up going to a support group. Apparently his wife is the talkative kind, you know?'

We both laughed at that. She'd have to be, since I don't think I'd ever heard more than two sentences escape Dwayne's mouth at a time.

'Anyone want to dance?' I yelled over the music.

'Sometimes, it helps to talk.' Trevor pushed on. 'If you want me to arrange for a visit over coffee or something, you just let me know.'

Scott was the only one of the three who would dance, but I didn't care who it was, I just needed someone to get me away from Trevor at the moment. And I think Trevor felt a little guilty for cornering me, because he did the next beer run, buying for the whole table. The rest of the evening progressed nicely, with the men keeping me supplied in beer and conversation, and no other uncomfortable subjects being brought up. Doug was back and forth a couple of more times, and finally put a phone call in to one of his on-call guys, getting tired of the interruptions. But he got called away once more before the new guy arrived and I pulled Scott out on to the dance floor again and kept him there for three songs in a row.

'That was fun,' Scott said, taking my hand and pulling me back toward the table.

'Come on, Scott,' I said, leaning backwards and trying to pull him back to the dance floor. 'Just one more dance?'

'That's what you said two songs ago,' he said.

'I promise.'

'Kate, I'm hot and I'm thirsty. We'll go have another drink and then maybe Doug will be back and he can take a turn.'

'Scott, please, this is my favourite,' I whined, as another song started.

'So were the last three,' he said, picking me up and tossing me over his shoulder. 'And the last three before that. I'm not falling for that again.'

'Spoilsport!' I giggled, pounding on his back. 'Now, put me down.'

Scott carried me back to the table and dumped me in my chair.

'There, you're down,' he said, sitting beside me. 'Now, which one of you buttheads drank my beer?'

'It's OK, Dwayne's gone for another pitcher,' Trevor assured us.

'Come on you wimps, one of you has to dance with me,' I pleaded with anyone within earshot.

'Kate, you're exhausting us,' Trevor said. 'Chill out and relax for a while.'

'I don't want to,' I whined. 'I want to dance.'

'I'll buy you a beer,' Scott promised.

'That only worked the first five times,' I laughed. 'I'm on to you now.'

'Well sit down anyways,' Scott said.

'I'd like to dance,' I heard a voice behind me say. 'If you would be willing.'

I turned around and saw a nice-looking man, somewhere around my age, holding out his hand for me.

'I'm Kate,' I said, taking his hand and following him across the dance floor.

'I know.' He smiled, taking me in his arms as a slow ballad started.

'You know?' I asked.

He reached into the pocket of his shirt and pulled out a red sponge ball, putting it on his nose.

'Recognize me now?' he asked.

'You're the clown, from the Plaza today?' I asked, pulling back slightly.

'I am.'

'Sorry, I didn't recognize you at all.'

'It's OK, I usually don't wear my red lipstick when I'm out on the town. People usually don't understand.'

I laughed. 'So what should I call you?'

'Well, ma'am, most people call me Buttons.'

I laughed back.

'But my friends call me Seth.'

'Buttons it is,' I joked.

'I got the feeling I was making you uncomfortable today. Again, I just wanted to apologize if that was the case,' he said. 'I've only been in Calgary for a little while and this is my first festival here and I really wanted to make a good impression.'

'Well, you did actually,' I said, thinking a crowded dance floor was as safe a place as any. 'I know it can get a little stressful with the crowds, and that we work a really long day, but I think it's important to try and maintain a professional demeanour.'

'I agree totally,' he said, twirling me.

'And I noticed that you watched me walk all the way back to the trailer.'

'I did,' he said. 'Well, actually, I didn't. I mean, I was watching that fellow that was following you. I just wanted to make sure you were all right. He just didn't seem like he was up to any good, you know? And with that Bishop fellow out there, I guess I was just a little overprotective.'

'Someone was following me?' I asked, alarmed.

'Yeah, that fellow that you were talking to in the merchandise tent.'

'Jeff?'

'I'm sorry, I don't know his name. But he came out the back of the tent and followed you across the Plaza. When you climbed up into the trailer he turned and went to the benches over there. I think he was hoping you'd come back out.'

'Well, thank you for watching out for me,' I said, as the music came to an end. 'And thank you for the dance, Seth.'

'Well thank you. Maybe we'll see each other again this week.'

'I'm sure we will,' I promised.

'I meant when I wasn't wearing makeup and there might be grown-up conversation involved rather than balloon animals.'

'Oh,' I laughed. 'Well maybe we will.'

I pulled away and headed back to the table, turning to see that he was watching me again, and he didn't turn away until I had joined my friends at our table.

'Has Doug come back yet?' I asked.

'No, he hasn't been back yet,' Scott said. 'Have a seat and I'll pour you some beer.'

'I don't think she needs more beer,' Trevor said, noticing me swaying as I stood there.

'She's off duty,' Scott said.

'She's standing right here,' I said.

'She's swaying right there,' Trevor repeated.

'Well, I don't want a beer anyway. I'm going to go find Doug. He's been gone far too long. I think he's been avoiding me.' I laughed, but I really did want to talk to him.

'I don't blame him,' Trevor said.

'Thanks,' I answered sarcastically. 'Now I really am leaving.'

'You want me to go with you?' Scott offered.

'I'll be fine. There's lots of people around.'

'OK, well we'll save your spot for you,' Dwayne promised, coming back with two pitchers of beer in each hand.

'But will you save any beer for me?' I called over my shoulder, as I turned to go.

I started to head straight for the security trailer, but soon realized it was too much trouble to try and push my way through the thick crush of people, after I was stopped several times by immovable crowds. I finally decided to head around the block, to the far side of the Plaza, where there was hardly anyone around, and then back down the street to the trailer. I had almost made it to the street when someone jumped out from behind one of the bushes and grabbed my arm. I screamed and turned to face my attacker.

'Hey, Kate!' Jeff greeted me, obviously drunk.

'Let go of me!' I said harshly, feeling very relieved it wasn't a serial killer but still threatened by the tight grip he had on my arm. I felt myself start to sober up quickly.

'Aw come on, Kate, let's go have a dance.' He smiled, putting a hand around my waist.

The feel of his hand on my bare skin sent a shiver up my spine.

'Jeff, I am not dancing with you, now let go of me,' I said firmly, trying to get through to him.

He started pulling me back toward the party, his grip on my arm tightening, as I tried to struggle from his grasp.

'Come on, one dance and I'll leave you alone,' he assured me, but neither of his hands released their grip. 'You're dancing with everyone else tonight.'

I tried to pull away from him, feeling myself begin to panic. I felt memories come flooding back, when a man had broken into my apartment and attacked me. I thought I was well over that, but the panic rising in my gut convinced me otherwise. I struggled to pull free and he turned angrily back to me.

'What is your problem?' he asked, his voice becoming menacing. 'Do you find me so totally disgusting?'

'I said I didn't want to dance with you, that's all.' I tried to be strong, but my voice had a nervous shaking sound that I couldn't manage to control, and my knees were awfully wobbly, from a mixture of beer and terror.

'OK, if you won't dance with me, how about a kiss?' he asked, grabbing my other arm and pulling me closer to him.

I tried to aim my knee for his groin, but I missed, throwing myself off balance and pulling him down on top of me. I screamed again as he pinned my arms over the top of my head and smiled at me for a moment, a cold evil smile that sent another shiver down my spine. And then he leaned close to me and I turned away. I felt his hot breath on my cheek.

'Now you're going to be mine,' he whispered into my ear, and then kissed me.

His leg jammed in between my legs, and his free hand moved down to the fly on my jeans. At the touch of his hand on my skin and the sound of the zipper being released, I felt a blind panic overtake me and I started flailing my arms and legs, trying to get him off me, trying to scream though his mouth was now pressing against mine. And then suddenly he was gone. Doug had grabbed him by the collar and picked him up. Jeff somehow turned and tried to throw a punch at Doug.

'Thank you for doing that,' I heard Doug say calmly, his arm pulling back to throw a punch of his own.

Then, before I realized what was happening, Jeff was back on the ground, with Doug on top of him, pulling his hands behind his back and handcuffing him. I pushed myself across the cold concrete, out of reach, and sat up, wiping my mouth with my sleeve, trying to get the taste of him off me.

'You bastard, let me up,' Jeff screamed from the ground. 'I'm going to have you fucking arrested for assault.'

Doug was ominously silent until Bruce and Tommy came running up to the scene.

'Take him to the trailer,' Doug barked. 'I'll be there in a minute.'

Tommy and Bruce wasted no time pulling Jeff to his feet and dragging him toward the trailer. Doug came over to where I was and suddenly I realized I was still sitting on the grass with my pants undone. I quickly zipped my fly but didn't have the strength to stand up on my own.

'Are you OK?' he asked, his tone changing to a much softer one.

'I think so,' I whispered.

'Are you hurt? Can you get up?'

'I'm OK,' I said, offering a weak smile.

'Let me help,' he said, putting his hands under my shoulders and gently pulling me up.

My knees still felt a little shaky, probably all the adrenalin running through my system, but I managed to stay on my feet. I guess I didn't have him totally convinced, because he didn't let go of me.

'We're going to go back to the trailer and call the police,' he told me, once he was sure I was OK.

'Let's go back to the trailer. I don't know about the police,' I said.

'This is one argument I'm going to win,' he informed me, still holding my arm as we walked.

'No. Doug, the festival doesn't need this kind of publicity. Hopefully he's cooled down a little and I can talk to him.'

'He attacked you, Kate,' Doug explained. 'Do we want

to talk about what he would have done if I hadn't found you?'

'I'm aware of that, Doug. But he was drunk and so am I. And how good is that going to look in the newspapers, huh? Drunken festival staff arrested during Trooper concert? Especially after I've flirted and danced with half the men here tonight. My name has been in the newspapers way too much this year and I'd rather not go for another headline just now, OK?'

'We can ask the police to keep this quiet,' he said.

'Right, and can we ask all the reporters who listen to the police scanners to keep quiet too?'

'It's not big news. There probably won't be anything they even think is worth writing about.'

'Look, I'd like to just try and find an easy and quiet solution to this incident. I don't want to spend the night at a police station swearing out a complaint against him either.'

At the trailer, Bruce had Jeff sitting in a chair, still handcuffed, with a hand on his shoulder, ready in case he decided to get hostile again. But at least Jeff seemed to have calmed down a bit.

'Take the cuffs off him,' I said to Bruce.

He looked at Doug, who grudgingly nodded his head in agreement, and Bruce took the cuffs off him. Jeff took a step toward me but Bruce's hand shot out and grabbed him by the shoulder, pulling him back down into the chair.

'I'm so sorry,' Jeff said. 'I don't know what came over me.'

'Jeff, the only reason I'm not firing your ass off this site is that you've been drinking way too much tonight. If I wasn't convinced that you are totally bombed and that's why you're acting so inappropriately, I would not hesitate to have you arrested. But if you show one second of inappropriate behaviour for the rest of this week, or if I catch you drinking on the site, or even hanging around after the market is closed, I will have you thrown out so fast it will make your head spin. Do we understand each other?' I asked.

'Thank you,' he said, getting up slowly as Bruce let him go, taking a step toward me and putting his hand out as a peace offering. 'I appreciate this . . .'

I pulled back, shaking suddenly at the thought of his flesh

81

touching mine again. 'You will also keep your distance from me.'

'I understand,' he said.

'Escort him out and make sure he gets in a cab,' Doug instructed Bruce, who immediately grabbed Jeff's arm and pulled him toward the street. 'Tommy, would you mind heading back to the party and letting Kate's friends know she's with me?'

'Sure,' Tommy agreed. 'I'll check on the volunteers while I'm there.'

'Thanks,' Doug said and then turned back to me. 'But I still think you're doing the wrong thing.'

'Back off,' I said, pushing him away from me.

'OK, well now that I've said my piece, are you really OK?'

I opened my mouth to speak, but instead, a sob escaped from my traitorous throat. And then there were tears rolling down my cheeks. Where was this coming from? And then Doug pulled me into his arms and held me to his chest. I wrapped my arms around him and let myself cry, not that I could have stopped if I had wanted to.

'Let's go into the trailer,' he said. 'We don't need to do this out here.'

I didn't let go of him as he walked me up the stairs and into the trailer. We just stood there, in the kitchen, Doug holding me and letting me cry.

'I'm sorry,' I said, when I finally started to calm down.

'It's OK,' he said, reaching behind me and grabbing a Kleenex.

He handed it to me and I wiped at my eyes, wondering how good I looked to him now.

'Do you want me to take you home?' he asked.

I felt fresh tears start and another sob tore out of me.

'What's the matter?' he asked.

'I don't want to go home,' I sobbed. 'Someone broke into my house and attacked me a while ago. I don't think I can stay there alone tonight.'

He wrapped his arms around me again.

'Don't worry,' he tried to soothe me. 'Do you want to sleep here tonight?'

'Can I?' I sobbed, sounding totally pathetic.

'Of course. You'll have to share the top bunk with me though.'

I pulled away quickly from him, shocked by his proposition.

'Doug, I can't sleep with you tonight,' I stammered. 'I'm sorry but I'm just a little upset and stuff and maybe it would be better if I just went home after all . . .'

'No, no,' he said quickly. 'It's just that I told Tommy he could sleep here tonight cause he worked a double shift and missed his last bus home. If I sleep out here on the couch, the night guys can't use the trailer for breaks. I just meant we'd have to share the space. I can hang a curtain or put some pillows in between us or something. I would never take advantage of you at a time like this.'

'I'm sorry,' I said, feeling myself blushing and fresh tears stinging my eyes again.

'But that doesn't mean I won't take advantage of you some other time,' he laughed, giving me one last hug. 'Why don't you go to bed now? I'll lock you in while I finish up for the night?'

'OK,' I agreed.

'Have you got something to wear?' he asked.

'I've got an extra T-shirt,' I said.

'You go change; I'll make sure the windows are locked. OK?'

I pulled a T-shirt out from my box and disappeared into the bathroom to change. When I came out, Doug had straightened the blankets on the bunk for me.

'Sorry, I'm not very good at making my bed in the morning,' he said, jumping down.

'That's OK, I never make mine either.'

'Do you need a hand getting up there?' he asked.

'I'm all right.'

'You get in, I'll get you some spare Kleenex,' he instructed.

I climbed up on to the bunk and pulled the covers around me.

'Here you go,' he said, handing me the Kleenex. 'And please, try not to cry on both pillows. I hate sleeping on a wet pillow.'

I laughed despite myself.

'Are you going to be all right?' he asked, this time being serious.

'Are you going to lock the door?' I asked back.

'I promise.'

'Then I'll be fine,' I assured him.

'Good. I won't be gone too long. The band is only playing for another half hour and the party should break up pretty soon after that.'

'Thanks,' I called after him as he left the trailer. I waited until I heard him lock the door before I settled into the bed.

I pulled the covers up tightly around me and fell into a fitful sleep. I tossed and turned, waking at every little noise and then gradually settling down again. I didn't know how long I'd been asleep when I felt a hand on my back. I jumped up, almost hitting my head on the ceiling.

'It's only me,' Doug whispered. 'I didn't mean to startle you.'

'Sorry, I guess I'm still a little nervous.'

'That's OK, but Kate?'

'Yes,'

'Can you move over a bit? I can't get in.'

'Sorry,' I giggled, as I slid over to the far side of the bed.

Doug climbed in beside me and drew the curtain around the bed. He settled himself in and pulled the covers over him. I could feel the heat radiating from his body as I lay beside him.

'Sorry I woke you,' he apologized.

'It's OK. I was only dozing.'

'Are you feeling better?'

'A little,' I lied.

'Good night then,' he said.

'Good night,' I whispered, sliding just a little closer, so I could feel him beside me.

We lay there in silence for a few minutes until I felt him turn toward me.

'Katie . . .' he asked.

I felt tears stinging my eyes again. Only Cam ever called me Katie. I don't know how he knew I was crying, but he gently pulled me close to him and held me.

84

'It's OK, you're safe,' he said softly, his fingers running through my hair as he tried to calm me. 'It's all over now.'

But I didn't know how to tell him that I wasn't crying about tonight anymore. So I didn't. I let him hold me and try to make me feel safe, while I cried over Cam. It took me a lot longer to cry myself out this time, but finally, exhausted, I fell asleep in his arms.

He pulled the collar of his leather jacket up around his neck, against the chill of the night breeze that was blowing across the Plaza, and he smiled when he finally saw what he wanted. He walked over to her, slowly, not looking like he was on any sort of mission. Just meandering, smiling to people leaving the concert, nodding to others, being as nondescript as possible. He finally got close enough to her to recognize her face in the dimness, and he stopped, knowing she could see his face too.

'Hi.' He smiled. He knew it was a good smile. It had worked countless times for him in his many searches for people to play with.

'Hi,' she answered back, a moment of fear being replaced with recognition.

'You know, you shouldn't be out here alone at this time of night.'

'I'm just waiting for a taxi,' she said. 'And I've got my phone ready for 911.'

She held up her cell phone and showed him that her hand was over the emergency call button.

'Well it's good to know you are being safe. It's been a long day, hasn't it?'

'I think there's going to be a few of us that are tired on shift tomorrow.'

'And a little hung-over,' he laughed, using that smile again. He noticed her thumb had moved off the emergency button of her phone and she flipped her hair back with a toss of her head. She was his.

'That'll just be our little secret,' she laughed.

'Look, your taxi seems to be taking forever, why don't you let me give you a ride home?' he asked.

'Oh, no, that's really nice of you but . . .'

'No buts. I would feel really bad leaving you here with *you know who* terrorizing the city. Please, allow me?' He held out his arm. She hesitated for only a second and then took it. 'I'm just down Ninth Avenue in that cheap parking lot, I'm afraid.'

'That's OK,' she said. 'A little walk might do me good.'

She kept up an endless stream of small talk as he walked her back to his car. And when they were there, he had a good look around to make sure they really were alone.

'Nice car,' she said, trying to impress him.

'Actually, it's a piece of crap,' he said. 'But that way I don't stand out.'

'What?'

'And thanks for the nice compliment,' he said, opening the door and taking her arm as if to help her into the car. 'But you don't have to work too hard to impress me, you know, because with or without compliments, I'm pretty sure you're going to see me naked tonight.'

'What?' she said, confusion taking over as she wondered at his change in mood.

And then he twisted her arm and had her face down in the passenger seat, her arm twisted painfully up behind her.

'You're hurting me,' she cried.

'I know,' he said, leaning over her and burying his nose in the back of her neck, enjoying the smell as she suddenly became covered with a light dusting of perspiration. He could almost smell the adrenalin kicking in to her system, as she tried to figure out how to get out of this. 'But am I scaring you?'

'What?'

He pulled her arm up a little higher, feeling her shoulder joint stretching to its limits, and then he pulled the duct tape out from under the passenger seat and taped her arms behind her back. Then he taped her ankles together and shoved her on the floor of the front seat, covering her with a blanket. But he left her eyes uncovered. He wanted to watch her eyes as he drove her back to his place. He taped a final piece of duct tape over her mouth and then slammed the passenger door, hurrying around and getting into the driver's seat.

'Well, Janice, how would you like to play a game with me?'

he smiled, as he turned the engine on and the radio blasted to life.

And he chuckled to himself as he saw her struggling to scream through the duct tape.

Wednesday

I woke up with a start.

'Good morning,' he said.

It took me a couple of minutes to remember where I was.

'How are you feeling this morning? You slept like the dead last night. You didn't even move when I had to get up to help out on the Plaza.'

And then I realized I was lying next to Doug, wrapped in his arms, his face smiling at me, very close to mine. I tried to pull away from him without seeming like I was trying to get away, but he was on to me.

'I'm sorry,' I said, not knowing which of my sins I was apologizing for.

'It's OK,' he said, reluctantly letting me go.

'Do you have any idea what time it is?'

'It's only eight o'clock,' he said. 'Still early.'

'I should get moving,' I said, feeling very uncomfortable with the situation, now that I was looking at it sober and in the light of the day.

'What's wrong, Kate?' he asked, not making any move to let me out of the bunk bed.

'I've just got a lot to do today,' I started.

'No, I don't think that's what's bothering you. Want to try levelling with me?'

'OK,' I finally gave in. 'I'm just feeling very uncomfortable. We have had a great working relationship this week. I don't want to ruin it. I shouldn't have stayed here last night; I should have gone to Sam's or something. But I wasn't thinking straight.'

'And you're afraid that now that I've spent the night with you, I won't be able to control myself around you?'

'Yes . . . no . . .' I didn't exactly know what the right answer was.

'Did you want to pick one of those answers and go with it?'

'Doug, I think you're a great guy. And we've had a wonderful little flirt and tease thing going for the past couple of days. But there is no way I would actually start a relationship with you right now.'

'Oh?' He sounded hurt.

'No, I meant not while we were working together. I'd be happy to give it the old college try after the festival is over. But I feel that by staying here, I may have taken this to a level that I'm really not comfortable with.'

'Kate, I don't think you have anything to worry about. I've shared a bunk several times with both Tommy and Bruce, and despite that fact, I still manage to maintain a very professional working relationship with them,' he teased.

'Well that sets my mind at ease,' I laughed.

'Good, now I'll let you out,' he said, unhooking the curtains and sliding off the bunk. 'You want to use the shower first?'

'I think I'll use the one in the theatre. I've got some clean clothes in my office, so I can try to make myself presentable,' I said, hopping down off the bed and slipping quickly into my jeans.

'Do you want me to walk you over?' he asked.

'No, I'm really feeling much better,' I assured him. 'I'll be back soon and then maybe we can make a bank run and do the night deposit we didn't do last night, before anything else gets in the way.'

'Sounds like a plan,' he said, climbing back up into the bed.

'Are you going back to bed?' I asked.

'I can sleep for at least another forty-five minutes and still be ready by the time you get back,' he said, and then drew the curtain back around the bed.

I started a pot of coffee brewing, grabbed my makeup bag and stepped out of the trailer just as Sam was about to knock on the door.

'Sam!' I said, shocked at seeing her standing there and feeling guilty all over again.

'Kate? You're here early today,' she said, not really believing it but offering me an easy out.

'Yeah, I actually have to go over some schedule stuff in the theatre office, so I thought I'd get that done first,' I stammered. Normally, I didn't have this much trouble coming up with a lie, but she had caught me totally off guard. 'Are you looking for me?'

'No, I just wanted to drop some muffins off for the security guys. I baked an extra batch for them this morning.'

'Well, the ones in here are still asleep. I don't know where the other guys are. Do you want me to leave them on the table?'

'Do you mind?' she asked.

'Not at all,' I said, taking the tray from her.

'Well, I better let you go,' she said. 'You want to get together later today?'

'Sure, how about around one o'clock? We could grab a bite to eat?' I asked, dreading where that conversation would go. Well, if I was really lucky the ground might just open up and swallow me before then.

'Great, why don't you meet me at Grounds Zero? I wouldn't mind getting away from the site for a while today.'

'Sure, one o'clock,' I agreed.

'See you then,' she said and turned to go.

I set the tray on the table and grabbed a chocolate muffin to take with me. A little chocolate always helped with guilty feelings. I could hardly wait to get to my office and have a cigarette and some coffee to work on the rest of it.

I stayed in the shower for a very long time but finally tore myself away when I realized I could stand here all day and not wash away all these mixed up feelings I had. Or the headache I had. I dried myself off and pulled on the clean clothes I had brought down from my office. I didn't have a big selection of summer casuals on hand, but I did have a khaki tank top with spaghetti straps, it was perhaps a little too low cut but that didn't seem to be stopping me this week, a pair of beige shorts and some clean socks and underwear. I put on my hiking boots, hoping my feet would feel better at the end of the day than they had been, and twisted my hair up into a knot on top of my head. I would let it down when it was dry and hopefully it would have some body to it. I added a little makeup and pulled a few wisps of hair out, to give me that casual wind-blown look we all work so hard to achieve. Satisfied, I trucked my dirty clothes up to my office, added my nametag and headed for the Plaza. Doug was waiting for me outside the security trailer and we headed off to start the day. We started at the festival office, where I loaded up my backpack with bank deposits and then we had a nice walk down the Stephen Avenue Mall. We stopped for an iced coffee on the way back, and then I got the float ready while he watched for subversives or whatever it was that he did. Today, I was going to do things differently; I was going to do tent two first and get it over with.

'Doug, do you mind sticking close to me in tent two?' I asked, as we got closer to the tent.

'Do you want me to take the cash box in for you?' he asked.

'I'd love you to, but I think I need to face this head on,' I said.

'I'll be right behind you,' he promised. 'Just waiting for him to make one inappropriate comment.'

'Well, let's try not to come on too strong unless he does something,' I said, trying to be the voice of reason. 'But I'm secretly hoping he does something stupid and you can knock his lights out.'

'Are you ready?' he asked, as we stood outside the entrance to the tent.

'Ready,' I said, taking a deep breath.

Doug lifted up the tent flap and we went in.

'Good morning, Jeff.' I smiled politely at him.

'Morning, Kate.' He smiled back, taking the cash box from me, acting as if nothing had happened between us last night. 'Are you ready for a record breaking day? I've talked to the team leaders at the other two market tents and we've got an official competition going. Just so you know, we in tent two are going to blow them away.'

'Great,' I said, quickly turning to go. 'Good luck with that.'

'Thanks for everything, Kate,' he called after me.

I didn't turn back to answer, finding myself hurrying away from him faster than I had planned. After we finished our cash drops, I headed back to tent one to try and get the new group of volunteers organized. Janice was scheduled but hadn't shown up. At least it would make my morning pass quickly and give me a good reason to avoid tent number two.

I was working the cash register, trying to explain to one of the new girls how to ring in the merchandise so it was coded properly, when I felt a shadow cross over me as someone came through the doorway. I looked up and saw bright red lips, rainbow wig and the star on the cheek. He was fluttering his fake eyelashes at me as he held out a bouquet of balloon flowers. I smiled, it was corny but it was sweet, and I took the flowers.

'Hello, Buttons,' I said. 'Thank you for the lovely flowers.'

'Well, thank you for the dance last night,' he said.

'You're welcome, but you didn't have to do this.'

'Shucks, it was nothing, ma'am,' he laughed. 'I just wanted to start today out on the right foot. And maybe end the night up with a drink?'

'Oh, that's really nice of you. But I'm short some volunteers today and at the best of times I haven't been able to predict what time I get finished at night.'

He looked down at the floor, studying his over-sized shoes, and pulled a handkerchief out of his pocket to blow his nose, but the material just kept coming and coming and coming.

'Well, if you would just calm down for a minute, I was going to say that maybe next week would be better for both of us?'

He looked up and smiled at me.

'That would give you more time to get your makeup off,' I giggled. 'Because I insist that when I go out with a man, I'm the only one wearing makeup.'

'Duly noted.'

'Stop by the trailer sometime and I'll give you a card with my numbers,' I said.

'I will do that,' he said, pulling some confetti out of his pocket and tossing it up into the air, and then he skipped off into the Plaza, pulling more balloons out of his pocket and looking for some kids to entertain.

I was flattered by the attention, but less happy with the confetti that was now filling the drawer of the cash register and the sly looks I was getting from the volunteer who was standing next to me.

'It's nothing,' I said, pulling out the money and shaking the confetti off it. 'And I've no time to talk about it.'

Grounds Zero was one of those great places that you could smell before you could actually see. They roasted their own coffee beans and there was always a smoky, aromatic haze hanging from the back of the Plex.

Gus was the owner and working manager of the place. He made a point of remembering everyone's name and always seemed to know what was going on before anyone else did. He was somewhere around sixty years old, a retired oilman who hadn't enjoyed retirement a lot. Gus always liked to drink coffee and eat, so Grounds Zero was a natural extension of those habits. I think his wife was just as happy that he was out of the house as Gus was.

I sat at one of the outdoor tables at Grounds Zero, waiting for Sam to join me. I didn't really need any more sunshine but Gus was another one of the multitudes of people I knew who seemed to feel they had to spend inordinate amounts of their time telling me how to run my life. He didn't like the summer heat much, so unless he was really intent on finding out what was up with me, sitting out here pretty much guaranteed he would leave me alone. That would only leave Sam for me to deal with. I had been growing an ulcer all morning thinking about what our lunchtime conversation might involve. Luckily, I looked up and there she was. At least the anticipation was over.

'Hey Kate, nice outfit,' she said as she sat down. 'And no, I didn't mean anything by that. No double entendres, no innuendo intended. OK?'

'I'm sensing a little hostility, Sam,' I told her, despite her protests otherwise.

'Well, Kate, every time I've tried to talk to you all week I've hit this defensive wall you seem to have erected. I was hoping we could just have a normal lunch.'

'I'm all for that,' I agreed.

'So I'm telling you in advance that I have no hidden agenda, I just want to chat like girlfriends do. You have to promise you'll take everything I say at face value.'

'OK, I promise,' I assured her.

'And not let your guilt for your behaviour this week get in the way.'

'Sam?'

'OK, so that was a little slip. From here on in we're good, OK?

'All right.'

'Good, I'm glad we've got that all straightened out.' She sat back and took a sip of the margarita I had ordered for her. Gus had got a new slushy machine in and was becoming quite creative with it. 'Now, tell me exactly what the hell it is you're trying to do with your life right now?'

'Excuse me?' I asked.

'Kate, this is not you. God, all week you've been walking around looking like the *I want to be fucked* poster girl. You won't talk to me; you broke up with Cam, and you're all over that security guy.'

'I've had a big change in my life and I don't think it's any of your business how I handle it.'

'It is my business,' she told me. 'I'm your friend. And I'm supposed to be here for you. Shit, it's probably my fault that you and Cam broke up in the first place.'

'No, it isn't. Cam and I can both take a fifty-fifty share in that. But there's no blame left over for anyone else.' I took a sip of my drink and wished I'd ordered a double, since it appeared I was to be the topic of conversation. 'And what do you mean, I look like the *fuck me poster girl*?'

'I haven't seen you display this much skin since I've known you. And I notice you've forgotten to put your bra on this morning. It's like you're oozing hormones.'

'Not hormones, pheromones.'

'Whatever. It's this total attitude switch you seem to be going through. I just don't think this is a healthy way to handle a break-up.'

'Probably not,' I agreed. 'But when have you ever known me to do anything the healthy way?'

'That's true. But Kate, I'm worried about you.'

'Well, I'm not. Sam, I am having fun right now. I don't know what I'm going to be like when the festival is over, but I've gotta get through this week somehow. This seems to be working for me.'

'What have you got on your arm?' she asked, abruptly changing the subject.

'Where?' I asked, twisting my arm so I could see where she was pointing.

'There, on the side, just below your elbow.'

'Oh, it must be a bruise,' I said, poking it to confirm my suspicions. 'Ouch! Yep, it's a bruise.'

'Does it have anything to do with the fact that you spent the night in the security trailer?' she asked.

'Only in a very roundabout way. I sort of got into a scuffle with a drunk last night.'

'Were you the drunk?' she asked.

'Well, I was a little tipsy until this guy jumped out of the bushes and grabbed me. I sobered up pretty quickly after that.'

'What?'

The shocked look on her face told me I probably shouldn't be telling her this stuff. Oh well, too late now.

'Kate, you do know there is a killer on the streets of Calgary right now, don't you?'

'It's OK, it was nothing serious. Doug was there in no time and managed to save me.' I smiled, trying to lighten the moment. 'That's why it pays to be nice to the security guys.'

'How do you manage to attract so much drama into your life?'

'I don't know. But I was really shaken up and that's why I stayed at the trailer last night. I was a little freaked out and I didn't want to go home alone. The guys were all perfect gentlemen.'

'Why didn't you call me, or come over to my place?' she asked.

'I don't know. I wasn't thinking straight. I am willing to admit that this morning. Now that I'm thinking a little more clearly, I realized that's exactly what I should have done.'

'So you weren't avoiding me?' she asked. 'You're not pissed off at me?'

'No more than I ever am,' I teased.

'Good. Kate, we've been friends for so long and I was afraid you were angry with me.'

'Oh, Sam, no. If I lost you as my friend, I'd be done. I love you.'

'So what are you going to do with this Doug guy?' she asked, a smile on her face but a very serious tone in her voice.

'I could tell you what I'd like to do with him,' I offered.

'Save me the gory details.'

'I don't know what I'm going to do. I really think he's a nice guy. But he's probably five or six years younger than me. It would never last.'

'But . . .?' she prompted me.

'It might be a fun rebound relationship. A month or so of movies, dancing and great sex. It might help me move on.'

'Are you going to move on? From Cam?'

'You like Cam better than you like me, don't you?' I asked.

'Some days. But I like the two of you together a lot.'

'I don't even know where he is,' I sighed. 'And I wouldn't have a clue how to find him. I guess I have to assume it's over since there's nothing else I can do.'

'Do you want it to be over?'

'I don't know, Sam. It just all happened so fast, I feel like I was watching it, not living it. I just know that every night when I go home, I say a little prayer as I stick my key in the door that he will be there waiting for me. Hasn't worked so far.'

'Can I do anything to help?' she asked.

'Like what?'

'I don't know, call his family, see if they've heard from him?'

'It's pointless. If he comes back, he'll do it when he's good and ready. And I guess whether I'm still hoping he comes back will depend on how long it takes him. I just don't want to spend all my time pining or sitting in the window with a candle burning.'

'But there is a middle ground,' she pointed out.

'Funny, that's what I thought I was on – the middle ground.'

'Try putting a bra on first.' She smiled. 'That might bring you a little closer. I'd say right now you're still swimming in the deep end.'

'Well, I'm a good swimmer.' I smiled.

Gus came out with a coffee in his hand, pulled up a chair and joined us.

96

'So Kate, where's Cam these days?' he asked, hitting the nail on the head just like he always did.

'Look at the time,' I said, feigning surprise as I looked at my watch. 'I'm late for my cash run. Will you two excuse me if I get back to work?'

I didn't really wait for an answer as I stood up and tossed some money on the table.

'Kate, before you go,' Gus said, grabbing my arm to keep me there a minute longer.

'What is it?' I asked.

'I heard that Jeff LeCroix is volunteering for you at the festival this week.'

'Yeah, he is working in the festival market. Why?' I was expecting an attack on my character or at least the third degree about Cam's absence. I was curious as to why Jeff's name had come up.

'I just wondered if you knew that Jeff worked for me once, as a waiter. Only lasted a day, though.' he said. 'Seems the cash register was a little short that day.'

'No, I didn't know that, Gus. Thanks. Now I'm really late, I have to go,' I said again, thinking I had better check up on tent two.

'Go ahead, Kate,' Sam said. 'I'll catch up with you later.'

'I'll be here if you want to talk,' Gus added.

'OK, thanks guys,' I called over my shoulder as I headed down the block.

I radioed security from the corner and met Tommy at tent one. We picked up the money from all three tents and Tommy dropped me off at the security trailer. I locked myself in and started trying to balance the money to the cash register tapes. Tents number one and three were a breeze. Ten minutes and I had both deposits ready to go. Tent two wouldn't balance again. I pushed it away from me and had just lit a cigarette when there was a knock on the door. I lifted the curtain and saw Doug standing at the door. I reached over and flipped open the lock. He climbed in and poured himself a coffee.

'You want one?' he asked.

'Please.' I nodded, passing him my empty cup.

'You look stressed again, Kate,' he said as he passed me my coffee and sat across the table from me.

'I'm having problems with tent two's cash again.'

'It's short again?' he asked.

'Yep.'

'Well, I had a volunteer report that she thought she saw the cashier put some money in his pocket instead of the cash drawer,' he informed me.

'And that would be Jeff?' I asked.

'That would be,' he confirmed. 'But she's not certain enough to accuse him. I've got Bruce and Tommy watching him and that tent, but so far they haven't seen him do anything out of the ordinary.'

'But he knows you're watching him,' I said.

'Oh, I'm sure he does.'

'Well, I can't let this keep going on. I'm going to have to take him off cash,' I decided.

'Finish up the deposit and we'll go do that now,' Doug told me.

'Yeah,' I agreed half-heartedly.

'Do you want me to tell him?' he asked.

'No, I've got to do this. But I want you with me, if you don't mind?'

'I'll be there,' he promised.

I locked the money up and finished my coffee.

'Ready?' I asked.

'Let's go,' he said, holding open the trailer door for me.

He paused to lock the trailer and then we headed straight for tent number two.

'Hi, Jeff, can I see you outside for a minute?' I asked.

'I'm a little busy right now, Kate,' he told me, ringing up a purchase for a customer.

'Sue, would you take over the cash, please. Jeff, now?'

I walked around behind the tent, with Jeff following me. I could see anger in his eyes, but he was working hard not to let it show anywhere else.

'Jeff, I want you to know I'm not accusing you of anything, but there have been some problems with the cash in your tent and I want Sue to run the cash register from now on,' I said, not pausing for a breath.

Anger flared up in his eyes, but he took a deep breath before opening his mouth.

'You don't think I . . .' he began.

I paused as Buttons the clown led a parade of kids past the tent. He smiled at me but I just turned back to Jeff.

'I don't think anything right now,' I said. 'The tent has been really busy, and there's lots of people around. So I just want to try out a new cashier for a while. Besides, this will free you up to supervise.'

'I think you're being really unfair,' was all he could say.

'I'm sorry you feel that way, but that's my decision,' I told him.

'Fine,' he said, turning around and storming back towards the entrance, muttering something under his breath.

'I'm sorry, did you say something?' I asked, my animosity growing as I followed him.

'I said that whatever you decide is just fucking fine with me,' he almost spat at me.

'Jeff, I'd like to know right know if you can or cannot deal with this. If not, I'll find someone who can.'

'You know, Kate, I thought you said last night that you were going to let my little slip pass.'

'Your little slip?' I asked, incredulous at his choice of words.

'However, it seems to me that you are being slightly vindictive here. Have you thought about your motives in doing this to me?' he asked.

I felt Doug take a step toward Jeff. I reached a hand out behind me and stopped him.

'Jeff, I am this close to having you thrown off the site. Now your choice is to either go back into that tent and do as I ask, or leave. Care to make a decision?'

'I'll go back and work. But don't think I won't be bringing this up with the festival director,' he calmly informed me before walking back into the tent.

I stood there breathing hard, feeling anger burning in the pit of my stomach.

'You have way more patience than I do,' Doug said. 'I would have thrown him out of here long ago.'

'If he were staff, I would have done it in a minute but he's a volunteer. One has to tread very carefully with volunteers. Big time public relations trouble if he starts saying I treated him inappropriately. Or saying that I was drunk.'

'Remember, Kate, you had witnesses last night. I think we can prove that he was out of line first.'

'Yeah, a witness that I was seen dancing and drinking with and then with whom I spent the night. Can you imagine how that's going to play out?' I asked.

'Damn, I hate the way this is working out.'

'Let's get back to the trailer,' I said, not waiting to see if he agreed with me or not.

'I'll get Bruce and Tommy to keep a closer eye on that tent,' Doug said, hurrying to follow me.

'I've got a better idea,' I said. 'Can I borrow your cell phone?'

He pulled it from his belt and handed it to me. 'Don't you have a cell phone?'

'At home.'

'Don't you carry your cell phone?' he asked. 'They work better that way.'

'To use a cell phone one has to remember to charge the battery. And to charge the battery, one has to remember where they put the battery charger.'

He raised his eyebrows but withheld his comment. 'Who are you calling?'

'A friend,' I said, sitting on one of the benches and dialling Graham's number. 'Hi Graham, it's Kate.'

'Hey Kate, I didn't think I'd hear from you this week.'

Graham was very young, only nineteen, and he wanted to be an actor more than anything else in the world. He had worked for me as an usher until he finished high school, when his parents had hoped he would get over the acting thing and head off for college, but Graham thought that just being near the theatre was an education for him. He didn't care if he was seating people, hanging up coats, or serving drinks, he just wanted to be there. He was tall, blonde, and quite well built for someone his age. I suspected he worked out more than he would admit to. He looked vaguely like a young Kenneth Branagh and he was convinced that was who he was going to be when he grew up. He was pretty good too. I had seen him in some children's theatre and been dragged to a couple of his high school productions. He sang, he danced, he acted, and he dreamed of seeing his name up in lights. When he had graduated and my former assistant quit, I decided to take him on full time. Graham was a smart-ass but he worked hard for me.

'So what are you up to?' I asked. 'I thought you were going to go camping this week?'

'Surrounding myself with wine, women and song,' he laughed. 'I haven't had five nights in a row off in ages and I'm trying my best to spend each night with a different woman.'

'Did you and Mandi break up?' I asked.

'No, but she's got some great costumes here . . .'

'Graham, remember that whole conversation about too much information?'

'OK, OK. Well, you never call just to see how I'm doing, so why are you bothering me while I'm on vacation and at my sexual prime?'

'Well, how would you like to spend the day with me?' I asked.

'Kate, don't you think I'm a little young for you?'

'Actually, I need a favour. Did you ever meet Jeff LeCroix when he worked at the theatre?' I asked.

'No, he must have been before my time' Graham told me. 'Is he the one that you told me about? The one that always asked you out?'

'That's him,' I confirmed. 'You sure you never met him?'

'Positive. Why? What's up?'

'Can you come down here?'

'Does it involve any women?' he asked.

'Not directly. But I do need your amateur investigator skills. And of course you'll have to do a little acting too.'

'I'm in,' he answered excitedly.

'Great. Now I want you to come to the security trailer and find me. Come on to the Plaza from the east entrance. And if you see me anywhere else, pretend you don't know me,' I instructed him.

'You going to tell me what's going on?' he asked.

'When you get here,' I said. 'How long do you think you'll be?'

'I can probably be there in half an hour,' he said. 'Any specific dress code?'

'Very casual. Look like a festival volunteer.'

'Will do. Security trailer, use the east entrance, and I don't know you,' he repeated.

'I'll be waiting for you.' I turned the phone off and handed it back to Doug.

'So what was all that about?' he asked.

'Graham is my assistant at the theatre,' I explained. 'The way I figure it, Jeff isn't going to do anything stupid as long as you guys are watching him. But he doesn't know Graham. So I'm going to put Graham in the tent for the afternoon and see what he can find out. If Jeff is stealing, I'm sure Graham will catch him.'

'That's not a half bad idea.' He smiled. 'You've got a devious mind.'

'It comes from months of experience,' I said.

'You've had some experience with crime?' he asked.

'Well, I was shot, doesn't that count?' I said, raising my eyebrows in disbelief. I showed him the faint mark on my arm where the bullet had grazed me. 'And I already told you it was my theatre where the dead body was found in the washroom. And then my cousin is Carrie Palmer.'

'Oh my God, the one who shot her husband?' he asked.

'Well, it turned out it wasn't her,' I reminded him.

'That's a pretty tiny little scar,' he said, inspecting my arm.

'Well, that's all that's left of my scar,' I said. 'It's fading. It was much larger than that.'

'I'm sure it was,' he laughed. 'No wonder you were a little freaked out when Jeff attacked you last night.'

'Well, getting shot wasn't as bad as being stalked,' I said.

'Your life is starting to sound like a novel.'

'Well, Cam used to say that my biggest problem was that I insisted on sticking my nose in where it doesn't belong. He thought I brought a lot of it on myself.'

'Who's Cam?' he asked.

'Sorry, old news. Forget I mentioned him.'

'Is there anything I should know before I start planning our future together?' Doug asked.

'Only that I'm anti-commitment and if you keep talking that way, I may have to consider seeing Bruce or Tommy instead of you.'

'So you're just looking for a cheap fling?' he asked.

'Basically.'

'I can deal with that.' He smiled.

'Don't get your hopes up,' I said sarcastically, as we reached the trailer. 'I may grow tired of you by the end of the week.'

'I'll do my best to keep you entertained,' he promised.

'I'll look forward to it.'

'What time is your friend supposed to be here?' he asked, as I climbed back up into the trailer.

'About half an hour.'

'OK,' he said, checking his watch. 'I'll go earn a living now, but I'll be back by the time he gets here.'

'Bring Bruce and Tommy with you, so they can meet him,' I suggested.

'Good idea. See you in a bit.' He smiled back at me as he started off across the Plaza.

'Looking forward to it,' I said softly, thinking he wouldn't hear me as he turned away. But his smile grew even broader at that. Shit, I hated it when I did that. I had to work harder at editing what actually came out of my mouth.

Precisely thirty minutes later, there was a knock at the trailer door. I opened the curtain and saw Graham standing there.

'Come on in,' I yelled.

Graham climbed up the stairs and closed the door behind him.

'You guys forget to pay the light bill?' he asked, noticing how dark it was in the trailer.

'I closed the curtains because I don't want anyone to see us together,' I explained. 'Our little scheme is only going to work if you are totally undercover.'

'Does Cam know you're doing this?' Graham asked. 'You know how he doesn't like us to do this kind of stuff.'

'Well, I can't say I've mentioned it to him,' I said, trying to brush off his question.

'And I didn't notice him at the dance last night.'

'I am making my own decisions now,' I said coldly, and Graham wisely decided to leave that issue alone.

'So what's the story?' he asked.

'I'm pretty sure Jeff is robbing us blind,' I began. 'But the problem is that whenever security is watching him, he behaves himself. So I want you to spend the afternoon in the market tent with him, and see if you can catch him in the act?'

'Piece of cake.' He smiled confidently.

'Graham, I've got to warn you, this guy has been a little psycho this week. If you agree to do this, you have to know that he might try something.'

'How big are the security guards around here?' he asked.

'Big enough.'

'OK, then I'm fine with it,' he said.

'I've got a T-shirt and nametag for you,' I said. 'Why don't you put them on? The security staff will be here in a minute. I want you to meet them, so you know who to go to just in case you need any help.'

Graham stripped off his shirt and pulled on his festival T-shirt. Then he slipped on his nametag.

'I don't get to be Graham?' he asked.

'No, I figured if anyone recognized you, you could say you were Graham's brother and still pull this off.'

'But why'd you have to pick this name?' he asked, holding out the nametag.

'It was the first thing that popped into my mind when I was sitting at the computer,' I said.

'Liar,' he said, 'You are doing this to get back at me for something.'

'Herman is not such a bad name,' I said.

'Easy for you to say,' he said. 'You don't have to use it all afternoon. Now I'm going to have to come up with a cool nickname in the next two minutes.'

'You're whining,' I told him. 'I could have called you Ethelbert or something worse if I had been trying harder.'

'Thank God for small blessings.'

There was another knock at the door and I peeked out the curtain again.

'Come in,' I called when I recognized Doug and the guys.

They climbed up into the trailer and Doug immediately poured himself a coffee. I had never met a person who drank as much coffee as I did, probably why I was so attracted to him.

'Guys, this is my assistant, Graham. Graham, this is Doug, Tommy and Bruce,' I introduced them. 'I've told Graham, or should I say Herman, what's going on.'

'So what are we going to do if Graham catches him?' Bruce asked.

'I thought Graham could just say he's going for a break, and come and find one of you guys. And me. I have to admit I'm really going to enjoy throwing Jeff off the site.'

'And long overdue that is,' Doug added.

'So you guys need to stay far away from tent two,' I instructed. 'I want Jeff to think he's totally free and clear to do whatever he wants.'

'Well let's get him working,' Bruce said.

'I'll walk you over to the tent,' Doug offered.

'No, I'll go alone this time,' I said. 'You're only supposed to be with me when I'm doing cash runs. I don't want him to get suspicious.'

'I don't want you alone with him,' Doug protested.

'I won't be alone with him; I'll have Graham with me. Besides I'm just going to introduce Graham and then disappear,' I argued. 'Graham and I have had some practice with this. Just let us do our thing and get Graham in that tent.'

'I think she's got a point,' Tommy said. 'Besides, she's got a radio and we won't be far away.'

'A guy like that is too chicken to try anything in broad daylight with lots of people around,' Bruce pointed out.

'Fine. But I expect to see you out of that tent in under two minutes,' Doug finally gave in.

'Come on, Graham, let's get out of here before they change their minds,' I said, getting up and attaching the radio to my belt.

Graham followed behind me as I left the trailer and started for the market tent.

'Why are they so uptight about this guy?' Graham asked. 'I mean other than the fact that he's stealing.'

'I told you, he's kind of been acting psycho this week, drinking a bit too much and carrying on.'

'And that's all?' Graham asked.

'Well, no, but I'd rather not get into that right now, OK? What I'd like to do is have you catch him stealing, fire his ass out of here and be done with him forever.'

'I can do that,' Graham said.

'Jeff.' I smiled as we entered the tent. I noticed he had

repositioned himself behind the cash register again, but decided not to confront him.

'Hi Kate.' He smiled uncomfortably, waiting for me to chastise him.

'Jeff, thanks for switching cashiers this morning. I'm afraid you guys were over this time, so we're just going to chalk this problem up to the fact that you guys are the busiest tent at the festival. I know it's really busy, but officially I do have to ask you to just be a little more careful when you're giving change.'

'Sure. I'm glad you understand some of the challenges we've been facing in here.'

'Jeff, I can't stay because I have some problems in tent number one. I just wanted to bring Herman over and introduce you. He's going to be volunteering here with you for the rest of the week.'

'Should I be suspicious?' Jeff asked, winking conspiratorially at me now that we were friends again.

'No, look it has to do with one of the other tents and Herman just asked me if he could work somewhere else.'

'Well, nice to have you join us here,' Jeff said, extending his hand across the table and Graham took it.

'Call me Buzz.' He smiled at Jeff. 'All my friends do.'

'Well Buzz, welcome to the festival market.' Jeff smiled back at him. 'Are you any good at selling T-shirts?'

Graham laughed, 'I think I can help you out in that department.'

'Great, well I'll leave you to train him, Jeff, and I'll be back around four to close you down for the day.'

'Don't worry about us, we'll be fine,' Jeff called after me as I hurriedly made my way through the crowds and back out on to the Plaza. I didn't know what to do with myself while I waited to hear from Graham and I was afraid Jeff might see me hovering a little too closely around his tent and give the game away, so I went over to tent three and worked with the volunteers for a little while. When I was tired and hot I wandered to the food fair and bought myself an iced tea. Then I found an empty picnic table and sat down to enjoy it. I was about halfway through it and searching my pockets for a cigarette when Sam sat down beside me.

'I didn't expect you to be taking it easy at this time of the day,' she said.

'I'm actually working very hard right now.'

'You could have fooled me.'

'I'm practising a very important Klingon philosophy right now,' I explained.

'What?'

'Well, you know the famous Klingon proverb?' I continued.

'No, as a matter of fact I don't.'

'Revenge is a dish best served cold,' I quoted.

'Huh?' she said. 'I think that might have been Shakespeare?'

'Shakespeare stole a lot of his work from the early Klingon philosophers. I'm very disappointed that you've been my friend for so long and yet you refuse to learn any of the basic *Star Trek* trivia.'

'I've lived this long without it and I seem to be doing just fine,' she said. 'Do you think that you watch too much television?'

'I think you don't watch enough,' I said. 'You can learn a lot from TV these days.'

'Yeah, like Klingon philosophy because we know how handy that is in life.'

'Well you don't look like you're working very hard either,' I said.

'I actually think I've got my assistant starting to do things my way,' she said. 'Or at least he's just stopped arguing about it and is doing it his way behind my back. Typical festival, I'll have everyone perfectly trained by the last day.'

I finally found a cigarette in the bottom of my fanny pack but had no match in sight.

'Have you got a light?' I asked, hopefully.

'Actually I do,' she said, pulling a book of matches out of her pocket. 'I was just lighting the barbeques.'

'Bless you,' I said, lighting the cigarette and inhaling deeply.

'Now are you going to explain what you're talking about?' she asked.

'It turns out that not only is Jeff a total little scuzz-ball and jerk, he's also a thief. My deposits and inventory counts have been turning up short in tent two for two days but we haven't been able to catch Jeff in the act. So I've got Graham working in the tent right now. As soon as he sees anything we can nail him for, Graham's going to contact security, they're going to radio me, and I'm going to throw him off the site. This is going to make my day!' I smiled triumphantly.

'You're getting far too much pleasure out of this.'

'Sam, after last night, I'll be very happy to have some tangible evidence against him. Something that's not going to get me in trouble for the way I treated a volunteer.'

'Do I get to watch you throw him out?'

'Well, I wasn't exactly planning on doing it myself, physically.'

'You should have him arrested if he's stealing,' Sam suggested.

'I'd rather not,' I said. 'It's bad publicity. We don't need the police down here bringing the inevitable reporters with them.'

'I suppose you're right, but it also doesn't seem right that he's getting away with it.'

'I'll be happy just to have him out of here.' I smiled, thinking about it.

'Doug to Kate, over.' My radio broke into our conversation.

'And this might just be it.' I smiled, pulling the radio off my waist. 'This is Kate, go ahead, Doug.'

'What's your twenty, over?' he asked.

'My what?' I asked.

'He wants to know where you are,' Sam explained.

'How do you know that?' I asked.

'What's your location, over?' Doug came back on the radio.

'By the picnic tables,' I answered him.

'OK, I'm on my way, Doug out,' he said.

I finished my cigarette, stomping it out on the grass and reattached the radio to my belt.

'How did you know what a twenty was?' I asked Sam again.

'Come on, Kate, we're the same age. Didn't your family have a CB radio in the seventies?'

'No. My dad did but I never used it.'

'Really. I thought everyone did. Remember that song, we got a great big convoy, trucking through the night?' she sang for me.

'I've tried to block most of the seventies from my mind,'

108

I told her. 'Just thinking about all that polyester gives me the chills.'

'I bet you were a disco queen, weren't you?'

'At three years old?' I asked.

'Come on . . .'

'OK, I hustled a little. I was the wildest nine-year-old on the dance floor. What was your name?'

'Huh?'

'The name that you used on the radio,' I explained.

'You mean my handle. I was Chocolate Chip.' She smiled. 'Even back then everyone knew me for my cookies.'

'You mean you weren't Sex Kitten or something?'

'No, I saved that for my college years. Look, I better leave you and Doug to your business,' Sam said standing up. 'And I better get back to my business while I still have one. That boy may be working hard now but he has a big habit of disappearing for very long breaks when my back is turned. Good luck with your project.'

'Thanks, Sam. I'll come and find you when this is over and fill you in on the details.'

'I'll have a burger waiting for you.'

'With curly fries?' I asked.

'I'll do my best,' she promised.

Doug sat down at the picnic table beside me.

'Well?' I asked.

'Well, I think we got him. Graham found Bruce and told him that Jeff has been stuffing money in his pockets.'

'All afternoon?' I asked.

'I guess he's been trying to catch up since we're not watching him as closely anymore.'

'Let's go get him then,' I said, standing up and pulling him after me.

'All right, all right,' he said, following close after me.

Bruce, Tommy and Graham were gathered behind the market tent, waiting for Doug and I to appear.

'Well?' I asked, as soon as I was within earshot of Graham.

'This was way too easy, Kate,' Graham smirked, proud of himself.

'Quit patting yourself on the back for a minute and tell me about it,' I ordered him.

'He's not very subtle,' Graham continued. 'I've seen him stuffing money in his pocket three times in the last little while.'

'Really?' I asked.

'Really,' he confirmed. 'Every time we've had a big sale, most of it's gone in his jeans, not the cash drawer. He's pretty good at it, but not good enough to slip it past me. Especially when I've been watching for it all afternoon.'

'So, we can get him now?' I asked.

'We can get him now,' Doug confirmed.

'So what are we waiting for?' I asked, and started toward the tent, followed closely by the four men. I had a good adrenalin buzz going and I didn't want to waste it.

Jeff stood in front of the cash register, smiling and chatting with a customer, when we entered the tent. I stormed over to where he stood and slammed the cash register closed. He looked at me with shock registering on his face.

'Kate, what the hell . . .'

'Empty your pockets, Jeff,' I told him firmly.

'What are you talking about?' he asked.

'I said empty your pockets,' I repeated.

'What is this all about? You have no right to ask me to do that.'

'I believe you have been stealing from the festival. And I have witnesses. Now empty your pockets.'

'Who are these witnesses?' he demanded.

'I believe you've met my assistant manager, Graham?' I asked, a smile on my face as Graham took a step forward.

'You've been spying on me?' he asked, shock registering on his face.

'Empty your pockets.'

Jeff looked around frantically for a way out of the tent but Bruce was on the left of him and Tommy on his right, with Doug, Graham and I standing in front.

'There's nowhere to go, Jeff,' Doug said calmly. 'Now, empty your pockets and let's get this over with.'

Suddenly, Jeff dropped to the ground and was halfway under the tent before Bruce grabbed one of his legs.

'Run!' he screamed as he struggled to break free. 'Get out of here. They've got me. I won't tell them anything.'

Tommy grabbed Jeff's other leg and the two guards pulled him back into the tent, where he became suddenly silent. Doug and I ran around to the other side of the tent, frantically trying to catch the person Jeff had been calling out to. The Plaza was crowded with visitors and there was no way to tell who Jeff had been talking to. The only familiar face I saw was Buttons, the clown with the star on his cheek, skipping across the grass, sprinkling his confetti over the crowds. We returned to the tent where Bruce was holding Jeff while Tommy was emptying his pockets.

'What, are you trying for an insanity plea?' I asked.

'It is none of your business who I might be talking to,' Jeff snarled at me.

I turned and noticed Doug had his cell phone out and was dialling.

'Who are you calling?' I asked.

'The police.'

'I told you I didn't want to do that,' I protested.

'Sorry, Kate, this isn't your decision,' he said as Tommy and Bruce pulled Jeff away from the cashier's table. 'Check his backpack too.'

Tommy had pulled a wad of bills out of Jeff's pockets and several CDs from his backpack, all of which he handed over to me. I counted through it and found several hundred dollars worth of bills.

'Take him to the trailer,' Doug ordered and the guys hauled him roughly out of the tent and on to the Plaza.

'The police are going to meet us at the security trailer,' Doug told me. 'They won't cause much of a disruption. I doubt anyone will even notice they're here.'

'Fine,' I said, meaning it wasn't but I didn't have a choice.

'I'll meet you back at the trailer,' he said. 'The police will want to talk to you.'

'I'll be back there in a few minutes,' I promised.

Doug left the tent and jogged to catch up with Tommy and Bruce. I turned back to Graham and smiled at him.

'Good job, kiddo.'

'It was pretty easy,' he said modestly. 'He's not a very smart crook.'

'I really appreciate it. But now I'm left with a whole new

set of problems,' I complained, a plan slowly forming in my head.

'What's that?' Graham asked.

'I have no one to supervise this tent. What am I going to do for the rest of the week?'

'Oh no you don't,' Graham protested, knowing what I was thinking. 'This is my vacation too, remember?'

'Graham, there's no one else I can get on short notice,' I whined.

'No way, Kate. Remember I have plans for the week.'

'There's absolutely no night shifts involved. I'll have you closed down and out of here by five o'clock every night. I swear.' At least I hoped I would. I wasn't doing a very good job of sticking to a schedule so far.

'I should know better than to ever help you out with anything. You're never satisfied.'

'Graham, I'll owe you big time if you do this for me.'

'You already owe me more than you could ever possibly repay in two lifetimes.'

'So will you do it?' I asked hopefully, waiting as he thought it over.

'Of course I will, you know I can't say no to you,' he said finally.

'All right, then the first thing I need you to do is to close down this tent. We have to do a complete inventory and cash out. I need to know exactly what Jeff got away with. Have two people do everything together and sign off on everything.'

'No problem,' he promised me.

'You're a life saver.' I kissed him on the cheek and turned to leave.

'Kate,' he called.

'What?'

'I'm out of here by five, right?'

'Yes, Graham,' I said as I tried to leave again.

'And Kate,' he called again.

'Yes, Graham?'

'No extra duties? Just this one tent?'

'I promise. And if I try to take advantage of you, you just tell me,' I said and then turned again but thought better of it. 'Anything else?'

'Yeah, a new nametag,' he said, holding up the one that said Herman.

'All right, I'll get that done this afternoon, I promise. I'll be at the trailer waiting for the police. If you need me just stop anyone with a radio, I'm on channel 1A.'

'Got it.'

'And Graham,' I called back to him.

'Yes, Kate?'

'Try not to need me too often, I've been kind of busy this week.'

'Boy, that'll be nice to see for a change,' he said.

'What?' I asked curiously.

'I mean me watching you work,' he laughed at me.

'Lucky for you I'm still grateful to you right now. But you will pay for that comment.' And then I finally did head for the trailer.

As I got closer to the trailer, I saw an unmarked police car parked beside the trailer. I quickened my pace and was surprised to see Ken Lincoln standing outside the car door, drinking a Gatorade and talking into a radio.

Ken Lincoln was a detective with the homicide division of the Calgary Police Department. His first case as a detective was a murder that took place in the lobby of my theatre back in September, which seemed like a lifetime ago. Ken had permanently changed my idea of what a police detective should look like. I had definitely had the Lieutenant Colombo, older man, rumpled raincoat image firmly implanted in my mind thanks to too many years of watching television. This detective was young, slim, with thick black hair covering his head and no sign of bald spots. He walked with a bounce in his step and certainly didn't look like he suffered from overwork or long hours of sitting at a desk. He also dressed much better than I ever expected to see a cop dress.

'Ken,' I called and waved to him.

He waved back, finished talking on the radio and leaned into the car to put it away.

'What are you doing down here?' I asked. 'Hopefully it's pleasure and not business.'

'Well Kate, turns out it's going to be pleasure after all. I have to admit that when I heard your name over the radio, I came down here. Somehow I seem to associate you with homicide investigations.'

'Sorry to disappoint you,' I teased.

'Trust me, no disappointment. I've called a squad car, and they should be here soon. I'll stick around until they arrive and then I intend to find out where that wonderful barbeque smell is coming from.'

'I can help you with that one,' I said. 'My friend Samantha happens to be cooking the food that's casting that wonderful aroma over the Plaza.'

'Then I think I'm going to have to be very nice to you.' He smiled. 'So what's up here?'

'Did you talk with the security guys yet?' I asked.

'A little. But your version of a story is always much more interesting than anyone else's.'

'Very funny. Short version is that we caught this guy stealing money from the festival market. I was going to just kick him out of here, but when he tried to escape with the money, Doug decided calling the police would be a much better idea.'

'How much has he taken?'

'We found about two hundred dollars on him,' I said. 'But I'm missing over six hundred dollars in cash and merchandise in the last day or so.'

'He's done pretty well for himself.'

'And what'll he get for it?' I asked. 'Two hundred is only going to be one of those slap on the wrist sentences.'

'Maybe not. Just wait until we check his priors. If it isn't the first time he's done something like this, it might just make a difference.'

'Good.'

'Is there anything else going on with this guy, Kate? Your animosity is showing.'

'Well, he sort of attacked me last night.'

'He what?' Ken asked, his eyebrows rising in shock. 'Why didn't you call the police then?'

'He was drunk. And I was feeling pretty good myself. I just figured when he sobered up he'd regret it and be a good boy for the rest of the week.'

'And he didn't?' Ken asked.

'Once a jerk, always a jerk.'

A police cruiser pulled up behind Ken's car and Ken turned and waved to the officers.

'You want me to tell them about last night too?' Ken asked.

'No, Ken, I'd really like to just let that pass. Let's keep this on a professional level and forget all the personal stuff.'

'There's a personal relationship between you two?' he asked.

'No, only in his mind. He's been trying to go out with me for a couple of years.'

'But you've never gone out with him.'

'Not even for coffee.'

'Are you sure about it?' he asked.

'That I've never gone out with him?' I asked.

'No, about not pressing charges over last night,' he explained.

'No, I'd really rather not.'

'It's your call,' he told me. 'But I don't think you're making the right decision.'

'Ken, please?' I pleaded, as the two officers approached us.

'Fine,' he said. 'Hey guys, we've got the man and the security staff inside the trailer. Come on in and I'll introduce you. Kate, don't you go too far away.'

I watched them climb inside the trailer and sat myself down on the hood of Ken's car, waiting for them to come out.

'Wow, lots of excitement around here today.'

I turned and saw Buttons juggling some beanbags as he wandered over.

'Nothing to see here,' I said. 'Keep moving on.'

'Really?' he asked. 'Not even one little bit of gossip? I would be everyone's favourite clown if I could find out what was going on. There's going to be lots of questions in the festival lounge later.'

'Sorry, let's just try and keep the crowds down. Why don't you go try and get that group of kids away from the police car?' I asked. 'Seth, please?'

Buttons looked disappointed through his clown makeup, but did as he was told. I settled back down, watching the trailer, wishing I could see through the curtains and find out what was going on.

'So what's all the excitement about?' a voice behind me asked.

I jumped off the car. 'Sam, you scared the shit out of me.'

'Sorry,' she apologized, joining me as I settled myself back down again. 'I just wanted to be in on the adventure for once.'

'Well, Graham caught Jeff in the act, we found a bunch of money in his pockets and the police are in there now. Other than that I'm not sure what they're doing in there.'

'That much I could have figured out on my own,' she said, disappointed.

'Sorry, I'm out of the loop myself.'

'So why are there two police cars here?' Sam asked.

'Detective Lincoln was driving by when he heard my name over the radio, so he dropped by to see what was happening. I guess he figured that with me involved there was probably a murder close by.'

'I don't know why he'd think that,' she said, sarcastically.

'Well, Ken is anxiously awaiting a sampling of your cooking. Apparently the barbeque is pulling people in from around the block.'

'And I'm anxiously awaiting finally meeting him,' she said. 'And having a long conversation with him while I ply him with my barbeque burgers.'

'And what are you hoping to find out?' I asked.

'Nothing much. Just all the details that you edit out of these adventures you have.'

'Did you ever think I might edit my stories for a reason?' I asked.

'Of course, that's why I want to hear what he has to say. Find out what you've been hiding from me.' She had an evil grin on her face.

The trailer door opened and we both turned to see who was coming out. Ken came down the steps first, followed by the uniformed officers and Jeff in handcuffs. They led him toward the police cruiser.

'You bitch,' he screamed, as he passed by me, struggling to break free from the officers' grip.

Doug came out of the trailer quickly at the sound of the struggle.

'That's enough,' one of the officers warned him, roughly pulling him a little further away from me and toward the police cruiser.

'You're going to fucking regret this,' Jeff screamed, even as they shoved him into the back seat of the car. 'You're going to live to fucking regret this!'

Doug had a hand protectively on my shoulder and Ken positioned himself between Jeff and me until they had the door to the car closed. The two officers got into the car, pulled out on to the avenue and drove away. Ken finally turned back to face me.

'I can see why you didn't want to date him,' Ken laughed, trying to lighten the mood.

'He's out of here for good now,' Doug said, gently squeezing my shoulder.

'Do you need any sort of a statement from me?' I asked Ken.

'No, we've got enough with Graham and the report from the security staff,' Ken said. 'Now how do I get to the food?'

'Ken, this is my friend Samantha,' I said.

'Sam,' she said, shaking his hand.

'You're the cook?' he asked.

'The cook?' I repeated. 'She is only the best caterer in the city.'

'Wow,' Ken said. 'I never realized Kate had such good connections.'

'I'll admit to being a good cook,' she laughed, hopping off the hood of the car and linking her arm through his. 'Now, if you'll follow me I'll hook you up with the best barbeque ever and we can have a nice chat.'

'Chat?' he asked, as she began to lead him toward the catering tents.

'I have so many questions for you,' she said, pulling him further away.

'Please don't incriminate me,' I called after him.

Doug put his arm around me and pulled me close to him.

'Are you OK?' he asked.

'I'm fine,' I said. 'But I am getting just a little tired of that question.'

'Point taken. You want to go grab a coffee?' he asked.

'I'd love to,' I said, wondering what Gus would make of me walking in with Doug. 'But not at Grounds Zero. Let's go to Vaudeville's instead.'

'Sure, but you have to promise to answer some questions for me,' he said.

'Then I've changed my mind. I don't want to have coffee if there's strings attached.'

'Simple questions,' he said. 'Nothing incriminating. I promise.'

'And if I don't want to answer?' I asked.

'Then you don't have to answer, yet,' he said, holding out his hand for me to take. 'OK?'

I took his hand. 'I guess.'

'Boy, I haven't heard so much enthusiasm from a date since my ex-wife.'

'You've been married?' I asked.

'You're not the only one with secrets.' He smiled as we headed towards the outdoor patio around the corner.

'Look, a nice quiet corner table where we can have some privacy,' he said, hopping over the fence and grabbing the table.

I followed him over the fence and sat down beside him.

I pulled a cigarette out and offered him one.

'Thanks,' he said, pulling his lighter out of his pocket and lighting my cigarette and then his own.

A waitress came over and he ordered iced cappuccinos for both of us. I waited until she was gone before saying anything.

'Nice day,' I said, hoping to avoid any serious conversation that I was not ready to have.

'So, Kate,' he began.

'OK, Doug, whatever it is you have on your mind, ask away.'

'Do you have a boyfriend?' he asked.

'What makes you ask that?' I answered, avoiding the question. After all, I really wasn't sure what the answer was.

'A few things make me think that. But mostly the way your friend Sam looks at me,' he said.

'How does she look at you?' I asked, truly perplexed.

'Like I'm somewhere I don't belong.'

'That's not her decision,' I said. 'That's mine.'

'So am I somewhere that I don't belong?' he asked, leaning closer and draping his arm over my shoulder. 'You know, you always avoid answering this question directly too and that is highly suspicious.'

'There is no boyfriend,' I told him. 'There used to be. I think my friends are just starting to get used to the idea that he's gone.'

He took a strand of my hair between his fingers and started twirling it.

'Are you sure?' he asked. 'I don't want to be someone you use to try to make somebody else jealous.'

'God, I swear I would never do that,' I said.

'I'm not asking for any sort of guarantee for the future or anything, but I really don't want to be used. And I just feel like there's something you're not telling me.'

'I swear to you, Doug, I am a free agent right now. My friends will just have to get used to seeing me with other guys.'

'So why didn't you want to go to Grounds Zero?' he asked.

'Because Gus, the owner, is another friend of mine.'

'So you know how your friends feel about me?' he asked. 'Do they hate me?'

'I don't think so. They've all been giving me a rough time, that's all. I'm just getting a little tired of it.'

'So we're OK with this,' he asked, as I suddenly realized he was very close to me.

'We're very OK with this,' I agreed, feeling my pulse quicken despite myself.

'Good,' he said, finally ending the anticipation, as he leaned even closer and kissed me.

I was just feeling that nice little tingle in my stomach, as the soft stubble of his chin pressed against my face.

'Tommy to Doug, over.' His radio came alive, breaking the mood quickly.

'I'm going to be so glad when the festival is over and that thing is off your belt,' I sighed, pulling away.

He laughed as he pulled the mike up and answered the call.

After the events of the early afternoon, the rest of the day passed in relative tranquillity. I had the tents closed up, the bank deposits in the safe, and was sitting on a lawn chair with a beer, waiting for the Plaza to clear and someone to come join me. That was when my walkie-talkie went off.

'Festival office to Kate, over.'

119

I almost jumped when I heard my name, but recovered nicely and was glad I had not taken it off yet.

'This is Kate.'

'Kate, can you come up to the office to meet with the producer please, over?'

'I'm on my way.'

I stashed the beer in the fridge and grabbed a mint, not that it would help but it would make me feel better. I ran into the Plex and climbed the couple of flights of stairs to the tiny office, sandwiched in the corner of the Plus 15. The door was still open and the receptionist looked up and smiled at me.

'He's in his office in the back,' she said.

'Thanks.' I smiled, hurrying back. I had a sinking feeling I knew what this was about.

Trent Cranston was a fixture on the Calgary Arts Scene since writing his first play over twenty years ago. He had always been the hippy-type artist, long hair in a ponytail, blue jeans, and he was always protesting something. He had begun to become a little more corporate ten years ago, when he founded this festival, slowly losing the ponytail and trading the jeans for khakis. But he was still not the suit and tie kind of guy and his office was covered with pictures of the actors and directors he had worked with over the years.

'Hi, Kate, have a seat.' He smiled warmly at me; prematurely grey hair framing a face that had spent way too much time without protection in the sun.

'Hi, Trent, you look pretty good considering we're in the middle of festival week,' I teased him.

'The exhaustion usually sets in midday of day four,' he laughed back.

'So what can I help you with?' I asked, not wanting to avoid the inevitable any longer.

'It's the whole darned police thing,' he said, using that aw-shucks attitude that probably disarmed a lot of people.

'Yeah, don't you hate that when people steal from you and you have to arrest them?'

'You know, Kate, I actually do,' he said. 'I just have some forms here that the lawyers and insurance company will need filled out. If you could get these back to me tomorrow, that would be great.'

'Really?' I asked. 'You're OK with this?'

'Well, it's not my first choice, hiring a thief and having the police on site to arrest him. But shit happens, right?'

'Thanks.'

'Really, you handled it great; you kept it low key. I even noticed you got a clown in to distract the kids. You did a good job and I really appreciate it.'

'Well, thanks. I'll get these forms back to you first thing tomorrow,' I promised.

'Good. Enjoy your beer,' he laughed. 'You've earned it.'

I took the paperwork and stood up. I noticed the great view he had of the entire Plaza from his office, including the security trailer. I best remember that Big Brother was watching me.

'Well, you're welcome to join us any time.'

I made my way back to my chair, put my feet up, had my beer in hand and noticed the Plaza was clearing nicely. I was still looking forward to some company. Sam was the first to join me.

'Have you got another one of those?' she asked, pointing to my beer.

'Pull up a chair and I'll grab you one,' I said, climbing up into the trailer and grabbing a beer from the fridge. Sam had a chair pulled up beside mine and I handed her the beer. 'So how was your day?'

'Busy,' she said, kicking her shoes off and stretching her legs out. 'I don't think I'm going to do another of these festivals. I'm getting too old for all this work. I think I'll stick to those quiet black tie affairs from now on.'

'You'll be here next year,' I said.

'We'll see.'

'Hey, ladies,' Doug greeted us, pulling up a chair for himself.

'Want a beer?' I asked.

'No, I'll get one later,' he said. 'I'm glad to see you're here, Sam.'

'You are?' I asked, surprised.

'I am,' he confirmed. 'I was hoping you'd take Kate home with you tonight.'

'Why?' Sam asked.

'Well, Detective Lincoln gave me a call about an hour ago. Our friend Jeff is out on bail.'

'What?' I asked.

'Yeah, he had a lawyer down there waiting for him and he was out in record time,' Doug confirmed, shaking his head.

'He had a lawyer waiting for him?' I asked. 'Does that sound strange to anyone else?'

'Do you think Kate's in danger?' Sam asked.

'Probably not. But I'd feel a lot better if she wasn't alone tonight. Just in case he's still mad.'

'And what about tomorrow?' I asked, getting my back up. 'Am I supposed to move in with Sam and hide out?'

'No,' he said, trying to calm me down. 'I'm sure he'll calm down by tomorrow and realize that he better be a good boy until his trial.'

'So am I staying with Sam to keep me safe or to make you feel better?'

'A little of both,' he admitted.

'Don't even think about arguing about this, Kate,' Sam told me. 'You are coming home with me tonight and that's that.'

'I don't need babysitting.'

'Your little goddaughter will be happy to see Auntie Kate and you and Ryan can have a mad game of Trivial Pursuit. And I can sleep well because I know you're safe.'

'Fine,' I gave in, secretly relieved that they had convinced me. 'But only for tonight. You know I hate hiding out.'

'Give it up, Kate,' Sam warned me. 'I know you're happy to be coming home with me.'

'Well, maybe a little,' I admitted. 'But I'm serious that this is only for tonight.'

'We can cross that bridge when we come to it,' she said.

'Is she always this stubborn?' Doug asked.

'This is mild,' Sam said, checking her watch. 'We better get going.'

'I'll walk you to your car,' Doug said, standing up.

'You don't have to, we'll be fine,' I protested.

'Well, he can walk me to my car,' Sam said. 'If you happen to be with us, so be it.'

'Once again, ganging up on me. I'm getting really tired of this,' I whined.

'My five-year-old can't win an argument with me,' Sam said. 'What makes you think you stand a chance?'

And as we sat in the back yard, listening to the gentle sounds of the river flowing by, and with a big fire blazing in the fire pit, I was happy to be here. Ryan brought out the Trivial Pursuit game and set it up on the table on the patio and I found myself actually relaxing, if only for a moment or two.

He sat on the bench, admiring the houses built on the river, as he tossed breadcrumbs for the ducks. They were beautiful houses with privileged people inside, people who felt safe from the dangers of the world. But they have no idea, he thought, as he watched the husband put another log on the fire and then sit back down at the patio table, rolling the dice and then taking his turn at the game board. He liked it that they enjoyed playing games though, it seemed very appropriate considering that he, too, loved games and soon their paths would be crossing in a very up close and personal manner.

A young blonde walked by, dressed in jogging gear but obviously tired and on her cool-down phase. He shook out the last of his breadcrumbs, crumpled up the bag and shoved it in his pocket. He could smell her sweat and it was almost the same as when he smelled fear. It excited him and he had to see where she was going. He would control himself and not play with her, but he could follow her, find out where she lived, save her for later, after this game was over. He stood up, pulled at the collar of his leather jacket and followed her down the path.

Thursday

Spending the night at Sam's had probably been the best thing that happened to me all week. I played Barbie dolls with Bonnie, who was very bossy for a five-year-old, had a great dinner that I didn't have to lift a finger to help with, played a couple of games, which I managed to win, and went to bed fairly early. I had slept better than I had since Cam had left. I got up feeling very refreshed, smelling coffee and the breakfast cooking downstairs.

Sam and Ryan had a lovely house on the Elbow River that they had inherited from her parents and then completely redone. The spare room had a beautiful bed with goose-down duvets straight from a Hutterite colony, a nice little reading area, and its own en-suite bathroom. When the aroma of sausage frying and coffee brewing from downstairs had penetrated my dreams, I jumped into the shower and quickly scrubbed up. I had spare clothes from the office with me, so I got dressed, left my hair wet and in a ponytail and followed the wonderful scent down into the kitchen.

'Morning, Kate.'

'Ryan? Since when do you get kitchen duty?' I asked.

'Ah, I felt sorry for Sammi. She's working real hard at that festival so I figured I'd treat her this morning. And you of course.'

'Good save,' I said. 'I didn't know you knew how to cook.'

'They teach us one or two things at the fire hall, you know. Now take a coffee and join the girls on the patio,' he ordered, and I obeyed.

I let myself out the French doors and on to the tiled patio. There was a wonderful run of grass leading down to the river, a nice little play area for Bonnie and a very pretty wild English-style garden of flowers. Sam and Bonnie sat at the

124

wrought iron bistro table, Sam with a coffee in hand and Bonnie with a hot chocolate and the ever-present Barbie doll.

'Morning,' I said, closing the door behind me and joining them at the table. The air was warm, the scent of the flowers sweet and I decided I didn't ever want to leave this place.

'You're up early,' Sam said. 'I figured I'd give you at least another hour.'

'Well, it was the coffee. God, this is good.'

'It's Gus's latest beans. You'll have to let him know it's a hit.'

'Good morning Bonnie-belle.' I smiled at the little girl.

'Want to play Barbies?' she asked.

'Why don't you go give the duckies some breakfast?' Sam asked, handing her daughter a bag of breadcrumbs, which Bonnie took happily and went down to the water's edge.

'Sleep well?' Sam asked.

'Oh yes. And I think I may just call in sick today and spend the day sitting right here.'

'Sorry, I'd have to tell on you,' she said.

'And you call yourself my friend.'

'If I don't get to stay here all day, then neither do you.'

'Why do you leave?' I asked.

'Well, Kate, we might have inherited the house from my family, but someone has to earn the money to pay the taxes on it.'

'But Ryan's a rich firefighter,' I said, referring to her husband, who was busy crashing dishes around in the kitchen.

'Oh, yeah, I keep forgetting that,' she laughed.

'How'd you get him to cook?'

'He volunteered. Really,' Sam said, 'after ten years at the fire hall, he should be able to cook something. I mean he makes dinner there every night.'

'Does he?'

'Well, I may help a little bit by sending stuff in,' she admitted. 'I expect with me and Cam cooking all the time, neither of you guys usually gets a chance to.'

'That doesn't really bother me though,' I laughed.

Ryan joined us on the patio, holding a big tray of plates in front of him.

'That smells good,' Sam said.

125

'That smells wonderful,' I added. 'What are you feeding us this morning?'

'French toast with goat cheese and Sam's raspberry jam. And there's some deer sausage one of the guys at the fire hall made last fall.'

'I may just dump Cam permanently and live here,' I laughed, and then realized I was met with a cold, hard silence. 'Uh, that would have been funny if we were still together, right?'

'Bonnie, come on up for breakfast,' Sam yelled for her daughter.

Bonnie was surrounded by tame ducks, which quickly lost interest when they saw her packing up their treats.

'Sorry,' I said.

'No, don't worry about it,' Ryan said. 'Sam told me you guys were going through a spell right now. You'll get it all worked out.'

The rest of the meal passed quietly, with Sam glancing over at me with tears in her eyes. Ryan was off work today so he offered to clear everything up before he and Bonnie went off to school, and Sam and I drove in bright and early.

'Is there something you want to say to me?' I asked, trying to alleviate the tension that had been between us since breakfast.

'No.'

'Sam, please.'

'Kate, I'm not mad at you. I'm just so sad. For both of you.'

We made the rest of the short drive in silence. Sam parked and then she headed off for her kitchen and I made my way to my theatre office. I figured as today was the fourth day, everyone knew what they were doing; Jeff was off the site for good, it would be a good day to relax and enjoy myself, so I buckled down and got all my paperwork caught up, got the floats ready and hoped, with Graham here, that no other problems would crop up. I packed everything up, hooked my radio on to my belt and but didn't bother to turn it on, I'd do that when I was officially on the site. Time to head for the security trailer and see what was going on with them. I let my hair down now that it was dry, pulled on my baseball cap and was on my way. I decided to go the long way round and stop at Grounds Zero for a coffee.

Gus was already hard at work but looked up with a smile when he saw me come in.

'Hey Kate, I'm relieved to hear you got rid of Jeff yesterday.'

'You and me both, Gus,' I said, positioning myself on my favourite stool and not even bothering to ask him how he knew about that.

'What's it going to be this morning?' he asked.

'Two cappuccinos and two mochaccinos to go please.'

'You feeding those security boys?' he asked.

'Uh huh.'

'Good. I hope they're doing a good job of watching out for you.'

'They seem to be doing a pretty good job of it,' I told him.

'Good.' He smiled. 'You need to be extra careful today.'

'Why?' I asked. 'We got rid of the problem.'

'You don't know that Jeff's out of jail?' he asked.

'Yes, we found out yesterday afternoon,' I said. 'How the hell did you find out so quickly?'

'Do you really want to know?' he asked.

'No,' I admitted. 'You're better off keeping your air of mystery.'

'Well you just keep yourself close to those big strong boys today,' he instructed me.

'Oh, Jeff isn't going to try anything,' I said.

'Better safe than sorry, Kate,' he said. 'Did I ever tell you that the day after I fired him, someone broke my front window?'

'No, really?' I asked.

'Yeah and I don't think it was just a coincidence,' he said, turning and busying himself with the cappuccino machine.

'Well, let him break any windows he wants in the theatre if it makes him feel better,' I said. 'But I don't think he'll be stupid enough to come back on the site this week. And by the time the festival is over I'm sure he'll have cooled down a bit.'

'I don't know.' He put the cappuccinos in a box and set them on the counter in front of me. 'I think that Jeff is a little more crazy than he lets the world know. I know there were some family troubles after he left the Plex and went up to the Jubilee Auditorium. I just don't have a good feeling about him.'

'Gus, I bet during the cold war years you saw communists around every corner, didn't you?'

'Kate, I may be overcautious, but I still say that's better than being so cavalier about this. After the year you've had, I can't believe you're still so naive and trusting about people.'

'I am not naive,' I protested.

'You have this innocence that you try and hide with your cynicism, but it's there. Now this one time I think you should try and chip away at that innocence and stick nice and close to those security guards, OK?'

'I promise. Especially if it'll get you off my back. Now how much do I owe you?' I asked.

'Sixteen dollars and twenty-five cents. Do you want me to put it on your tab?' he asked.

'No, I actually have money on me today,' I said, pulling out a twenty and tossing it on the counter. 'Take advantage of the cash while you can get it.'

'Don't you want your change?' he asked, as I stood up and picked up my box.

'Put it against my tab, please,' I told him and headed out the door.

I wandered slowly toward the security trailer, enjoying the beautiful sunshine before the heat of the day hit. There was a nice breeze blowing and birds singing in the trees around me. It was too perfect, I thought, feeling chills running down my spine, something had to go wrong. Gus had made me totally paranoid.

'Kate!'

I looked up and saw Tommy jogging across the Plaza to join me.

'Hey, Tommy, how's it going?'

'Great now that I've found you.'

'I didn't know I was lost.'

He rolled his eyes. 'Yeah, something about us protecting you – to do that we actually need to know where you are.'

'Beautiful day, isn't it?' I asked, avoiding the topic.

128

'Nice quiet night last night, hopefully to be followed by a nice quiet day today.' He played along with me. 'And the only way it will be that way is if you manage to do what you're supposed to do.'

'That's not what I wanted to hear. But I'll try my darndest.'

'Would one of those coffees happen to be for me?' he asked.

'You bet.'

He picked one out of the box, opened it up and took a big gulp. 'This is way better than that crap we've got going in the trailer. Which is where you're headed now, right?'

'Yes.'

'Because if you don't check in with Doug right away I'm going to have to call in and report you.'

'I promise I'm going to the security trailer,' I repeated.

'Thanks for the coffee.'

'Actually, it's supposed to be a bribe,' I told him.

'I don't care.' He smiled. 'Unless of course there's something illegal going on, then I'd have to return the coffee and arrest you.'

'No, I'm just supposed to bribe you guys to babysit me today in case Jeff shows up.'

'I think we had that in mind already,' Tommy said, as we arrived at the security trailer.

'Morning, Kate,' Bruce said, throwing open the trailer and jumping down the stairs.

'She brought us our morning caffeine,' Tommy said, pulling the lawn chairs out and setting them up.

'Thanks, sweetie,' Bruce said, helping himself to a cup and having a seat beside Tommy.

'Where's Doug?' I asked.

'He's inside,' Bruce said. 'And he wants to see you for a minute.'

'What, am I in trouble or something?' I asked.

'Maybe he just missed you,' Tommy teased.

I climbed into the trailer with the two remaining coffees and closed the door behind me.

'Morning, Doug,' I smiled. 'I brought some cappuccino.'

'Where the hell have you been?' he asked angrily.

'Excuse me?'

'Sam stopped by and dropped off some muffins. She said you came in with her this morning and she hadn't seen you since. That was over ninety minutes ago!'

'I just stopped at my office to do some work,' I tried to explain, wondering why exactly I felt I owed him an explanation.

'And you didn't think to let anyone know where you were?' he asked. 'You had your radio with you for God's sake.'

'So why didn't you radio me?'

'We did,' he said angrily, pulling the walkie-talkie off my belt and holding it up under my nose. 'But you have to turn it on before you can hear us talking to you.'

I turned to the kitchen counter and set the coffee down. I opened mine and took a sip before answering him, trying to marshal my immediate reaction to lash out. After all, that hadn't seemed to work so well in the past.

'What is all this about?' I finally asked, trying to sound calm and quell the indignation.

'I was worried sick. We've been looking everywhere. I thought Jeff had turned up and grabbed you.'

'Are you really that concerned about him?' I asked, now feeling guilty.

'Yes. And I'm that concerned about you.'

'I can take care of myself,' I assured him.

'Kate, all I could think about was the other night when he attacked you. And you didn't do a very good job of getting away then.'

'I was drunk then. My wits are back about me again, I promise.'

'But he's bigger and stronger than you,' he pointed out.

'I'm sorry,' I said. 'I guess I just didn't think about it.'

'Kate, you've got to be careful for the rest of the festival. This is a big Plaza and no matter how good we are, I can't guarantee we can keep him out of here.'

'I understand,' I said. 'I promise I'll be careful.'

'And I want you to promise that you'll let me know where you are every minute.'

'Doug, I'll be careful, but I'm not going to hide under a rock. That's not my style. Just ask Detective Lincoln, he'll fill you in on how cooperative I can be.'

'Do I have to handcuff you to the trailer to protect you?' he asked, his frustration showing in his voice.

'No, but showing a little respect for how I feel about this wouldn't be out of line,' I suggested.

'How about you showing a little respect for the fact that this is my profession and maybe I know what I'm talking about.'

'Doug,' I began, a little more loudly, as I felt my control slipping away. 'Just in case you're missing any of the signs here, I think you should know that you're fucking pissing me off.'

'Well, join the club, Kate. That's how I've felt since I talked to Sam this morning.'

'Fuck this,' I said, throwing my coffee into the sink. 'This is not how I plan to spend my day. Thanks for starting it so well for me.'

I spun and headed for the door.

'Don't you dare walk out on me,' he yelled. 'I'm not finished.'

'Well you may not be finished but I've certainly had enough!'

I opened the door but he grabbed my arm roughly and pulled me back into the trailer, closing and locking the door behind him. I tried to pull away from him, but he just tightened his grip, pulling me very close to him.

'I don't like people to walk out on me,' he said.

'Let me go!'

'I'll let you go when I've said what I have to say.'

I tried to pull away, but I didn't have a chance.

'Fine, what do you want to say?' I asked, angrily.

'That if I were Jeff, you would be dead by now,' he said calmly and finally let me go.

I rubbed my aching arms where he had gripped me, tears stinging my eyes.

'So all that macho crap was to prove that I can't protect myself?' I asked, glaring at him.

'I think my point was well made.' He smiled. 'Are you ready to listen to me now?'

I took a step toward him and reached back to slap his face. He grabbed my hand and caught it just before I made contact with his cheek.

'Now, do you know how you can break free from this kind of a grip?' he asked.

'I am not in the mood for this right now,' I said, trying to pull my hand free. 'And I certainly don't feel like any self-defence demonstrations from you.'

This time he let my hand go right away.

'Why are you so stubborn?' he asked. 'Would it be so very hard to just let me look after you?'

'Yes,' I whispered.

'Why?' he asked, finally taking the coffee I had brought for him.

'It's one of my biggest problems,' I admitted. 'I don't like being dependent. I have a huge fear about not being able to look after myself.'

He poured half his cup of coffee into a mug and handed it to me, since I had thrown mine down the drain in my anger. I seriously hoped the coffee Gods would forgive me.

'Want to share?' he asked, changing the subject with his peace offering.

'Share the coffee or are you speaking in a broader sense here?' I asked.

'We'll start with the coffee,' he said. 'Kate, I'm not asking you to give up your freedom. This isn't even about our personal relationship. Fuck, we don't even have a personal relationship. We've been flirting with each other for three days. But this Jeff thing is strictly a professional concern.'

'See, now you're lying. This is what I was worried about. If this was strictly professional, you might have been concerned about me but you certainly wouldn't have been so emotional about it.'

'Maybe not,' he said. 'But why can't you just trust me?'

'Doug, I have problems trusting people I've known my whole life, how am I supposed to trust you after a couple of days?'

'I have great references,' he laughed.

'So, can you really show me how to get away if somebody has a hold of me like that?' I asked, still feeling a throbbing in my arm.

'I can.'

I set my coffee cup on the counter.

'How?' I asked.

He set his cup of coffee down and grabbed my arms again, only a little more gently this time.

'So what do I do?' I asked, as he pulled me close to him.

For a moment we stood there, toe to toe, and then he bent down toward me and kissed me. When he finally pulled away from me, it took me a moment to catch my breath.

'That's what I should do if Jeff grabs me?' I asked, still a little bit breathless.

'Well, it would certainly take his mind off what he was trying to do.'

'Did it take your mind off what you're doing?' I asked.

'Actually, it was all I could think about. I had to do it before I could think about anything else,' he explained. 'Should I apologize?'

'No,' I said. 'But maybe you should show me how to get away in case I change my mind.'

He smiled and I felt some of the tension I had been feeling leave me.

'OK,' he started. 'The secret to getting away is not what you've been doing. If you try to pull away, you're never going to win. He's bigger and stronger than you. If someone has you like this, you've got to twist and drop. That way you're working against his weakness, not his strength.'

'Like this?' I asked, doing what he had said and finding myself free of his grip.

'Good. See how that works?'

'I like that,' I said, suddenly feeling a little more in control again. 'Do it again. Just make sure you hold me as tight as you did before.'

When I finally came out of the trailer Bruce and Tommy were both gone, patrolling the Plaza, so Doug walked me to the market tents while we dropped off the floats for the day. We parted at the last tent, Doug heading out to do his rounds and me heading back to the trailer for a coffee. The only reason he let me go on my own was because the Plaza was still fairly empty and he could see me from almost any vantage point.

I poured myself a fresh coffee, grabbed a cigarette and a

magazine and settled myself into one of the lawn chairs. My volunteers were well under control, with tent two being run by Graham, and tents one and three each having a solid core of volunteers that had been here since the first day. There were always a lot of no shows at these events, so I was happy that most of the volunteers were returning and knew what they were doing. Because they were all happy with their responsibility, I got to sit here and have my cigarette and coffee in peace. And I enjoyed that peace and quiet for quite a while until someone approached and blocked the sun, casting me in shadow and ruining my chance for an even tan. I reluctantly looked up from my magazine.

'Graham, what's up?' I asked, dreading that he was going to tell me about some sort of problem that had come up.

'I just wanted a break. I figured you'd been alone long enough and could spare a little conversation.' He smiled. 'May I join you?'

'Sure, pull up a chair,' I said, closing the magazine and dropping it to the ground beside me.

'So, how's it been going?' he asked. 'Other than the obvious, of course.'

'It's been OK,' I said.

'You don't look so OK,' he pointed out.

'What do you mean?'

'You look kind of stressed or tired or something. Are you and Cam fighting?' he asked.

'What makes you automatically jump to that conclusion?' I asked.

'I know you too well, Kate, you can't hide what's really going on from me.'

'Well, things are up in the air for me and Cam,' I admitted. 'But that's all I have to say right now. Remember how I try and keep my personal life personal?'

He laughed out loud but then silenced himself right away when he saw the look in my eyes.

'I just want you to know that I'm here if you need me,' he tried to recover.

'Thanks, Graham. That means a lot to me.'

'I take it you're feeling a little pressure from some of your other friends?' he asked.

'So how are sales going?' I asked, trying to change the subject.

'OK, I get the point,' he said. 'But when you're ready to talk, just remember me. And sales are going great.'

'Good, no problems?' I asked.

'Absolutely none. You've got great volunteers and they're working their buns off.'

'It's your influence, I've had nothing but problems in that tent since the week started.'

'Well Kate, think about who you had in charge.'

'Let's remember that I didn't put him in charge, the volunteer coordinator did. I just walked into this mess on Monday. And I have to meet with the festival producer this morning so it will be nice to be able to give him a good report.'

'It'll be fine,' he said. 'You've dealt with worse than this before. But I've been reading the festival schedule, and since I'm doing such a big favour for you, I want to try and catch some of the performances every day, so you're going to have to cover for me, OK?'

'I can't really say no, can I?'

'No, you can't. So today, I want to catch Lunch Box Theatre at noon on the main stage. And then there is a U of C demonstration of sword fighting after that. Are you OK with those?'

'I'm fine. You'll have to remind me though. I might get caught up in doing my nails or braiding my hair,' I said sarcastically. 'Since now that you're here I won't have to work.'

'Kate, it's only funny if it isn't true!' he laughed, racing back to the tent before I could pelt him with anything.

Though Trent Cranston may have been quite forgiving about the way I handled the situation with Jeff yesterday, the head of the Plex security, Lazlo Hilleo, was much less impressed.

'You totally ignored every resource we have in place here. You could have put the festival right on the front page of all the newspapers with all the wrong headlines! You've already done that often enough for the Plex, Kate, we don't need to become known for our crime stats.'

Lazlo Hilleo is head of Building Services, which includes security. He had been a cop for a couple of years, but he likes everyone to think he had been on the force for much longer.

No one knows why he left the police department after such a short time. There's a pool worth over five hundred dollars to the person who finds out why.

Lazlo loves rules and regulations, he is obsessed with numbers, logbooks, and signing things in and out. All these picky rules just create more paperwork for the rest of us. Lazlo also likes to be the one to talk to the police and to the press, something I had denied him yesterday. He needed to feel he was in charge. Unfortunately, Lazlo and I had never gotten along very well, as I tend to react poorly to authority.

'The festival hired me because I'm good at what I do.' I tried to remain calm. 'I handled the situation the best way I knew how. It would have been a lot quieter if Jeff hadn't lost it. He was the one who blew this all out of proportion. And do you care that he was trying to hurt me?'

'Kate, we have an entire infrastructure in place in this building. I understand you are used to working nights and making decisions on your own, but it really is best if you don't bring your staff in to spy on people and if you don't call the cops on to the festival site unless you consult with me. I'm sure the festival would appreciate it too.' He smiled at Trent Cranston, sitting quietly behind his desk and taking in the situation. 'At least it would give the marketing director a little time for some spin control. Do we understand each other?'

'The decision to call the police was totally mine,' Doug admitted. He had been sitting quietly beside me, as I had asked him to come to the meeting with me. Until now. 'Kate wanted no part of that.'

'And I do understand why you decided to do it,' Lazlo agreed, lulling us both into a false sense of security. 'But the second call you should have made was to me! I'm hooked up to more telecommunications equipment than the phone company. Did you forget I was on radio? Or did someone neglect to give you one of my two cellular phone numbers?'

'OK, I understand you're upset,' I broke in. 'But is there a point here somewhere, or are you just blowing off steam? I'd just like to know whether to take this personally or not.'

'I'm blowing off steam. Because if I don't, I'm afraid I'm

going to recommend to have both your asses removed from this festival site right now.'

'Fine, you want me to go, I'll go,' I said, standing up and grabbing my bag.

'Sit back down, Kate,' Trent told me. 'Let's just all calm down here.'

'I'm not finished!' Lazlo yelled.

'I think you are,' Trent said quietly. 'We're not going to fire anyone's ass because it's the middle of festival week and there's no way I could replace either of them on short notice. And also because this didn't turn into a disaster and the press aren't down here in droves, we're just going to say it turned out OK and let everyone off the hook,' he continued. 'If anything else happens this week, we all promise to keep you in the loop, Lazlo.'

'I have heard that before,' he said, indignantly. 'You artists have no respect for the need for authority.'

'Do you want me to memo you when I take a shit this week?' Trent said, finally losing his cool.

'Fine,' Lazlo said. 'But one little slip . . .'

'Fine,' I said, grabbing my bag and standing up again and thinking I should try and be grown up about this. 'I'm sorry; I should have spoken with you. You're right about everything. Are we done here?'

'We're done,' Trent confirmed, not waiting for a consensus.

I turned around and stormed out of the office. I heard Doug behind me, but I didn't slow down to let him catch up with me.

'Kate,' he called. 'Wait up.'

I didn't answer.

'Kate,' he called again, running to catch up with me.

'What?' I asked angrily.

'I wanted to say I'm sorry,' he said.

I stopped and turned to face him. 'For what?'

'That you had to go through that. It wasn't your fault. I made a bad decision when I didn't inform the Plex security that I had called the police on to the site, and you had to suffer for them.'

'Don't patronize me,' I almost spat at him, turning and storming down the corridor again.

'I'm not patronizing you,' he called after me.

I stopped, turned around and stormed back to where he stood.

'Not patronizing me?' I laughed. 'You made the decision and now the little lady had to listen to that bad security manager swear at her. Fuck, I've heard worse than that on good days. Perhaps you'll open that chauvinistic mind of yours and remember that this was all my idea. I'm responsible for my own decisions and I'm perfectly capable of living with the consequences, OK?'

'It was my decision to call the police.'

'OK?'

'Fine,' he gave in.

'You don't have to fucking protect me or try and take the blame for me. Do you understand what I'm saying?' I asked.

'I understand that you're upset and perhaps now is not the best time to try to discuss this.'

'Funny, I didn't think I was discussing anything. I thought I was telling you how it was.'

'I'm sorry, I guess I was wrong about you,' he said.

'See, I told you this is what I was afraid of,' I said. 'You're making this personal again.'

'I am not making this personal.'

'Fuck, I can't deal with this right now,' I said, frustrated. 'I've got to go somewhere and think.'

'I don't want you to be alone. Jeff is out there somewhere, remember?'

'Like any of you will let me forget!'

'Why don't you let me walk you down to the security trailer?' he asked. 'You can lock yourself in there for as long as you want to be alone.'

'That is not exactly what I had in mind.'

'Then I'll send you home with Sam?' he tried.

'Just stop it,' I yelled. 'Stop making decisions for me. Stop talking to me. I need some silence so I can think for a few minutes.'

'Well, if you don't want me to make decisions for you, maybe you could try making one. Where do you want to go? I'll get you there and then I'll be more than happy to leave you alone!'

I pulled my keys out of my pocket.

'Fine, I've made my decision,' I said, running for a door leading to a service corridor. I opened the door, let myself in and then pushed it closed behind me.

I saw Doug running for the door, but I managed to shut it just as he got there. He didn't have keys to the Plex and I was now safe from everyone who was annoying me.

'Kate,' he screamed, pounding on the door. 'Kate, don't do this! Let me in!'

I didn't wait around to see what else he might have to say. I started down the stairs to the basement and a short cut I knew to my office. There was a package of cigarettes in my desk and I could have a pot of coffee going in a couple of minutes. I was feeling better just thinking about it.

I sat in my office until my coffee pot was empty and my ashtray was full. I was feeling much calmer and definitely more in control. I was also feeling guilty about screaming at Doug the way I had. I had a lot of unresolved anger inside me right now, and I had taken the opportunity to direct it all at him. He deserved some of it, but not all. I turned off the lights and locked up the office, resolving to find him and try to apologize before I had to cover for Graham so he could watch his shows. I didn't find Doug but I did let Bruce know where I was and what I was doing. And then I spent several hours working in the market tent for Graham. The crowds were smaller today, the Plaza fairly quiet, but it gave me a chance to chat with everyone and keep my mind off the things I didn't want to think about. Tommy helped me close up the tents and Graham stayed and helped as well. Then I headed for the theatre, to get my backpack and take one last look around for Doug before I headed for home.

I wandered out of the theatre and down the street. I thought I would find him on the Plaza, or maybe at the security trailer, so I was surprised when I rounded the corner and saw him sitting on the patio at Vaudeville's. His back was to me and he was alone. I could have snuck around the way I came and avoided him, but I just felt I should face up to this and apologize to him for my behaviour today. I took a deep breath and then headed for where he sat, stopping a few paces behind him.

'So, now that you've seen my bad side, did you still want to go out with me?' I asked.

He turned around and looked at me.

'I wondered if I'd see you again today.' He smiled up at me. That was a good sign.

'Can I join you?' I asked.

'Please,' he said, sliding the chair beside him out for me.

I hopped the fence and sat down.

'You've been drinking,' I commented, checking out the empties on the table.

'I gave myself the night off,' he said. 'I thought I'd earned it.'

'I guess you have.'

'Let me buy you a beer,' he said.

'Just one, and then I'm going home.'

'Waitress,' he called, holding up his bottle. 'Two more of these, please.'

'I thought I should find you and apologize,' I said.

'That's very magnanimous of you. That was my word today, by the way. Do you like it?' He smiled at me.

'It's a lovely word.' I humoured him.

'We're a great pair, aren't we? Patronizing and magnanimous.'

'I think I should take your calendar away, you could get dangerous with those big words.'

The waitress brought a couple of beers to our table. I took a big drink from my bottle and lit a cigarette before I continued.

'I want to apologize,' I began.

'Good.'

'But I want to qualify what I'm apologizing for.'

'That's what I expected,' he sighed.

'What do you mean?'

'I mean that I hoped you would come by and apologize, but I knew I would never just get a straight *I'm sorry* from you. You have to explain and qualify and never let yourself be open for even one minute.'

'But I was right. It was just the way I handled it that was wrong.'

'Kate, have you ever been wrong?' he asked.

'I beg your pardon?'

140

'Have you ever been wrong? Even once in your life? Or is it just the way you handle things that's wrong sometimes? Or is it just flat out everyone else is always wrong and you're always right?'

'I think I resent that.'

'Well maybe it's time somebody pointed out the truth to you,' he said. 'Maybe it's time you took a long look at the way you deal with people. You have such potential. You're such a great person until you open your mouth.'

'Excuse me?'

'I was right, you know. I wasn't patronizing you when I said it was my fault. I'm in charge of security and I have strict protocols I follow. But I got totally caught up in your little idea and threw everything out the window. I should have stopped you dead in your tracks before we let this little plan get underway. I should have gone straight to the festival staff and talked this over with them. But I didn't. So, therefore, it was my fault. Your idea, but I deserve the blame for following along.'

'You don't know me very well,' I said haughtily. 'Once I get an idea, nobody can stop me.'

'Oh don't give yourself so much credit,' he said. 'Of course I could have. This isn't your theatre where you run the show. You're just a small cog in a big wheel here. So, I didn't stop you, it's my fault. Now that's the end of that argument, all right?'

I took another drink of my beer and didn't bother to answer him.

'I'll take your silence as agreement since it seems to be so hard for you to admit you were wrong.' He smiled. 'Now, I do understand why you lost it this afternoon. After the blast that good old Lazlo gave us, I felt like letting off some steam too. However, I have years of security training so I know how to keep my cool in times like that.'

'OK, I take back that patronizing remark,' I said.

'Good.'

'But I'm replacing it with arrogant.'

'I can live with arrogant,' he said.

'I don't have to sit here and take this, you know.'

'Then why are you?' he asked. 'You're free to go anytime.'

'Maybe I will,' I said, rummaging through my bag to find some money for the beer.

'There's just one thing before you go,' he said.

'What?' I asked.

'Give me your hand.'

'Why?'

'Kate, just give me your hand,' he said, holding his out for me to take.

I took his hand, figuring this was the only way I could get out of here without creating a scene.

'What is it?' I asked.

Before I knew what was happening, he slapped his handcuffs over my wrist and attached the other end to the arm of the chair.

'What are you doing?' I asked.

'I've decided I don't want you to leave yet. I think we need to talk.'

'You're drunk, Doug, and you've lost what little good sense you might have ever had. Let me out of these things right now!' I demanded. 'We can talk tomorrow.'

'Want another beer?' he asked, ignoring me and holding his empty bottle up for the waitress to see.

'No, I want to go home,' I insisted.

'I'll make sure you get home soon,' he said. 'But I think we should talk for a while longer. We had a big blow-out this afternoon and we need to smooth it out. If nothing else, we still have a few more days we have to work together. Wouldn't you rather we be friends than enemies?'

'OK, I'll save you the trouble. We're friends. I'll be nice to you for the next couple of days, all right? Can I go now?'

'So now I'm arrogant, but you're becoming insincere. I want the truth, not just to be pacified.'

I leaned back in my chair and lit another cigarette. I pulled at the handcuffs a couple of times, but he had really locked me in and, unless I took the chair home with me, I wasn't going anywhere.

'OK, you want the truth?' I finally asked. 'The truth is that bondage is not going to endear you to me. And it's certainly not going to make me open up and share my feelings with you.'

'You forget, I've got the night off. I'm sure after we sit here for a couple of hours and drink a few more beers, you'll be ready to chat.'

'You're serious about this?' I asked. 'You're not going to let me go?'

'I'm serious,' he said, smiling again.

'Fine, then I'll have another beer,' I said.

'OK, that's the attitude. I'll go get you one. I have to hit the little boys' room anyway,' he said, standing up.

'I thought you didn't want me to be alone?' I asked. 'What if Jeff comes by?'

'Well, I doubt he'd try anything here. There are too many people around. But I'll leave my radio here just in case. If you see him, call for Bruce. He's at the security trailer and can be here in less than thirty seconds. I'm sure you'll be fine.'

'I'd rather you let me go?' I tried, holding my shackled hand up hoping he would change his mind and let me loose.

'Right, and have you gone when I come back out?' he asked. 'I don't think so. I think the radio will be just fine.'

'Have I told you that you're really pissing me off?' I asked, pulling at the handcuffs again and accomplishing nothing more than hurting my wrist.

'Kate, everything I do is going to piss you off, I've come to accept that.' He leaned forward and kissed me on the forehead. 'I'm just working on different degrees of anger right now. And so far, this seems to be an acceptable degree for me to live with. I won't be gone long.'

He took off into the restaurant, leaving me stuck in my chair. My beer was empty so I reached over and grabbed his. I took a drink and stared at the radio sitting in the middle of the table. I wondered if I called Bruce on the radio, if he would maybe unlock me. But I wasn't sure if he could get here before Doug got back. Then I felt a hand on my shoulder. I turned, hoping to see Bruce or Tommy, or maybe even Sam, anyone who was on my side. But my heart began to race when I saw Jeff standing behind me, staring menacingly down at me.

'Take your hand off of me,' I said, calmly.

'Kate, I have my hand over a nerve bundle that can cause

143

you so much pain if I decide to apply pressure, that you will pass out. Do you want me to prove it to you?' he asked.

'No,' I said, not knowing whether to believe him or not. 'What do you want?'

'I like you this way,' he laughed. 'You're much more compliant. I guess I should have tried handcuffing you.'

'What do you want?' I repeated, my heart pounding. I looked into the restaurant and saw Doug standing at the bar, chatting with the bartender.

'He's not coming to your rescue,' Jeff whispered in my ear, glancing in the direction I was looking. 'He hasn't even gone to the bathroom yet. I'm very observant, you know. I feel it's important to my freedom to keep track of this kind of stuff.'

'You've just lost your freedom,' I told him. 'This has got to be a violation of your bail agreement.'

'Actually, Kate, it's a violation of the restraining order you had the festival file against me. I think that's probably more serious than anything else.'

'I never filed a restraining order,' I protested, wondering what he was talking about. 'I don't know anything about it.'

'Well that detective friend of yours served me with it as I was leaving the Remand Centre. Don't tell me you forgot about it already.'

His face was pressed against mine, his breath warm on my neck, and chills raced down my spine.

'Detective Lincoln must have arranged it. I swear I didn't know anything about it,' I assured him, hoping to keep him talking until Doug finally made his way back to our table.

'Yeah, well I don't believe you and I don't think that was a nice thing for you to do to me,' he said. 'That really pissed me off. It was bad enough having me arrested, but that restraining order was the final straw.'

'So what are you going to do to me?' I asked.

'What I would like to do to you is take you somewhere and beat some bloody manners into you. But that would only be a few minutes satisfaction for me. I decided I wanted to do something that would make you suffer a little longer. Make you think about how you treated me.'

'Lots of talk, Jeff, but you're not really saying anything,' I said, trying to see if my false bravado might scare him off.

144

He squeezed a little tighter and I felt a stab of pain that took my breath away. Then he released his hold a little.

'See, now you're getting rude again,' he whispered into my ear, his lips brushing my cheek. 'You've got to learn to be nicer, Kate. Especially when you're not in control.'

'I'm sorry,' I gasped, still feeling the echo of the pain.

'Good. Now you don't exactly expect me to tell you my little plan, do you? That would ruin my surprise. And that would take away all my fun. And all your anticipation. Which really is the best part, isn't it?'

'Why don't you tell me when you plan to do this then?' I tried.

'Tomorrow or the next day. I have until the end of the week, don't I?' he pointed out. 'Tonight, you get to go home and toss and turn and wonder what it is I could possibly do that would make you suffer guilt for the rest of your life. It's going to be a long night for you. And then sometime in the next couple of days, you'll know. And it'll all be your fault. If you'd just left me alone in the market, none of this would have happened. If you'd just had a simple coffee with me, none of this would have happened. Now, you'll have to weigh the difference between your selfishness versus what's going to happen to some poor soul out there.'

'Jeff, this isn't funny,' I said, wishing someone would come to my rescue. Unfortunately, we looked like any other couple at the end of a long work day.

'It isn't meant to be funny, Kate. So I'm happy you don't see any humour in it.'

'I refuse to accept any of your actions as my fault.'

'Well, we'll see how you feel when this is over. It was your behaviour that prompted me to do this, you know. So you just sleep on that tonight, Kate. And then spend tomorrow looking for me. But no matter how hard you look, you'll never see me.'

His hand moved from my shoulder and slipped under my shirt, playing with the strap on my bra. He felt me stiffen with fear and laughed, leaning close and kissing my neck.

'See, for a simple little kiss like that you could have avoided all of this,' he said.

I wondered what would happen if I screamed right here

145

and now. Surely he couldn't hurt me too badly before someone came running. And then I saw Doug coming out of the restaurant, two beers in his hand. He looked in my direction and stopped dead in his tracks for a second.

'Doug!' I screamed.

Jeff looked up and saw him standing there, released me and took off across the street. Doug dropped both beers and ran. He hopped the fence and was across the street, trying to catch up with Jeff, who had disappeared into the crowd. I grabbed the radio and turned it on.

'Kate to security,' I screamed. 'Jeff is here. Doug's chased him into the Plex. Help him!'

'Kate, where are you, over?' Bruce came back right away.

'Don't worry about me,' I screamed. 'You've got to catch Jeff.'

I saw Tommy running across the street and into the Plex.

'Tommy's gone after him,' Bruce confirmed on the radio. 'Now tell me where you are, over?'

'I'm at Vaudeville's, on the patio.'

Bruce came tearing around the corner to where I was sitting. He saw the handcuff holding me to the chair, pulled out his key and released me.

'Did he do this to you?' he asked.

'No, it's a long story. Please just go help them catch him,' I said, trying to push him across the street.

'I'm not leaving you alone,' he insisted.

'You can't let him get away,' I repeated.

'I think it's too late.'

'What do you mean?' I asked.

He pointed across the street, and I saw Doug and Tommy crossing the street, headed back to the restaurant.

'What happened?' I asked frantically. 'Where is he?'

'I lost him,' Doug said. 'I chased him up to the Plus 15 and into Palliser Square.'

'What do you mean?'

'I lost him. He vanished into the parkade behind the Tower,' Doug repeated. 'Are you OK?'

'No, I'm not OK,' I said. 'He's going to do something tomorrow or the next day. We've got to find him and stop him.'

146

'Kate, calm down,' Doug ordered me. 'Bruce, I want you to find Trent Cranston and Lazlo and brief them on what's happened. Tell them we're calling the cops, but we're off site, so no one needs to panic. Tommy, you head back to the security trailer, call the cops and wait for them there. Bring them here as soon as they arrive. OK?'

They both nodded agreement and took off in two different directions. Doug stepped back over the fence and pulled me close to him.

'Are you OK?' he asked.

'Let me go,' I said, trying to push away from him. The other patrons in the restaurant had finally turned their looks away from me, until I started struggling with Doug, and suddenly all eyes were back on me again.

'Calm down,' he whispered.

'How dare you leave me trussed to this chair with him out there? How dare you?' I asked again, not knowing what else to say.

'I'm sorry. You have to believe me when I say that I really didn't think he would come back here. He knows we've got a restraining order against him.'

'Oh, so you knew about the restraining order too?' I asked. 'That's what set him off, you know? Why didn't you at least tell me about it?'

'Kate, that was Detective Lincoln's idea to make it part of his bail agreement. He came back and talked to the producer about it and then talked to the judge about it. I swear I had nothing to do with it. He promised he was going to tell you about it later.'

'When?' I asked. 'Sometime tomorrow, next week, next month? Why do all you overprotective men feel like you can just come in and take over my life like this?'

He made the wise choice not to answer me. I plopped myself back down in the chair and lit a cigarette. An uncomfortable silence fell over our table.

'Do you want a beer or something?' he asked, finally breaking the silence.

'Sure.'

He signalled to the waitress and sat down beside me.

'What did Jeff say to you?' he asked.

147

'He said he was going to do something that would make me regret firing him for the rest of my life.'

'Did he say what?'

'No, just that it was going to happen before the festival was over.'

'Here's the cops,' Doug said, glancing down the street.

I turned to see Ken Lincoln and a couple of uniformed officers walking down the street. Ken hopped the fence, pulled an empty chair from another table and sat with us.

'Ken, what are you doing here?' I asked. 'Hear my name on the radio again?'

'No, I was asked to take this investigation on as a special favour to a friend. Payback for getting you out of jail last fall. So Jeff decided to push the limits on his restraining order? Want to tell me what happened?' he asked.

'Want to tell me why you kept the restraining order a secret?' I asked, still angry.

'Because I knew you'd overreact,' he said. 'Want to answer my question now?'

'We were sitting here having a beer. Doug went in to order another round and use the facilities and Jeff snuck up behind me.'

'Why didn't you run?' he asked. 'There are lots of people around here.'

'Well, I did a stupid thing . . .' Doug began.

'We were fooling around,' I jumped in. 'And I was hand-cuffed to the chair. I couldn't go anywhere. Besides, Jeff had a good grip on me, I don't think I could have gotten away from him, handcuffs or not.'

'What did he say?' Ken asked.

'He told me that he was going to do something at the festival before it was over. Something that would make me feel guilty for firing him, for the rest of my life.'

'Anything else? Anything that might give us a hint as to what he's thinking?' Ken asked.

'No, just that he wanted me to suffer. He said he hoped I tossed and turned all night trying to figure it out, and then tomorrow I would start to regret what I did.'

'Not much to go on. What made him leave?'

'Doug came back out on to the patio,' I said. 'Jeff took off and he and Tommy chased him across the street, through the Plex and into the mall in Palliser Square.'

'Where did you lose him?' Ken asked Doug.

'At the exit on the other side. He just disappeared into the crowd in the parkade.'

'Why don't you guys go over and see if anyone saw anything?' Ken asked the other two cops. 'I'll meet you back at the security trailer when you're done.'

'Yes sir,' they said, before crossing the street and taking the stairs up to the Plus 15.

'Did he hurt you or threaten you, Kate?' Ken asked, turning his attention back to me.

'No, I'm fine,' I lied, not wanting to get into any more details than that.

'Well, why don't I believe you?' he asked.

'Probably because I've sort of warped the truth before,' I admitted. 'But I swear that's all.'

'Except . . .?' Ken asked.

'Except for the fact that his hand sort of wound up inside my blouse. But it was no big deal. He tried it just as Doug came back out on to the patio. Jeff took off before anything else could happen.'

'Kate, you've got to learn to tell me the truth,' Ken said. 'All of the truth. At one time.'

'I'm sorry,' I said.

'I'm going to try to add sexual assault on to the charges. Maybe we can keep him in jail a little longer this time.'

'If you can catch him,' I said.

'If we can catch him,' Ken agreed.

Sam drove me home and made sure I was locked up safe and sound in my empty apartment before finally leaving. She had really wanted me to stay at her house again, but I had really wanted to be at my place tonight, with my things, and try to get a good night's sleep. Try being the operative word. A hot bath didn't work, neither did eating, nor the couple of glasses of wine I finally drank. I finally got my comforter from the bed, put on a CD and curled up on the couch with a third glass of wine.

I reached over for my glass of wine and realized I must

have dozed off for a couple of minutes, because the CD was finished. There was a knock on the door. I set the glass back on the table and climbed out from under the comforter, wondering who could be calling at this time of night. I looked through the peephole and was surprised to see Doug standing there. I unlocked the door and let him in. We both stood there in silence for a few moments.

'I'm sorry to bother you at this time of night,' he began.

'It's OK,' I assured him, self-consciously tugging at my T-shirt and wishing I was wearing something a little less revealing. 'What's up?'

'I just came by to . . .' he started and then changed his mind. 'No, there's only one reason I came by.'

'Why?'

'To do this,' he said, taking me in his arms and kissing me. I wrapped my arms around him, feeling I should fight him off but not able to. Then he picked me up in his arms and carried me to the couch. He set me down gently, sitting beside me and staring silently into my eyes. I couldn't stand it any longer and pulled him to me, kissing him hungrily. He pulled away for a moment and smiled.

'I'm so happy that . . .' he began but I cut him off.

'Don't talk,' I said, reaching up and unbuttoning his shirt. 'I don't want to talk right now.'

He pushed my fumbling fingers away and undid his shirt himself, tossing it on to the floor. I reached down for his belt buckle, feeling my heart begin to pound faster in my chest . . .

A knock on the door startled me and I sat upright on the couch, reaching to pull my T-shirt down when I realized it was down and I was alone. Thank God it was only a dream, I thought, feeling a little sad though. I had a quick drink of wine and tried to shake the image of Doug from my mind, when there was more furious pounding at the door.

'I'm coming,' I yelled, trying to untangle my legs from the comforter.

I checked through the peephole, feeling a sense of déjà vu when I saw Doug standing there. I unlocked the door.

'This is surreal,' I said.

'Pardon?' he asked, letting himself in and locking the door

behind him, making me feel slightly uncomfortable.

I tugged at my T-shirt, reliving my dream.

'What are you doing here?' I asked, taking a step back from him.

'I'm sorry to bother you at this time of night,' he said.

'This is too freaky.'

'What?' he asked.

'I was just thinking about you.' I fudged the truth, not wanting to admit I was actually dreaming about him.

I led him into the kitchen, turning on as many lights as I could on the way there.

'Can I make you some tea or coffee?' I offered, trying to busy myself and stay as far away from him as possible.

'No, thanks.'

'So what's up?' I asked, both anxious for and dreading his answer.

'Ken Lincoln called me. He didn't want to call you and freak you out, so I told him I'd come over and fill you in and make sure you were OK.'

'What's wrong?' I asked, feeling my stomach sink.

'Jeff turned himself in earlier this evening. Turned up at the police station with his lawyer and said he'd heard that they were looking for him.'

'Well, that's great.' I smiled.

'Not so great. He has a really good lawyer, Kate.'

'Don't tell me this,' I said, sitting across the table from him.

'He's out. They couldn't hold him. And then he called me and told me to tell you he was still thinking about you. I wanted to make sure you were OK.'

'Fuck!'

'Kate . . .'

I threw the chair back from the table and stormed over to the sink. He followed me. I think he was afraid I was going to hurt myself.

'Kate . . .' he tried again, as I slammed some dishes around in the sink.

'What the fuck is wrong with the police?'

'I don't think it's exactly productive to debate our judicial system right now. I think it would be much more productive to try and figure out what we're going to do tomorrow.'

'I don't want to think about tomorrow,' I said, slamming a pot into the sink and turning the water on. I put way too much soap in and pulled the plug out as the bubbles started to flow over the counter and on to the floor.

Doug grabbed a dishtowel and helped me wipe up the floor.

'Now, could we just sit down for a minute and talk?' he asked. 'Or do you need to bang a few more pots around?'

'What is there to talk about?' I asked, backing myself into the corner literally. 'They can't protect me from him.'

'I am not going to let anything happen to you.'

'But he's not going to come after me directly. He's going to do something but not to me.'

'Kate . . .'

'Look, it's late, I need to get some sleep,' I said. 'You better go.'

He took another step toward me and wrapped his arms around my waist. A picture from my dreams, of me in his arms, flashed through my mind, sending tingling feelings into places I didn't even want to acknowledge right now.

'I'm not going to leave you alone tonight,' he said gently. 'I don't trust him.'

'Doug, I'm a big girl and I've got great locks on my door,' I said, thinking about pulling away from him but not actually doing anything to make that happen.

'I don't trust him, Kate. I'm worried that this whole thing about something happening at the festival is a ruse and that he's going to try something with you tonight.'

'Fine, I don't have the strength to argue,' I said, gently unfolding his arms from my waist. 'But this isn't the night to start something between us, OK? There's a blanket and pillow on the sofa, it's all yours.'

I headed for the stairs and my bed and turned around half way up.

'Doug,' I called down to him.

'Yes?'

'I'm sorry. I want you to know that I'm not really mad at you. I'm just totally frustrated with this whole situation. I know you're just trying to help.'

'I understand,' he said. 'Sleep well.'

He turned off the kitchen light and went into the living room. I didn't move from where I stood.

'Doug,' I called softly, feeling much braver in the darkness.

'Yes?' he said, poking his head around the corner and looking up at me.

'Do you want to come up?' I asked, not believing the words that were coming out of my mouth.

'Katie, I would love to,' he answered quickly. 'But you were right. We both need to get a good night's sleep and be clear headed tomorrow, OK?'

'Good night,' I said, climbing the rest of the way upstairs and burying myself under the covers. I lay there, thinking about what might have happened if he had agreed. I think I felt relieved but at the same time, I still wondered what it would have been like. And those thoughts kept my mind off Jeff for a while, just long enough for me to finally fall asleep.

A shiver ran up and down his back. The air was warm and humid that evening, sweet from the flowers that dangled off the balconies. He wasn't looking for someone to play with tonight. A game had already begun. It had started this afternoon but he didn't want to ruin the anticipation. Because tomorrow, he would watch her as she tried to win his game. And then he would watch her die.

Friday

I woke up before the alarm rang, something that didn't happen very often in my life. I reached over and shut it off before it could ring, turning back over and enjoying the warmth and safety of my bed for a few more minutes. I heard a gentle snoring coming from the living room and felt a smile creep over my face. Even though it had only been a week, I realized I missed the smells, the feel and even the sounds of a man in this place. I had thought I could never adjust to living with a man in this tiny apartment, and now it seemed so strange to live here alone again. It was comforting to know there was someone else here with me and I suddenly realized I didn't like being alone anymore.

Content for the moment, I pulled the covers tightly around me and I found myself starting to doze off. I knew that if I let that happen I would wake up hours from now and miss half the day. Reluctantly I threw the comforter back and climbed out of bed. I put my robe on, tying it tightly around my waist, and threw Cam's robe over my arm before going downstairs. Doug was sleeping soundly and I watched him for a moment, smiling again and feeling my thoughts stray to Cam. I tried to push him out of my mind as I leaned over the man who was actually sleeping in my apartment right now, their images blurring for a moment in my mind. I put a hand on his chest and shook him gently.

'Doug,' I whispered. 'Time to wake up.'

His eyes opened slowly and I watched him struggle for a moment, as he tried to remember where he was.

'Kate?' he asked.

'Are you awake?' I teased. 'Or are you dreaming?'

'Is it Friday?'

'Yes it is.'

'OK, I know where I am and what day it is,' he joked, sitting up and pushing the blanket away. 'I must be awake.'

'I brought this for you,' I said, tossing him the robe I was carrying.

'You always keep a man's robe around?' he asked.

'It is the twenty-first century,' I said. 'Women have been liberated.'

I turned quickly toward the kitchen as he stood up and wrapped the robe around him.

'I'll make some coffee,' I offered.

'I could use some.'

'Do you want to use the shower first?' I asked. 'The coffee should be ready by the time you're finished.'

'And breakfast?' he asked.

'I can manage pouring cereal into a bowl, but I'm afraid that's about as far as my skills go in the morning.'

'That'll do,' he said. 'Besides, I'm sure Sam will have something wonderful waiting for us at the site.'

'I'm sure she will,' I said, thinking he was starting to sound like me.

'OK, I'll be quick,' he promised.

'Help yourself to any of the towels on the shelf. And there's a razor and stuff in there too if you want to use it,' I added, wondering if he was going to ask why I seemed to be totally set up for male company.

'Thanks, Katie,' he said, avoiding the subject.

'And Doug, please don't take this the wrong way, but I don't like to be called Katie.'

'I'm sorry,' he said, sounding fine but looking slightly hurt.

'It's OK. With a name like Kate, it's an occupational hazard.' I tried to ignore the look in his eyes while I turned to make coffee. Cam was the only one who ever called me Katie and it just stirred up too many uncomfortable emotions when Doug called me that.

Doug came out of the bathroom clean and damp and smelling of Cam's aftershave. More uncomfortable memories. He still had Cam's robe on and I felt my eyes begin to fill with tears. I blinked them away, thinking happy thoughts as I poured coffee for both of us. I sat him at the table with a

155

bowl of cereal and his cup of coffee and I hurried into the bathroom. I always found the shower was a safe place to cry. When I came out he was fully dressed and I was greatly relieved. I wrapped my robe tightly around me and headed upstairs. I pulled on a pair of shorts and a tank top and then threw a sweatshirt on over the tank. I decided to braid my hair before putting on a baseball cap. I slid on my Birkenstocks and headed downstairs.

'Are you going to have something to eat?' he asked.

'No, I'm pretty much coffee and cigarettes in the morning,' I said. 'It takes my digestive system longer to wake up than the rest of me.'

'You need your strength.'

'I'll eat when we get to the Plex,' I said. 'I promise.'

'Kate, are you OK?'

'No, actually I'm scared. If there was anything I could do to avoid living this day, I would do it.'

'Everyone would understand if you stayed home today,' he said, offering me an out.

'I can't. Somehow, I feel like if I'm there, then maybe I can do something to stop him. But if I stay home, he's won. He's scared me away from what I love to do, and even if nothing else happens, he's won. So I have to be there, no matter what.'

'I understand,' he admitted. 'I'd feel the same way. But we're going to stick very close together today.'

'I have no problem with that at all,' I promised.

'Well, my car is downstairs, shall we go?' he asked.

'Do you want another coffee or anything?' I asked, realizing I hadn't been a very good hostess.

'No, I'm fine.'

'OK, then I'm ready too,' I said. I turned off the coffee and the lights and grabbed my pack from the corner. I slugged back the last of my coffee and turned to him. 'Let's go and get this over with.'

We rode to the festival in silence. He parked his car and walked me to the security trailer. I made a fresh pot of coffee while he went to find Tommy and Bruce. Sam had left a tray of muffins on the table and I picked at one but didn't really have much of an appetite. The door to the trailer opened and

I jumped, turning and screaming at the same time, until I recognized Graham climbing up the stairs.

'Whoa, Kate, it's only me,' he said.

'Sorry,' I said, wiping up the coffee I had spilled on the counter in my panic. 'I guess I'm a little jumpy today.'

'A little?' he asked.

'OK, a lot.'

'You should probably have this door locked if you're in here alone and that freaked out,' he suggested.

'I thought it was locked,' I told him. I was angry that I had forgotten to check it but I wasn't going to admit that to Graham.

'Did you get any sleep last night?' he asked, helping himself to a muffin and plopping himself down at the table.

'A little,' I told him. 'Doug came over later. Ken Lincoln called to let him know the police had Jeff but couldn't hold him. Both Ken and Doug wanted to make sure I was OK and decided I needed a babysitter.'

'So where was Cam?' he asked innocently.

'Cam's away this week,' I snapped at him. Then I realized I had been snapping a little too much at everyone this week and tried to soften my tone. 'Actually, I think he's moved out.'

'Kate, I'm sorry,' he said. 'I guess you could have really used him around this week.'

'Yeah, I could have. But that's all water under the bridge now. I've survived.' I poured a coffee, grabbed a juice out of the fridge for Graham, and then joined him at the table, deciding I might try a muffin after all. 'I really don't want to talk about that today. We've got other more important things to worry about for the next couple of days, OK?'

'Subject closed,' Graham agreed. 'You don't have to hit me over the head with a two by four.'

'I swear, when this week is over, I'm going to take you and all my other friends out for a drink, tell you what happened, answer your questions and listen to your bad advice. Get it over with all at once and then I don't have to listen to it again.'

'You know, Kate, the intrinsic nature of friendship is that you talk to your friends about what's going on in your life.'

'Well, the extrinsic nature of my friends is that they want to take over my life and run it for me.'

'That's not really true,' he told her.

'What do you mean?'

'No, you're not in the mood for true confessions. And I'm not in the mood to risk my life by telling you my observations on your life.'

'Tell me what you were going to say,' I insisted. 'I won't hold it against you.'

'Maybe we should use the handcuffs, just in case?'

'Graham!'

'Well Kate, I think you struggle really hard to be independent. But when someone cares about you and does things for you, which would happen in any normal caring relationship I might point out, you think they're trying to take away your independence and take over your life. You struggle so hard that you end up overreacting to everything.'

'I do not,' I defended myself.

'You called me patronizing when I sent you flowers for your birthday a couple of years ago.'

'I didn't call you patronizing,' I argued.

'Yes you did.'

'I believe I said you were looking for patronage, hoping I would give you a job. Besides, you got my birthday wrong.'

'You weren't born on Labour Day?' he asked.

'Nope.'

'Damn, I thought I had a good source on that one.'

'Are we done here?' I asked.

'No we're not. What about Cam? You fight with him about every little thing he tries to do for you,' Graham continued.

'You're right.' I gave in, but not in the way he wanted.

'I am?' he asked, total surprise on his face.

'Yes, you are right. And would you like to know what you're right about? That I don't want to discuss this right now!' I pushed away from the table and headed for the door. 'I'm going for a walk.'

'Should I go with you?' he asked.

I resisted the urge to scream at him about being overprotective in light of our recent conversation.

'You probably should, but I'm just going to walk over to the catering tent and find Sam. There's nobody on the Plaza right now, so I'm sure I'll be OK.'

'Not a problem,' he gave in too. 'Do you want me to get the floats ready for you?'

'No thanks, Graham. I'll find one of the security guys later. I think I need to keep busy today.' I smiled at him, hoping he would realize I was trying hard to be understanding. 'But I do appreciate all you've done for me this week.'

'Say it with money, Kate,' he laughed. 'I'll be looking for that nice little bonus at the end of the week.'

'You've got it,' I said, turning around and heading out of the trailer. 'Hey Graham, I swore I'd be a good girl, so give me a three minute head start and then would you radio security and let them know where I'm going?'

'Ten four,' he laughed.

I didn't really want to see Sam right now either but I knew nobody was going to let me be alone today. So I started to walk toward the catering tent, but I took the long way, heading around the perimeter of the Plaza. I must admit, though, that as soon as I got down wind of the catering tent, the aroma of fresh baked pastry drew me there faster. I plopped myself down on one of the picnic tables and waved over at Sam who was busy arguing with her assistant again, which was becoming her theme of the week. I lit a cigarette and waited patiently for her to join me. She didn't let me down, bringing a plate of banana bread with her. She had a big pat of whipped butter on the side and I greedily spread it across a nice thick slice of still-warm bread.

'Good morning to you too,' she said, sarcastically. But I knew she was secretly pleased when people enjoyed her cooking.

'Don't push me, Sam, I'm having a rough week.'

'Yeah, well me too,' Sam said.

'What's wrong with you this week?' I asked. 'As long as your answer doesn't involve me.'

'This assistant I hired. He is such an asshole. He argues with me about every single little thing.'

'Fire him.'

'And he keeps disappearing on me.'

'Fire him.'

'It would be easier if he weren't such a hard worker when he was around. And that he can think. It's hard to find people

159

with common sense, you know. But I'm getting so totally frustrated with him.'

'Then fire him,' I said, again.

'Get real,' Sam finally acknowledged me. 'It's Friday. Do you know how many people are going to be here today?'

'Yeah, I know. But it felt good to think about firing him for a minute there, didn't it?' I asked.

'Yes it did,' she said. 'But look how well it worked out for you, firing one of your volunteers.'

'Yeah, thanks for bringing that up.'

'Well, it's over as of tomorrow,' Sam reassured me. 'Only another two days and you can go home, lock yourself in your apartment and screw up your life all on your own.'

'OK, you're just dying to know what happened and blame it on me, aren't you?' I asked, angry that everyone seemed to think I needed to talk about Cam when all I wanted to do was push him out of my mind. 'Well I didn't leave him, Sam, I'm the one that's still here. Have you seen Cam all week? I don't think so. He's cruising the Caribbean without me.'

'What happened?' she asked quietly, ignoring my anger.

'He wanted to go on a cruise, I wanted to do the festival.'

'You couldn't work it out. Did you try to talk to him about it?'

'There's was no talking to him. He had his mind set. He didn't understand that I'm going into summer, which is my slow season. I couldn't turn this down because I needed the money. But he wouldn't listen.'

'You know, he called me and asked me about the cruise,' Sam said. 'I told him I thought it was a good idea.'

'And just why the hell would you do that?' I asked, dropping my banana bread and preparing to bolt.

'Kate, it was before I told you about the festival and he never said anything about when he wanted to go. I didn't think it would be a problem and with the whole summer to pick from, I didn't think he'd settle on this week. But I feel really bad about it, like it's my fault.'

'It's not your fault, it's his. He wouldn't even listen to me. We could have gone after the festival.'

'But I think I know why he was so set on doing this,' Sam said. 'Would you like to know?'

160

'I don't think so,' I said, knowing she was going to tell me anyway.

'He was going to ask you to marry him on the cruise.'

'What?' I asked. I don't know what I had imagined she was going to say, but that was about the farthest thing from my mind.

'It was this big romantic plan he came up with. He called and asked me what I thought about it.'

'What did you tell him?'

'I said I didn't know if you were ready for it yet. That maybe he should bring the subject up and see how you reacted. But I guess he just decided to go for it.'

'Why didn't you say something to me?' I asked her.

'You wouldn't talk to me about this all week,' Sam reminded me. 'If you'd said something before the festival I would have told you to go and found someone else to do this.'

'You're always standing up for him,' I lashed out at her. 'Suddenly this is all my fault. Do you like him better than you like me?'

'For God's sake, are you three years old?' she asked, fighting to hold in her own temper. 'I'm not even going to dignify that with a response.'

'Fuck,' I whispered. 'Why does he want to go and ruin everything we have by getting married?'

'Kate, that's generally the next step that two people who are in love take. You're the only one I know that would think it was unnatural.'

'Well, it's too late now.'

'No it isn't,' she insisted. 'He's got to come back at some point. You've got his clothes. And when he comes back to get them you sit down and work it out, like grown-ups!'

I picked up the banana bread and turned it over, staring at it while I tried to formulate my thoughts.

'It's too late.'

'No it isn't, Kate. You can't just throw away all the time you two have invested in each other.'

'Come on, Sam, surely you've noticed that I've been all over Doug all week? There's definitely an attraction there. How dedicated am I to Cam if I'm so ready to take off after another guy?'

161

'Or maybe it's how somebody like you reacts to rejection. Maybe you had to run out there and prove to yourself that you were attractive to somebody when you thought Cam dumped you.'

'I'd like to think I'm a little more evolved than that,' I protested.

'We all would.'

'It's too late,' I told her again. 'I've already moved on. He left, Sam. If I make up with him, how will I ever trust him not to just leave the next time we have a fight? I'll be scared to say what's on my mind. It just won't work.'

'Wait until you see him again.'

'The next time I see him will be to get my keys back.'

'We'll see,' she said, but I knew in my heart there was nothing that could convince her.

'There's Doug,' I said, spotting him coming across to us. 'I've got to go pick up the floats with him.'

'Be careful,' Sam warned me as I got up. 'What you do over the next couple of days will affect your life forever.'

'I'm supposed to be the melodramatic one,' I joked, trying to lighten the mood.

'I mean it,' she called after me. 'You need to try thinking before you act for a change, Kate.'

I waved her off as I hurried to meet Doug.

'Why the big hurry?' he asked. 'I was hoping to get a piece of whatever smells so good over there.'

'Banana bread,' I told him. 'You can get some after we do the floats.'

'You're a little testy,' he felt the need to point out to me. 'What happened?'

'Nothing,' I said, trying to shake off the mood and put on a good front for him. 'I guess I'm just a little jumpy about today.'

'Nothing is going to happen,' he assured me, putting his arm around my waist and giving me a quick hug as we walked. 'People like Jeff don't usually do anything. They're all talk, a little aggressive sometimes, but when push comes to shove, they usually don't back up their threats.'

'Usually?' I asked.

'Kate, I've seen his type before and I'll almost guarantee we won't hear from him again.'

162

'I'd sure like you to be more certain,' I said. 'I just can't seem to shake this feeling I have.'

'You have to think about where that feeling is coming from. Everything's just piling up around you right now. The city is all worked up about the Bishop and all that stuff, and then Jeff comes along and it all plays with your mind, you know? But that's where it all is, in your mind.'

'Are you sure?'

'Trust me, it'll be all right,' he said, opening the door to the Plex for me.

'OK, I'll trust you,' I said, following him up the stairs. 'You better be right though.'

Sam had been right, it was crazy busy today. People started showing up almost before we had the tents open and they didn't seem to stop coming. Between the beautiful weather and the great acts on stage all day, I was sure we were going to break records. I was bopping along to Billy Klippert's band as they rocked on the stage, when I realized it was almost noon. I had all the tents well manned and under control so I decided to take a break and grab some lunch. The catering tent was lined up at least a hundred deep but I noticed the hotdog stand on the corner had a much shorter line. Gus probably would have fed me too, but I liked the hotdog guy, he didn't know me and didn't ask me any questions. He took my money and handed me a hotdog and a huge kosher dill and moved on to his next customer. I liked that in a restaurateur. I took a bite out of my dill and sat on the cool marble stairs of the Plex, in a spot of shade for a change. This was part of the historic building that had originally stood in this spot, the part that they had been able to save. We in Canada seemed to love our historic buildings, since being fairly new to country-hood, we didn't have that many. The problem here was that not all of them stood the test of time. Luckily, a lot of the Plex had incorporated the old and built the new in modern stark contrast to it. You either loved it or hated it. Sort of like the Louvre with its pyramids by IM Pei. Always a good topic for a heated conversation.

I was engrossed in my pickle and surprised when someone sat down beside me.

163

'Ken?' I asked. 'What are you doing here? Is my life in imminent danger?'

'Nope,' he laughed. 'Some of us cops actually like music, you know. I figured I'd have my lunch break down here and listen to the band. I haven't seen him since he was on Canadian Idol.'

'What do you think so far?'

'I'm reserving judgment as I've just arrived.'

'Ever the diplomat.'

'Do you mind the company?' he asked.

'Oh, not at all,' I said with my mouth full as I finished the dill pickle. 'I can highly recommend that hotdog vendor too, great pickles.'

'Kate, do you know what hotdogs are made out of?' our resident health nut asked.

'Nope,' I laughed. 'Nor do I want to!' I added quickly before he could begin his lesson.

'But they sure smell good.'

'Live a little, Ken.'

'Promise you won't tell?' he asked.

'Swear. And bring me back an orange soda please,' I called, as he trotted over to the vendor.

He came back with a giant bratwurst, buried in onions, sauerkraut, mustard and ketchup. He tossed me my pop but he had bought a bottle of water for himself. Oh well, Rome wasn't corrupted in a day.

'Boy, when you go off the wagon, you go all the way,' I teased.

'I don't know what came over me,' he laughed, straining to get his mouth around the bun.

'The smell.'

'Mmmm,' he said through a full mouth.

'Huh?'

'I said, it's not that I don't like this stuff. It's just that I don't think it's particularly healthy for you.'

'Everything in moderation,' I said. 'Isn't that the rule?'

'Well, when you ever do anything in moderation, you let me know how that works out.'

'Are you saying you're a junk food-aholic?'

'Recovering,' he laughed, finishing the hotdog and leaning back on the step.

'Gives me hope. So what's keeping you busy these days?'

'Well, not you for a change.'

'Yes, my resolution is to stay away from all murders for the period of at least one year.'

'Good resolution. We're all pretty busy with this Bishop thing though.'

'How's that going?'

He just gave me the look. 'You haven't been around me enough to know I neither can nor will answer that question?'

'Well, you know me, never give up.'

'It's going.'

'Is it your investigation?' I asked.

'No, there's a task force set up. But, Kate, that's really all I can say. We don't want to give away anything we may have found out and we don't want to panic the public.'

'The public is pretty panicked already, I should say. Do you know how long it took me to get a cab the other day? Everyone's scared to go out at night.'

'Well, right now, that's a pretty good attitude,' he said. 'But you have to remember, it's not like this guy kills two or three people a day. So far, he's only killed four people that we know of. And that's over a year.'

'But he's escalating.'

'And how do you know that?'

'I read the papers.'

'We have never talked about when the people were killed. Only when we found the bodies.'

'I read between the lines,' I said. 'And I'm learning from Gus. Sometimes when you just throw a statement out there, people will confirm it for you, Detective Lincoln.'

'It is hopeless talking to you.'

'Funny, a lot of people say that.'

'Well, just be careful and use common sense.'

'I am always careful,' I said, and then remembered who I was talking to and what he knew about my past behaviour.

He gave me that look again and was about to open his mouth when my radio squawked to life.

'Doug to Kate, over.'

'Saved by the bell,' Ken laughed.

'Kate here.'

165

'Don't forget to use over, Kate,' Doug reminded me. 'They need some change in tent one. What's your twenty, over?'

'I'm at the entrance to the concert hall. I can meet you at the festival office in two minutes . . . over.' It felt so weird to say that.

'All right, I'll be there. Doug out.'

'Sorry, Ken,' I said, getting up and stretching my legs. 'Duty calls. Enjoy the concert and say hi to your lovely wife for me.'

'Will do,' he promised.

It was two o'clock in the afternoon the next time I had enough time to myself to stop and look at my watch. And so far Doug's prediction was proving to be right. No problems. The biggest crisis I'd had all day was running out of child-size T-shirts and the purple puppets, which were proving to be the favourites. I had Graham out front of the tent alternating between juggling and walking the 'dogless' leash, trying to move some of the other products. He was having a blast with the kids and they were having fun too. And it was going so well that I started moving merchandise from the other tents. Another successful day, which I needed after its inauspicious beginning. It worked so well that I got volunteers walking around the Plaza with festival Frisbees and I moved the neon friendship bracelets and shoelaces to one of the other tents. The volunteers starting braiding them in their hair and wearing them as chokers and they started selling like crazy too. The kids were lapping it up and the parents were coughing up the money for it. If the day continued as it had started, I was going to break all of last year's records. And if I was really lucky and my evil plan came to fruition, I would have no merchandise to inventory at the end of the festival. Of course, it helped that it was a glorious day out. The temperature topped out at 32 degrees Celsius, with a nice breeze blowing, to take the edge off the heat.

I had been running since lunchtime, replenishing stock, so Graham and the other volunteers didn't have to leave their tents. They were selling well and having fun and I didn't want Graham, especially, to feel like he'd done all the heavy work this week. I finally decided to take a little break. I bought myself a snow cone and parked myself on a lawn chair in the shade of the security trailer. I was enjoying the moment alone, watching a group of kids being entertained by a clown with a water pistol, when I felt a hand on my shoulder. I jumped out of the chair and turned to see Doug standing behind me. Guess I wasn't as relaxed as I had thought.

'Why does everyone insist on sneaking up on me this week?' I yelled at him.

'Sorry,' he said. 'I wasn't thinking . . .'

I settled myself back into the chair, glad I had been able to save my snow cone.

'It's OK, I guess I'm still a little jumpy.' I smiled up at him. 'You going to join me for a few minutes?'

'No, I just thought I'd come by and check on you.'

'I'm fine,' I assured him. 'Enjoying my first break of the day.'

'Second break,' he said.

'Are you spying on me?'

'Essentially, yes.'

'Isn't that against the law or something?'

'It's what they pay me to do, actually. And I couldn't help but notice that you are sitting here alone,' Doug chided me.

'Both Sam and Graham know where I am and I have my radio on,' I explained. 'I'm just fine.'

'I just wanted to make sure.'

'Besides, you appear to have been correct, though I hate to admit it. It is a nice peaceful day and it looks like the festival is going to end without further incident.'

'I told you so.'

'Well this is one I told you so that I'm happy to take.' I smiled up at him. I was lying of course, I was still absolutely sure something was going to happen. But I thought I owed him one win this week. 'You sure you don't want to hang around? I'll buy you a snow cone.'

'No, I need to get back out on to the Plaza,' he said. 'I'm trying to keep those kids out of the pool.'

'Oh give them a break. It's a hot day, I would be playing in the fountains if I weren't so busy.'

'No lifeguard on duty,' he explained.

'You're such a stickler for the rules,' I laughed.

167

'If you'll recall, that's also what I get paid for.'

'Oh yeah.'

'Look, I'll check back with you in an hour or so,' Doug said. 'Make sure you keep your radio on, OK?'

'I promise,' I assured him, as he ran off after a kid on a skateboard.

I turned back to watch Buttons the clown soak all the kids and found myself laughing out loud. He turned his water gun to me, but I gave him a look and he turned it back on the kids. I was totally engrossed when I felt another hand on my shoulder. This time I didn't jump, but turned calmly, expecting to see Doug checking on me again. But it wasn't Doug.

'Excuse me, do you work here?'

She was a young woman, probably about twenty-five or so. She had short dark hair and was wearing a light summer dress and sandals. A typical festival-goer. What caught my attention was the frantic look in her eyes.

'Yes, I do,' I said, dropping the snow cone and sitting up straight. 'Can I help you with something?'

'Yes, my little boy is missing. He was just with me a couple of minutes ago and now I can't find him. But there's so many people here, it's hard to tell. Is there some sort of security here that can help me look for him?'

I stood up and turned on my radio, which I had actually turned off while I was on my break. I was glad Doug hadn't noticed that.

'We've got a great lost child program,' I assured her, trying to sound more certain of myself than I felt. My mind was racing, trying to remember what I had read in my orientation package. At least I knew what step one should be. 'Come with me to the kids' tent and we'll get a description of him on the radio. I'm sure we'll have him back to you in no time.'

'No, I have to keep looking for him. I just want you to help,' she said, starting off for the far side of the Plaza.

I raced after her and put my arm firmly on hers, steering her towards the kids' tent and the volunteers that specialized in this.

'I'm Kate Carpenter,' I introduced myself, trying to keep my voice light. 'I'm the market manager here at the festival. Now you need to come to the kids' tent with me and tell us what your son looks like and what he was wearing so the security guards and volunteers know who they're looking for.'

'Thanks for your help.' She smiled weakly at me. 'I'm Cindy Peters. My little boy's name is Ben. And he's never been alone before. He's probably really scared right now.'

I picked up my pace as she stopped fighting me and started to follow my lead.

'How old is he?' I asked once again, now finding myself racing to keep up with her. But at least she was headed in the right direction.

'He's only eight. He's too young to be on his own down-town. Or anywhere. My husband says I'm overprotective, but I think he's just such a little boy and I need to watch out for him all the time and . . .'

'Cindy, it's OK. We'll find him. There are lots of volun-teers around here today. No one's going to let him get into trouble,' I assured her. 'All we have to do is get him back together with you.'

I led her into the tent and luckily one of the women came over and helped her into a seat, taking her off my hands. She was sitting down, in front of one of the volunteers that I knew from the theatre, frantically wringing her hands and blinking back tears of panic.

'Hi Louis.' I smiled at the volunteer behind the table. 'This is Cindy Peters. She has been separated from her little boy. Why don't you take a description of him and I'll get on the radio with what I got while we were coming over here.'

Louis smiled reassuringly at Cindy and pulled out his lost child form. He started going through the questions with the boy's mother. I noticed that not only was he getting a good description of the child but Cindy was calming down a little, more focused now that she was doing something concrete to help her little boy. I took a few steps away and switched my radio to channel one.

'All personnel on this channel to channel five please,' I said calmly, and then repeated my request on all the other chan-nels. I gave everyone a few moments to get switched over and then continued. 'This is Kate and I'm calling a code one. We have an eight-year-old boy named Ben Peters separated from his mother. She is at the kids' tent. Description to follow, over.'

'Kate, what's your twenty, over?' Doug's voice came over the radio.

'I'm at the kids' tent with the mother,' I replied.

'I'll be there in a minute. Don't move, over,' he commanded.

Louis handed me the first page of the description and began going through the next page with the mother. I got back on my radio.

'The child is described as approximately four feet tall, dark brown hair, hazel eyes and very tanned. He is wearing denim shorts, a blue striped T-shirt and yellow sneakers. He does have a lost child tag attached to his belt loop. His full name is Benjamin Joseph Peters. He is eight years old, over.'

Doug was suddenly behind me.

'How long has he been missing?' he asked.

'She said about five minutes, that was before we walked over here. Probably ten minutes all together now,' I told him.

'How'd you find her?'

'She came up to me outside the security trailer. I brought her here right away.'

'Good job.' He turned to his radio. 'This is Security one, all security report, over.'

'Security two, I'm at the north-east corner, over,' Bruce answered.

'Security three at the centre stage, over,' Tommy answered immediately.

'Start sweeping the area,' he ordered. 'Festival market, report in, over.'

'It's Graham,' he said, on the emergency radio we had in all the tents. 'I've got the main tent closed and the volunteers are starting to search. I'm just on my way over to tent two to send some more recruits out, over.'

'OK, call me if you hear anything.' Doug continued through his checklist. 'Festival catering, over.'

'This is Sam,' she said, cutting in on his transmission. I didn't even know Sam had a radio. 'I've got my designated volunteers out around this area, over.'

'Thanks, Sam. Plex security, over?' he called, switching his radio over to another channel.

'Nick here, over,' the voice replied.

'Nick, this is Doug, we've got a code one. Who can you send to help, over?'

'I've got three guys on the way,' he said. 'We'll get the description and start searching the building, over.'

'OK, I'm at the lost kids' tent. I'll watch for your guys, over.'

'Plex security out, over.'

Doug switched his radio back to the emergency security channel.

'Security two and three, report in please, over,'

'Nothing here, over,' was the reply from both of them.

'OK, we're at ten minutes,' he informed them. 'You got ten more and then we're calling the police. I'm going off channel for a minute to inform the festival but I'm standing right next to Kate, so call in if you get anything, over.'

'You're calling Cranston?' I asked.

'Protocol, Kate, you know what we have to do.'

'I don't think I want to be here for that conversation,' I joked half-heartedly.

Doug switched channels and moved a couple of steps away while he tracked down the festival producer. I moved closer to the distraught mom, listening to Louis continue to question her from his lists, hoping to find some new piece of information. Not only would we have a really good description of the child and the events leading up to the incident if we had to call the police, but it kept the parents busy too. I could see Mrs Peters fighting to maintain control as she answered the questions, hoping that something she might say would lead us to her son. I wished I had something to keep me busy right now, rather than waiting for my radio to make a sound.

'They're sending Trent Cranston over,' Doug said quietly. I hadn't noticed him come back beside me. 'He's on stage right now, hosting the sing-along.'

'He's not going to be a happy man.'

'This isn't the kind of publicity he wants,' Doug agreed. 'That's pretty obvious.'

'What time is it?' I asked nervously.

'Quarter past. I'm going to go do one last check in and then I'll call the police.'

171

'I'm going to go for a quick walk around,' I said. 'If you don't need me here. I feel like I should be doing something.'

'Go ahead,' he assured me. 'But you watch yourself as well. This doesn't mean that you're safe from Jeff. He might be lurking out there somewhere.'

'I'll be fine,' I said, checking the time on my watch and hurrying out on to the Plaza. I spent five minutes wandering and staring at every child I saw, wishing his face would morph into the one that I was looking for. There were volunteers everywhere, doing exactly what I was doing. I kept checking my watch, willing time to stand still, but it didn't and as the last few minutes of our search ticked away, I hurried back to the kids' tent.

'Well?' I asked, knowing full well if he had been found I would have heard it on my radio.

'Nothing,' Doug confirmed. 'I'm calling the cops.'

'Is Cranston here yet?'

'Nope.'

'Don't you want to wait a few more minutes and let him make the call?' I asked.

'No. The protocol is clear and approved by the festival. I'll call the police and Cranston can deal with the media.'

'I just don't know if we should get the police down here again.'

He pulled me harshly a few steps away from the kids' tent, hand tightly on my arm.

'Kate, this is a kid here. We're not screwing around with this. What are you thinking?'

'I'm just thinking of the festival . . . oh God, I don't know what I'm thinking. I'm insane. Do what you have to do, Doug.'

'I just want to talk to the mother first, let her know what we're doing.'

'Let me,' I said.

'Are you sure?' he asked.

'Yes,' I confirmed. 'But I wouldn't mind if you were standing right behind me.'

'Cindy?' I said, approaching the woman and crouching down to be at the same level as she was. 'I'd like to introduce Doug Walsh. He's head of security for the festival.'

'Have you found him?' she asked, hopefully.

'No, we haven't,' I said, putting my hand on her knee. 'Cindy, we have a very strict lost child protocol in place at the festival. I just wanted to let you know that we have to call the police now and let them know what's happening. We don't want you to be scared when you see the police arrive.'

'The police?' she asked, her eyes growing larger. 'Oh my God, my little boy.'

'No, it doesn't mean something has happened to him,' I said firmly. 'But it's a crowded plaza and we're right downtown. The police can help us block off the streets and things. So we need to notify them right away so they can help, OK?'

She nodded her head but couldn't muster any words. I turned and nodded to Doug who already had his cell phone out. He took a few steps away while he dialled.

'Cindy, is there anyone we can call for you?' I asked. 'Can we call your husband?'

'He's at work,' she managed.

'I know. But do you think maybe he should be here with you?' I asked. 'Louis, did you get his number?'

'I've got it,' Louis confirmed.

'Can we call him, or maybe you've got a friend or some family with you here today?'

'No, it was just me and Ben here today. I don't think I can tell my husband. How can I say that I've lost our baby?'

'Cindy, it's OK, we'll call him for you.'

'OK,' she cried openly now.

'Louis, can you give Doug the husband's phone number?' I asked. I pulled a chair over and sat next to Cindy, putting an arm around her shoulder.

'You're doing really good,' I told her. 'Now, when the police get here, they're going to want to go over everything with you again. Are you ready for that?'

'No,' she admitted. 'But I'll do whatever I have to do.'

I heard sirens in the distance and gave her shoulder a squeeze.

'They've called your husband,' Louis told her, taking the seat on the other side of her. I vaguely recalled that Louis was the father of two young kids and was glad he was here to help.

'Can I get you anything?' I asked. 'Some coffee or a glass of water or something?'

'I really want a cigarette,' she laughed. 'I quit over five years ago but I really want a cigarette.'

'That I can help with.' I smiled, pulling two from my package and giving her one. I lit it and she coughed as she inhaled, but took a second puff anyway.

'Cindy, I'm just going to see what's going on and I'll be back in a couple of minutes,' I told her, giving her shoulder a quick squeeze before I hurried over to Doug.

I followed his gaze and watched a patrol car and an unmarked cruiser pull up on to the edge of the Plaza. Ken Lincoln got out of one car and hurried over to where we stood, joined by two uniformed officers.

'Ken, you again?' I asked. 'Twice in one day.'

'Well, once again I heard the festival call over the radio and I figured you might be having more problems with Jeff. I thought I'd come and see what I could do.'

'Well, it's not Jeff this time,' Doug explained. 'We've got a little boy that's been missing for over twenty minutes. Here's the paperwork.'

'Well, I might as well stay and help now that I'm here,' Ken said. 'Where are the parents?'

'The mom's sitting over there,' Doug pointed her out. 'The father's on his way over.'

Ken handed our questionnaire over to the uniformed officers.

'You go talk to the mother,' he instructed.

'We've done a very thorough search of the Plaza and Nick, in the Plex, has his guys searching the building,' Doug continued. 'But they haven't come up with anything. We're just going to expand the perimeter to the street and I'll get my guys on to the dumpsters and recycling bins now.'

'What about inside?' Ken asked.

'The Plex security said that nothing has turned up. They've done all the public areas and they are expanding to the basement and secure areas.'

I shuddered at the thought of that poor little boy in a dumpster somewhere and knew it was time for me to get out of there.

'If you don't need me here, I'm going to go looking again,' I told them.

'Stay on your radio,' Doug ordered me.

'I will,' I promised, heading off in the general direction of the market. I thought I'd check in with my people and make sure they were looking. I also thought I should close up all the festival markets and then everyone could get out and help with the search. I still checked the face of every little child I saw, still hoping he would turn up and this would be over.

About halfway to the market, I stopped, my eyes drawn to the back of tent two. There was someone standing by the picnic tables, staring back at me. I couldn't recognize him from this distance, as his face was covered in shadow, but I could tell he was watching me. I slowly began moving closer. His eyes never left mine as I got close enough to recognize him. I hurried, getting closer and closer, my heart suddenly pounding in my chest.

'What are you doing here?'

'What's all the excitement about?' he asked, not answering my question.

'I said what are you doing here?' I demanded, my tone bordering on hysteria.

'Just wanted to see how the festival was going,' he answered, a mean sneer creeping on to his face.

'Have you done something?'

'I don't know what you mean.'

'What have you done?' I screamed at him. 'What have you done to that little boy?'

'I told you I'd make you regret what you did to me.' Jeff smiled, slowly, after checking to ensure that no one was within earshot of us. 'You should have left me alone, Kate.'

'You stole that child?'

'I'm just here to pick up my jacket. I left it here yesterday.'

'You bastard,' I hissed at him.

'My, you are touchy,' he laughed at me. 'Having a bad day?'

'Jeff, where is he? What have you done with that little boy?'

'Why don't you look for him? I thought you liked working with kids? Not up for a little game of hide and seek?' he asked.

'What is wrong with you? Tell me where he is!'

'Fine, if you want to suck all the fun out of this game, go

175

ahead. But you're not going to ruin it for me. I'm sure he's just hiding for a while, Kate. I'm sure he'll turn up sooner or later. He'll probably be gone just long enough to make you realize how wrong you were to treat me the way you did. And the joy is that there is nobody around to hear me say that. Even if you started screaming for the cops right now, I'd just stand there and tell them I was here to enjoy the festival and there's nothing anyone can do about it. Isn't this a fun game?'

'You bastard,' I snarled at him.

'Come on, Kate, start screaming, call the cops over. Let's play this out. I'm starting to enjoy this.'

'I'll do better than that,' I whispered, feeling a rage growing in the pit of my stomach.

'What will you do?' he asked. 'Come on, I've waited for this for days. And remember, if I go to jail or if anything bad happens to me, you'll never finish this game. What can you possibly do to me that is worse than you having to live with the disappearance of a little boy?'

'I'll kill you, you bastard,' I screamed, launching myself through the air toward him.

I lost all sense of reason as I flew at him, and knocked him off his feet and landed on top of him on the ground. The look of surprise on his face was almost enough to stop me, but not quite. My hands went around his neck and he was trying to break free of the grip I had on him, battering my face with blind, panicked slaps and punches. I don't know if anything made contact because I couldn't feel or hear or see anything except my hands around his throat, trying to choke off what little air he was getting.

Suddenly I was off him. Strong arms on both sides of me pulled me away. I struggled to get back to Jeff, but couldn't break free.

'Kate!' Ken screamed, inches away from my face, finally breaking through my fugue.

'He did it,' I sobbed. 'He did it.'

'What are you talking about?' he asked.

But I couldn't talk, I was an out of control hysterical woman, crumpling to the ground and sobbing uncontrollably.

'Get her back to the trailer,' Ken ordered Doug and then

turned back to the uniformed men surrounding Jeff. 'Cuff him and put him in the cruiser for now.'

I lost track of the rest of Ken's commands as Doug half dragged me back to the security trailer. He sat me on the couch and poured me a coffee, waiting for me to regain my senses.

'He did it,' I finally said, choking back another sob. 'He stood there and told me he did it so I would regret what I did to him.'

'What else did he say?' he encouraged me.

'He said that no one could prove anything and I'd just have to live with this.' I sipped the scalding coffee and wiped my eyes with the sleeve of my shirt. 'Oh God, what if he's hurt that little boy?'

'He wouldn't do that,' Doug said. 'He's not stupid. He's just got him hidden somewhere. He wants to play with you, Kate, not go to jail for the rest of his life.'

I tried to stand up but my legs were still shaky and almost crumpled under me.

'Where do you think you're going?' he asked.

'I've got to talk to him. I can reason with him. If he thinks I've suffered enough, he'll give Ben back.'

'Kate, let the police handle this.'

'I can't, I'm responsible,' I shuddered. 'It's all my fault.'

Doug put his arm around me and held me tightly.

It had been a devastating afternoon and evening. We had searched everywhere. When we gave up on the Plaza, I helped the guys in the Plex, but all to no avail. The police had canvassed everyone on the site and no one had noticed anything, but as there had been around 25,000 people down there that didn't surprise me. I sat outside the security trailer, having shut down the market ages ago, but I couldn't seem to make myself leave the site. But tonight was not a night for company or beer. I watched the security team and a bunch of volunteers covering every inch of the park, desperately searching for some sort of clue. Graham was out there with them too, but I couldn't manage to put one foot in front of the other at this point of the evening.

Ken Lincoln had taken Jeff back down to the police station

177

and several very skilled and very angry police officers were doing everything in their power to draw some information out of him. At last report, there was still no news. Jeff was apparently enjoying this all so much; he hadn't even called his lawyer yet.

Sam had tried to take me home with her when she had finally left, but I just couldn't leave the site. Jeff was right, I didn't think I was going to be able to live with myself if we didn't find this little boy safe and sound. I just sat in the lawn chair and stared out at the Plaza, watching the flashlights bobbing around.

'I brought you this.' I heard a gruff voice behind me and smelled the enticing aroma of mochaccino drifting across the cool night air.

I turned and saw Gus standing behind me, a take-out cup in his hand.

'Gus, what are you still doing here?' I asked. 'This is way past your bedtime.'

'Oh, I just decided I might stay open tonight and keep the coffee going for the police and volunteers. You know, we all have to do our part.'

'I know that,' I sighed, taking a big sip of the coffee and feeling the warmth flow through my veins.

Gus sat down in the chair beside me, following my gaze out into the Plaza.

'What are you doing here, Kate?' he asked.

'I'm just watching them search,' I said.

'Is it helping?'

'Not them, but it's helping me.'

'You feeling guilty about this?'

'Yeah. No. A little.'

'Well, you should.'

'Gus?'

'Isn't everyone else telling you it's not your fault?' he asked me.

'Yep.'

'Well, you know me, I like to be different. Besides, you took offence at what I said, didn't you?'

'Yes I did.'

'Then you don't really think it's your fault, do you?'

178

'I guess not,' I said. 'Fuck, Gus, how come you know everything that happens in this building, you know every secret, everybody's history, every time someone sneezes. We can't keep a single thing from you ever and yet here we sit, looking for this poor little boy, and you have nothing to say? How come you don't know who did it or where he is?'

'I'm not psychic,' he said quietly. 'I just ask the right questions of the right people.'

'And I guess Jeff hasn't been hanging around your coffee shop much?

'Nope.'

'Too bad. Maybe you could have found something out sooner and spared us all this trouble.'

'You going home tonight?' Gus asked. 'I can give you a ride.'

'I don't think I can bring myself to leave just yet,' I told him.

'Why don't you let me walk you up to your theatre? Isn't there a nice comfy couch in the Rodeo Lounge? Maybe you could sleep on that tonight.'

'That's a really good idea,' I agreed. 'I suddenly feel really tired.'

'Yep, you look tired, Kate.'

'It has been a long day, Gus.'

I found a blanket in the green room, double-checked all the doors to make sure I was locked in and then I turned out the lights and curled up on the couch. There were no curtains on the windows, and I watched the headlights of the cars on the street below me reflect off the glass and play on the ceiling. I was bone tired but couldn't fall asleep. My brain kept flashing all these different images at me, images I didn't want to see or think about. I finally gave up and sat up, thinking that maybe a beer from the fridge might help me sleep. And then I had an even better idea. I knew something that would help me sleep even better.

I folded my blanket and straightened the cushions on the couch. Then I slipped back into my shoes, pulled my hair back into a ponytail and grabbed my keys. I headed out into the main corridors of the Plex. I knew there were security cameras in the building, but I also knew that most of the guys were out searching and I doubted these were being monitored as closely as they usually were. Besides, I wouldn't raise too many suspicions, I belonged here. Still, I felt slightly guilty roaming the corridors at midnight and I stuck close to the walls, making my way quickly and quietly to the festival office. The office was dark. Everyone was down at the security trailer, which had become the headquarters for the search, so I wasn't surprised to find the office empty. I let myself in, quietly locking the door behind me, and made my way over to the volunteer coordinator's area. I sat in the chair and pulled at the file cabinet drawer. It was locked. I figured it might be.

'Kate,' I heard a voice whisper and saw someone move in the cubicle beside this one. I stifled the urge to scream but jumped about three feet off the chair.

'Graham, what the hell are you doing up here?' I demanded, trying to slow my breathing back to near normal.

'Obviously, the same thing you are.'

'I'm just checking to make sure everything is locked up for the night,' I tried.

'Yeah, well Kate, you can bullshit me and we can waste the night away or we can do this together and get it done.'

I paused, trying to think of something, an excuse, a story, something Graham would believe that would get him out of the office and leave me to my task. But if the truth were known, I was kind of relieved not to be alone. I gave up.

'The file cabinet is locked,' I said.

'I know, I already tried it,' he admitted.

'Luckily, I think I know where the key is,' I said, opening the desk drawer and opening the box of breath mints that was inside. 'Success.'

'How did you know that's where she hid the key?' he asked. 'I've been looking for half an hour.'

'I saw her get it one morning when I was getting the floats out of the safe.'

I opened the file cabinet and rifled through the files until I found the one I was looking for. I pulled it out, opened it up and then looked up at Graham.

'All right, I've got it. What now?'

'We go down to the stage door, tell them we're going home, call a cab and no one ever knows the difference.'

'Good plan. But next week, we need to talk about the way your mind works and maybe get you some help!'

I scribbled down the address, replaced everything the way I had found it, and followed Graham down the stairs. We said a quick good night to the security guard on duty and got into the waiting taxi.

The cab let us out and we stood on the front stairs of the building, waiting for it to pull away so the driver wouldn't see where we were going. As soon as it was out of eyesight, we crossed the street to our real target, at the end of the block. I stood at the front door and pulled on it. Of course it was locked. All apartment buildings were locked. Mine was locked. How stupid was I, thinking we could just walk in.

'Shit!'

'Kate, it's OK.'

'It's not OK. We can't just start ringing buzzers at this time of night.'

Graham reached into his pocket and pulled out a set of keys.

'Are those . . .?'

'These are the keys to Jeff's apartment.'

'How?'

'Jeff left them in his jacket pocket, which he left at the market tent. Good thing I found them and that we decided to return them on our way home tonight.'

I kissed him on the cheek before I swiped the keys from his hand. 'I love you a whole bunch right now.'

We let ourselves in and took the stairs up to the third floor. We made our way down to the correct apartment door and tried the keys. It took three tries before the door opened. We snuck in quietly, closing and locking the door behind us before we turned on any of the lights.

'Hello?' I called.

'Shh! Kate, what are you doing?' Graham asked.

'Making sure the police haven't let him go and that's he's not sleeping in the bedroom,' I said.

'He's still there, I talked to Detective Lincoln just before

181

we left,' he explained. 'Now be quiet, you're making me nervous.'

'Sorry.'

'So, what are we looking for?' he asked.

'I don't know. A clue? Just something that doesn't look right, something that might say where he likes to go, where he might hide a kid?'

'OK, well that's easy.'

'Yeah, it sounded good in my head when I was thinking about this. You take the living room, I'll take the kitchen,' I instructed.

I dug right in, opening one of the drawers and rifling through what seemed to be a hundred post-it notes. An hour later I had been through his grocery receipts, coupon book, post-it notes, and chequebook record from two years ago. I intimately knew the contents of his fridge and knew that his oven needed cleaning. I knew he drank too much soda pop, as his pantry had more empties than food. I knew he preferred canned cream of tomato soup to almost everything else. But I didn't know a single damned thing that was actually helpful. Graham was busy at his computer desk in the living room so I moved into the bedroom.

The bedroom was very tidy. I opened the closet doors and found his trousers hung neatly and his shirts arranged by colour. His sweaters and underwear were all folded neatly and in the dresser drawers. There was nothing hidden in amongst them. Nothing at all. I went into the en-suite bathroom and opened the medicine chest. This was more exciting but not very revealing. He had all the assorted hair care and body care products, though he did seem to have a lot of body lotions. He also had some Prozac, some Valium and a couple of other things that I wasn't sure what they were for. I found some needles but they were beside a bottle marked insulin. I hadn't realized Jeff was diabetic. But I got a little suspicious when I noticed a box marked insulin and opened it up. Inside were vials filled with fluid, but instead of insulin one said Ketamine and another said Demerol. None of those were normal home medications and I couldn't come up with a single good reason why he would have those here. Only bad reasons. I gave up in the bathroom and went back into the bedroom. I decided to check under the mattress and then go see how Graham was doing. I threw back the comforter and sheets and then actually laughed out loud. Graham came racing around the corner, ready to save me.

'What?' he asked.

'Oh my God,' I laughed, pointing at the bed. There, on the pillowcase, was an ironed-on image of my face. 'He sleeps with me every night.'

'That is just pathetic,' Graham said.

'Man, that is going to give me nightmares for weeks.'

'What are you doing with the bed?' he asked.

'I was just going to check under the mattress, see if there was anything hidden.'

'Let me help you,' Graham said, taking one end of the mattress and helping me lift it up. 'Nothing there either.'

I dropped down to my knees and looked under the bed.

'Oh my God,' I whispered.

'What, more pillowcases?' he laughed, plopping down on the bed.

I reached under the bed and pulled out a box. When it came out into the light, we could both clearly see the familiar packaging with the bright red lettering running across the top of the box. Monopoly.

'So, everyone has board games,' Graham said.

I reached back under the bed and kept pulling them out. Chess, checkers, Yahtzee, Uno, Trivial Pursuit, Balderdash, Pictionary, they just kept coming.

'Oh this is bad,' Graham said.

'This is very bad,' I said, opening the chess game to see if there were two bishops. There weren't. 'There is no way he's the Bishop, he's not crazy enough.'

'You know what they say,' Graham said. 'It's always the quiet ones. The ones that no one ever suspects.'

'We've got to get the police up here,' I said, running for the phone.

'No,' Graham said, taking it out of my hands and hanging it back up again. 'I don't want to go to jail.'

'Jail?'

'Breaking and entering, Kate.'

'We had keys, Graham.'

183

'But we didn't have permission, Kate.'

'But we suspected something was wrong, so we came in.'

'And the police are going to let you get away with that one?' he asked. 'Ken Lincoln would lock you up himself.'

'Well, we've got to get the police up here somehow,' I insisted.

'Yes, but you can't let them know we've been up here. They might think we've contaminated the crime scene.'

'Shit, why didn't you bring any of this up before we got here?' I asked, punching his arm in frustration.

'Because I thought we'd find something.'

'OK, I'm going to call Detective Lincoln,' I said, picking up the phone again.

'And what are you going to tell him?'

'I don't know yet,' I admitted. 'I'll improvise. Now shush.'

Ken picked up his phone on the second ring.

'Detective Lincoln,' he said briskly.

'It's Kate,' I said.

'Kate, I don't have time right now.'

'I was just calling to see if there was anything new?' I began.

'Look, Kate, we're just on our way to Jeff's apartment to search it. If it's important, give me the number where you are at and I'll call you later.'

'No, it's not that important, Ken. I'll catch you tomorrow.' I hung up the phone and turned to Graham. 'Shit!'

'What?'

'They're on their way over here to search the place,' I said. 'We need to get this mess cleaned up and get out of here.'

We quickly pushed all the stuff back under the bed and I remade it, while Graham raced out to the living room to shut down the computer and cover up his tracks. I peeked out the front window and saw the police cars pull up out front. I hit the light switch and grabbed the keys.

'Graham, they're here!' I whispered, opening the front door and waiting for him to catch up with me. It didn't take him long. We hurriedly locked the door and raced down the back stairs, not stopping until we were out the back door of the building and trying to catch our breath in the back alley. Suddenly, a set of car headlights switched on, lighting us like actors on a stage. I held my breath and heard Graham do the same as the passenger side door opened.

'Get in,' a harsh voice whispered across to us. 'Now!'

As my eyes adjusted to the light, I recognized the silhouette sitting in the driver's seat and I pulled Graham around to the passenger side of the vehicle. We got in and closed the door, the car slammed into reverse and we sped quickly out of the alleyway.

'What are you doing here?' I asked.

'Kate, I can't even talk to you right now,' Doug said, through clenched teeth. I could almost feel the anger, as he tried to keep it from boiling over.

The only thing he managed to ask was for Graham's address. We drove in silence and dropped Graham off and then we drove in an even colder silence to my apartment. He stopped the car and sat, engine idling, waiting for me to get out. I guess I wasn't going to get my personal escort tonight.

'Look, Doug . . .' I tried again.

'It's late.'

'Please, can we just talk for a minute?'

'We'll talk tomorrow,' he said, in a not so promising voice. 'I've got to get back to the festival now.'

I got out of the car. He watched until I was safely in the building and then slammed the car into gear and raced away. Well, this night hadn't exactly gone the way I had planned. I did manage to make it up to the apartment and get the doors locked behind me before the tears started, though.

It was good to see her upset. Good to see her cry, he thought. The game was in his control. He pulled the collar of his jacket up and smiled to himself as she turned the lights out in her apartment. It wasn't checkmate yet, but it was definitely check.

Saturday

I had tossed and turned at home for a couple of hours and then gave up. I took a cab back to the Plex and curled up on the sofa in the Rodeo Lounge. Somehow it eased my mind to be here, close to the action, even though I couldn't really do anything to help. I managed to fall asleep and rest for a couple of hours. I woke up early and had a long, hot shower, and then dressed. I wandered down Tin Pan Alley and past the security desk, where Nick and his crew looked like they hadn't slept much either. I found my way to Grounds Zero and ordered a coffee from one of Gus's staff, with Gus himself nowhere to be seen.

'He's home sleeping,' the waiter explained. 'He was here until about two o'clock in the morning, feeding all the volunteers. His wife came and got him and then refused to let him come in this morning. She said we could have him back after he'd had some sleep.'

I smiled, wishing I had someone like that looking after me this week and blinked back another one of those errant tears. I paid for my coffee and made my way back around the front of the Plex to the Plaza. I climbed to the top of the stairway overlooking the Plaza. I expected to see security, volunteers and police everywhere. What I saw looked like a perfectly normal day. The booths and kiosks were all full of people, bustling around, trying to get everything ready for opening. Volunteers circled the Plaza, picking up litter and helping out where needed. Graham was running around with a trolley loaded with supplies, refilling the stock in the market tents. And the lawn chairs were set up in front of the security trailer, though the guys must have been off making their rounds, as they all sat empty. It all seemed surreal.

I climbed down the stairs slowly, looking down at the chalk

186

drawings the kids had been making on the sidewalks this week. My heart wanted to cry, to free some of the emotion that was building inside me, but I couldn't yet, not until this was over. I felt so lost without Cam here, by my side. Without the one person I could share all this with, who would understand how I was feeling and would just be able to touch my shoulder or cheek and make me feel better. I didn't know what to do. I stood there frozen for the better part of a minute until someone came up and stood beside me.

'It's hard to believe anything bad is even happening here, isn't it?'

I turned and saw Seth standing beside me, no clown make-up, just blue jeans and a festival T-shirt.

'It's unbelievable,' I agreed.

'So is there any news other than the screaming headlines?' he asked, pointing to the newspaper box and the front page headlines.

'I don't know, I'm just getting here myself.'

'Do you want to maybe go back to the coffee shop and let me buy you a scone to go with that coffee?' he asked.

'No, I want to get to work. I need a smoke though, have you got a light?'

'I don't smoke, Kate.'

'Sorry?'

'I don't smoke. I don't have a light.'

'Oh, sorry, I don't know why I thought you did.'

'Probably because most theatre people seem to smoke.'

'We'll do coffee some other time,' I promised. 'When I'm a little more fun to be around.'

'I'm going to hold you to that. I really would like you to meet my girlfriend. She's just moved here and I think you two would get along really well together.'

I turned and looked at him, embarrassed that I thought he had been trying to pick me up all this time. And disappointed that he hadn't been trying to pick me up all this time. But I tried to hide all that and give a grown-up type answer.

'I'd love to meet her.'

'Well, I'll go hang around the festival lounge for a while,' he said. 'I've noticed you're never there.'

'No, I guess I haven't managed to hang around much.'

'There's some interesting people, you know? There's that Canadian Idol guy. And I met those stilt walkers from Hungary. And even most of the volunteers are pretty cool.'

'Seth, I kind of have some problems going on this week that are distracting me a little, I'm afraid.'

'Well, I hope you'll at least try and make the closing night party?'

'I'll try,' I said. 'Look, I have to get going. I'll see you around, OK?'

'I hope so.'

I had noticed Sam working in the catering tent and I headed over there for my best friend, the only person that might understand how I was feeling right now. I saw her busy, working away, trying to mould some bread dough into some shape it obviously didn't want to be. I decided for once not to interrupt her and just sat with my coffee at the picnic table beside the catering tent. I sat there for ages, smoking and sipping my coffee, before she saw me. She finished what she was doing, gave some instructions to her assistant and came out, bottle of water in hand, to sit across from me.

'I see your assistant made it in on time today.' That was my pathetic attempt at small talk.

'Yeah, he actually beat me here today. Everyone wants to be around the scene of the crime, I guess.'

'Not me.'

'It's going to be a hot day, huh?' Sam asked.

'Yep.'

'Any news?'

'None since last night. I haven't gone looking for any updates yet though. I figured no news was no news.'

'Well, I suppose good news would have found you.'

'What is happening here today?' I asked.

'What do you mean?'

'Why are all these people here? Why is everyone getting set up?'

'Because it's the last day of the festival,' she explained to me, as if I was a slow child.

'But what about that poor little boy?' I asked. 'We can't just carry on like nothing has happened.'

'Kate, the police have looked everywhere for him. Whoever

took him, took him far from downtown. The Plaza is clear and the festival must go on.'

'It's not right.'

'Kate, why don't you just go home for the day?' she asked me. 'It looks like Graham has everything well in hand.'

'Go home? Sam, I can't go home until they find him.'

'Kate, they might never find him. Child abductions are horrible things, but the fact is that every hour that goes by makes it more and more likely that they will never find him.'

'Don't say that. Don't ever say that again. We have to be positive.'

'Kate, I know you've had a really bad week and you've got more emotions swirling around that little heart of yours than you know what to do with, but right now, you've got to get it together. No one here has time to worry about how you're feeling. They've all got their own stuff to deal with, including the search for this little boy, which has not been called off yet, by the way. So you need to either leave this Plaza and go home, or you need to get it together and act strong and helpful, like everyone else is trying to do.'

I looked at her, tears stinging my eyes, but I realized she was right.

'All right,' I said, blinking rapidly and trying to dry my eyes.

'For sure?'

'Yes, you're right. This isn't about me.'

'Kate, now you've got me really worried. No one in the entire history of the world has ever won an argument with you in this short a period of time. Are you sure you're all right?'

I tried a smile on and found it didn't actually hurt or cause my face to crack.

'I'm fine. But I know I'm not going to be any help this way. And it is up to me. It's my fault, right?'

'It's not your fault.'

'No, I didn't really mean it like that. I meant I'm the catalyst that brought everyone together. Without me being here Jeff would have just been a normal volunteer and no kids would have gone missing . . .'

'And maybe World War Two happened because of you?'

189

she asked sarcastically. 'Or that earthquake in Afghanistan?'

'Maybe I can do something about making it all end,' I said, ignoring her sarcasm. 'And you're right, meanwhile, we have to get through this day and see what happens.'

Sam shook her head at me.

'Maybe you need food. I'll get you some breakfast and see if we can't clear that up.'

'Just give me whatever you've got for the security trailer and I'll take it to them.'

'I would appreciate that,' she called out from inside the tent. 'But I'm going to throw something extra inside for you. Make sure you're the one that gets it.'

I put my cigarette out, tossed my empty coffee cup into the garbage can and took the bag from Sam. I worked my way slowly back to the security trailer, checking in with all the market tents and making sure everything was going OK. Graham, as always, had everything under control and was making me look good, so I left him to it and took breakfast to the security trailer. None of the guys were inside or outside, which made me happy, so I got the coffee started and unpacked the muffins. Sam had put some chocolate croissants inside the bag for me and I greedily bit into the first one, enjoying the taste of the chocolate and the aroma of the brewing coffee. I pulled out my paperwork for the day and had almost forgotten about yesterday. Almost, until the trailer door opened and Doug walked in, looking worse than I felt.

'Please don't tell me there's bad news?' I asked.

He flopped down on to the bench seat, seeming to have the weight of the world on his shoulders.

'No news,' he said.

I poured him a coffee and we sat in silence as I continued sorting through my box for the day.

'Shall we do this now or save it for later, after passing the day in an incredibly uncomfortable silence?' I asked.

'What are you talking about?'

'OK, let's pretend that you really don't know what I'm talking about and I'll give you an opening. So Doug, how was it that you just happened to be in the back alley at Jeff's apartment building last night just as Graham and I came out the back door?'

'You don't want to do this with me,' he said, avoiding eye contact.

'No, I do want to do this with you. I love confrontation.'

'Well, Kate, Gus told me he'd tucked you into bed at the theatre,' he started sweetly. 'So I got Nick to let me in so I could check on you. When you weren't there, I called you at home and there was no answer. When I checked at the security desk, they said you and Graham had hopped into a cab. Luckily, I have a really good friend at the cab company, and when I found out where you were going, I figured I better get over there quickly. I pulled up out back just in time to see the lights go off in Jeff's apartment when the police lights started flashing outside. I was sure hoping you were smart enough to come out the back way. But even if you weren't, I figured you would need somebody to bail you out of jail.'

'I thought we were being really clever,' I said.

'Yeah, well, that's the thing about you. You think you're smarter than all of us. But we do this for a living, OK? We know how all this works, Kate, and we have ways that we handle things. And do you know why we have all these specific methods and means of doing things? It's so that we don't screw up the court cases or let the bad guys get away. Or so that we don't let innocent albeit stupid civilians get hurt.'

'I wouldn't get hurt.'

'What about if Jeff had been let go? What about if he walked in while you were searching his place?'

'We checked. I'm not totally stupid, you know?'

'I'll believe that when I see some actual proof of it.'

'Well, we made it out safe and sound,' I said. 'So I guess it was a success.'

'You made it out because you were incredibly lucky. Did you notice that there were probably ten cops that went up to that apartment? They didn't go alone, Kate, they all have guns. They know that shit can go terribly wrong in these situations.'

'Well, it won't happen again.'

'You can't just say that. You have to mean it. You have to really mean that you are not going to get involved in anything. That means that if something happens this afternoon, you have

191

to call Detective Lincoln and tell him, and then go home and leave it be.'

'I will.'

'I wish I could believe you,' he said.

'I wish I could believe it, too.'

'Do you think it's going to help the investigation if we have to send people out to search for you, Kate?'

'No.'

'And Jeff is a creep. Detective Lincoln told me about the pillowcase.'

'I know,' I said, thinking about the games. I didn't want to tell Doug about those, he was already pissed off enough at me. If he thought Jeff was the Bishop, he really would lock me up today and I would not get out until sometime next week. But I wondered if Ken Lincoln had said anything about that to him.

'Normal people don't do things like that.'

'I had a Donny Osmond pillowcase,' I offered, trying desperately to charm my way out of this.

'I'm going to go out on patrol,' Doug said, ignoring me.

'Should we still talk some more?' I asked, not feeling really at ease yet.

'We'll talk more, I promise,' he said.

'I hope so.'

'Anything I need to watch for today?' he asked, getting up and rinsing out his coffee cup.

'Nope.'

'Anything I need to do?'

'Find that missing little boy,' I sighed.

'Kate . . .'

'Never mind. I'm sorry I said it. We're going to have a good day at the festival.'

'We've done all we can for him, you know? The police will find him.'

'I know.'

'The police are trained for this. They will find him,' he repeated.

'They may not.'

'I think they will,' Doug said. 'Jeff isn't a normal paedophile or child abductor. If he's the one responsible for this, he's doing it just to taunt you. It has nothing to do with that little boy.'

'If he wants to take a round out of me, why doesn't he just come and do it?' I asked.

'Because he doesn't have enough guts to face you.'

'This is so frustrating.'

'Yes it is.'

'Oh well, I need to get my mind off this for a while. I think I'll go help Graham move some inventory around.'

'Should I come with you?' he asked.

'No, I just need to burn off some energy,' I said. 'I don't think I'll be very good company right now. And I promise I'll stay close to Graham.'

'And that is supposed to make me feel better?' he asked, a hint of a smile finally creeping on to his face.

He kissed me on the forehead, a breakthrough.

'Call me if you need me, huh?' he asked.

'And you call me if there's any news, huh?'

I found Graham by the now famous tent two, unpacking boxes of puppets and hanging them on the display rack. I took the empty boxes and started tearing them apart, flattening them for disposal. Graham had been using a utility knife, but I was happy to rip at them with my bare hands. Graham was wise to my moods and just turned back to his unpacking. When I was finished, he sent me down to the storeroom, to fetch and carry more for him. I was happy to throw some more boxes around; it was definitely helping to burn off my frustration. I finally felt a little better when we had all the stock up for the last day's events and had the tents ready to go.

I was just counting the float out and putting it in the cash register in tent two when I looked up and saw Ken Lincoln standing there.

'Sorry, we're not quite open yet, Ken,' I told him. 'Take whatever you want and I'll settle with you later.'

'I need to talk to you,' he said.

'Sure, I'm almost done here, why don't I meet you . . .'

'Graham,' Ken called. 'Take over here please, Kate is coming with me.'

He took my arm and led me across the Plaza and into the near empty corridor of the Plex.

'What is the matter?' I asked, pulling away from him and rubbing my arm. He was pacing back and forth in front of me and I was starting to get worried.

'So, last night, we searched Jeff's apartment,' he started. 'But I told you that already.'

'Yes, when we talked on the phone you said you were on your way over.'

'Well, we went up and had a real good look around.'

'Did you find anything?' I asked innocently.

'Did you?' he asked.

'What do you mean?'

'Well, funniest thing. When I pushed redial on his phone to find out what the last number was that he had called, do you know what number came up?'

'No.'

'My cell phone number.'

'No way.'

'Yeah, that's what I thought too. So I checked my last cell phone calls and do you know what I found?'

'No.'

'I found that the call from you came from Jeff's apartment.'

I stared up at him, but wisely kept my mouth shut.

'So, why don't you tell me a really good story so that I don't have to arrest you and take you to jail right now?'

'I don't have one,' I whispered. 'I found Jeff's keys and then made a really stupid decision.'

'That is probably the first time you've ever said anything so true to me.'

'I'm sorry.'

'Kate, sorry isn't good enough. If we tried to prosecute, his lawyer can say that you tampered with the evidence, or planted something. This is serious stuff. And what you did was breaking and entering, not to mention interfering with an ongoing police investigation. Do you know what could happen to you?' he asked.

'I have a bit of an idea,' I admitted.

'How long were you there?' he asked.

'Well, not really too . . .'

'Kate, it is of the utmost importance that you answer me truthfully right now. I swear, if I think you are lying I will arrest you. Do we understand each other?'

'Yes.'

'OK, how long?'

'About an hour, maybe a few minutes longer.'

'And where did you go in the apartment?'

'I checked the kitchen, the living room and the bedroom.'

'Did you take anything?'

'Nothing. Only his keys, the ones I used to let myself in with.'

'Kate?'

'Honest to God,' I insisted. And I pulled the set of keys out of my back pocket and handed them to him to prove it.

'Did you look under the bed?' he asked.

'Yes,' I said, looking at the floor.

'So you saw the games.'

'I did.'

'Kate, it is really important that you don't tell anyone about them. Not anyone. This investigation may have reached a turning point and we cannot risk a leak.'

'I promise.'

'We might have the Bishop,' he reiterated. 'Make sure we don't lose him.'

'I swear,' I said. 'I don't want him back on the streets either. I won't whisper a word of this to anyone.'

'OK, now I want you to stay where I can find you.'

'I will,' I promised again, very eager to please him. 'And thanks for not telling about my little indiscretion last night.'

'Not telling?' he asked.

'Yeah, not telling that I was up in the apartment before you guys.'

'Kate, I'm not keeping that a secret,' he said.

'What?'

'We can't risk the investigation and then a trial on the fact that you might be found out.'

'What's going to happen?' I asked, feeling my legs grow weak under me.

'I spoke with the lead investigators on both the Bishop task force and the one searching for the little boy. They said they would trust my instinct on this. So, for now, you're free and

I'm really hoping you don't do anything else because this could be my career.'

'I'm sorry, Ken,' I said.

'Yeah, well you need to prove that by staying on the straight and narrow today. I'm not kidding when I tell you that if I think anything is going on with you, I will take you to head-quarters and turn you over to the Bishop task force.'

'I believe you.'

'I'll be back later. You better be here when I get back.'

'I'll be here,' I said, but it was to his back as he was storming off down the corridor. I headed slowly back out to the Plaza, crossing over to tent two, where Graham was anxiously awaiting my return.

'What was that about?' he asked.

'He knows I was at Jeff's apartment just before they got there,' I admitted.

'Crap. Are we in trouble?'

'I didn't tell him about you,' I said. 'There's no need for both of us to get in trouble.'

'Kate . . .'

'I mean it, Graham.'

'Are we in trouble?'

'I'm in a whole mess of trouble,' I said. 'But I think Ken is still on my side. He didn't arrest me.'

'Well, that's a good thing.'

'But we can't say a thing about anything we found in that apartment. Not a thing.'

'I won't.'

'I mean it, Graham, not to your mom, not to your girlfriend. Not to anyone.'

'OK, Kate, I get it.'

'If anything gets out, Graham, he is going to have me arrested for interfering with a police investigation.'

'Oh.'

'Yeah.'

'OK, not a word. As a matter of fact, I'm going to try real hard to forget we were even there.'

'Good.'

'So how do you want to run things this morning?' Graham asked me.

'I don't know,' I admitted. 'I think I'm going to have to work really hard to get my heart into this today. I don't seem to be there yet.'

'If you need to just go home and be alone or anything, I think I can manage here,' he offered.

'No. What would I do there? Sit and stare at the walls? I'll stay here with you guys and we'll get through the day and then maybe we can all go out and get drunk or something. As long as I'm still a free woman.'

'OK.'

I turned when I felt someone come up behind me and saw Doug.

'You ready to get your floats for the day?' he asked. 'Or would you like me to come back in a little while?'

He was still a little on the somber side.

'Tommy got them from the office for me, but I have to get to the other tents,' I explained. 'And I think I'm ready to do that.'

We were strangely silent as we walked across the Plaza, and slightly uncomfortable with each other, unlike our previous behaviour over the last week. He leaned over to unfasten the tent flap for me at tent one, but stopped before opening it.

'Are you going to be OK today?' he asked.

'I'll be fine.'

'No, I meant will you really be OK?'

'Doug, it's been a long week and I don't know if I'll be OK or not. But I'm going to get through today. I always get through the day.'

'Good. Even though I'm still a little ticked, Kate, I want you to know that you can call me if you need me. You do know that, don't you?'

'Yes, I do.'

He paused, still not opening the tent flap for me.

'What?' I asked, growing a little impatient.

'Nothing,' he sighed, pulling up the tent flap to allow me entrance. 'I guess I was just hoping that you might wonder how I was doing.'

And then he turned and walked away. I looked at him, my heart stinging with the thought that I hadn't asked him that. What kind of a horrible selfish woman was I really? Was I destined to drive everyone who cared about me away from me? Luckily, before I could wallow in too much self-exploration and self-pity, a volunteer called me and I shook my head to clear it and took the float in to him. I always get through the day. I got the other tents set up and opened and then headed back for the familiarity of Graham's tent.

'Kate, I'm sorry but I forgot one box of masks downstairs. Can you watch things while I run down and get it?' Graham asked, once we had everyone set up.

'I'll go,' I offered. 'I still have some energy I'd like to burn off.'

'You sure?' he asked me.

'Yep.'

I left the tent and started across the Plaza.

'Kate!' I heard someone yelling behind me.

I turned and saw Doug running to catch up with me.

'What's up?'

'The police just called,' he said.

'Good news?' I asked.

'Well, not really news. They want to know if you're willing to talk to Jeff. He said that if they bring him down here, he would tell you where the kid was.'

'Of course I'll talk to him.'

'I figured you would,' he said. 'I already told them you agreed to it. They'll be here in a half an hour.'

'OK, I just have to run down to the basement and bring some masks up for Graham. I'll be at the security trailer in ten minutes.'

'See you there.'

I raced down the stairs, some happiness creeping back into my stressed little brain. Jeff was finished with whatever silly game he was playing and we were going to find the little guy and get him back to his parents. And then I was going to kill Jeff. I was willing to risk going to jail, but I really wanted to kill him at this exact moment in time. I continued down the stairs, realizing the elevator would have been faster but finding a new-found spring in my step. I passed by basements and sub-basements, past 'warning asbestos' signs and finally to the storage cages. I was in such a hurry I even forgot to get creeped-out by the dark and dank basement, like I normally

198

did. Until I heard a noise in the cage beside me. I turned around slowly to see what had made that noise and then screamed as the distorted blackened eyes and red slash of a clown mouth descended upon me from above.

Back up in the sunshine, things were much less spooky and a glass of water and a seat in the sunshine had finally settled my pounding heart. I saw the police car pull up and park on the street at the edge of the Plaza. I looked Doug in the eye, tried to leech some of the calm and courage he seemed to feel from him, and then I strode purposefully over to where the cruiser was parked. Jeff was just getting out of the back seat, hands cuffed in front of him. A smile broke across his face as he saw me approach him. I answered him back with a great big smile of my own. I stopped right in front of him. We stood face to face and toe to toe, two police officers on either side and Doug behind me.

'I want her alone,' Jeff said.

'That's fine,' I assured everyone, and they all cleared back four or five feet. But I could still feel their eyes boring into my back, which was a comforting feeling.

'OK, I'm here,' I said. 'Tell me where he is, just like you promised.'

'Oh, I will,' he promised. 'But why don't you tell me how you've been feeling for the last day or so first?'

'Jeff, I believe we had a deal.'

'Kate, come on. I'm in handcuffs; I'm going to jail. Give me a break. Give me my two seconds of happiness, knowing that I actually made you suffer a little bit.'

'I've been feeling sick to my stomach since that little boy went missing,' I admitted. 'I haven't been able to sleep or eat. And I've hated myself for the things I have been thinking about doing to you.'

'Oh, don't ruin it for me,' he laughed.

'Well, it's true. But overall, you've accomplished what you wanted to. I've been sick and upset and feeling totally helpless.'

'Guilt will do all of that to you,' he sneered.

'Oh, you've got me figured out so wrong,' I sneered right back. 'I'm sick to my stomach with worry and sick to my stomach that I would even know someone who could do something like this. But I don't have any guilt. Maybe your mother should be the one you're talking to about guilt. Did she not breastfeed you?'

'You better be nice to me. I don't have to tell you where he is,' he said, holding up his cuffed hands. 'What are they going to do if I reneg on my agreement, arrest me?'

'Did the kids pick on you at school? Were you strange and different and never fit in?' I taunted him.

'Shut up, you bitch,' he whispered.

'Or was it your father? Did he neglect you? Was he disappointed in you? Or worse, did he pay too much attention to you?'

'Fuck you then! I'll never tell you where the kid is! Live with that, you superior . . .'

'No, fuck you, you asshole,' I spat back at him. 'You never took the kid!'

'What are you talking about?'

'We found him this morning. He got away from his mom and followed a clown down into the basement. He went exploring, trying to find his way out and he got locked in the storage cages downstairs. He's never seen you or heard of you and right now he's with his mom safe and sound and probably still eating. He was pretty hungry. It was just an accident.'

'But I made you flinch, didn't I?' he asked, getting a little of his calm demeanour back.

'Yeah, you made me flinch,' I admitted. 'And for that, there is just one thing I'd like to say to you.'

'Oh yeah, what's that?'

I had a smart comeback ready for him. Really I did. But I admit that I have some problems with anger management and I guess that's why I hauled back and hit him as hard as I could. Now, I don't know if my punch was that great or if he just wasn't expecting it, but the next thing I knew he was on the ground holding his nose and two police officers were holding me back.

'You asshole,' I screamed, finding more anger inside. 'Letting everyone think that you had done that.'

'Kate,' Doug said firmly, taking me from the police officers and pulling me a couple of feet away from Jeff. 'Kate, get it under control. It's over.'

I didn't want to. I wanted to hit him again. My hand was sore but my psyche felt slightly restored. But I took a deep breath and tried to find that inner peace that everyone always talked about. I had to settle for a slightly slower heartbeat and a slightly smaller urge to hit him again. Feeling me begin to settle, Doug let me go and helped the police officer pick Jeff up off the ground. His nose appeared to be bleeding profusely and I admit I took great pleasure in that.

'Come on, Doug, we're done here,' I said, turning and starting back to the Plaza.

'Do you know what's really funny?' Jeff yelled after me.

I ignored him and kept walking.

'What's really funny is that you haven't even discovered who's really missing yet. That stupid kid getting lost was just a bonus. It let me stretch the game out a little longer. But someone else has been missing for almost four days now and nobody has even noticed yet. How do you feel about that?' he yelled after me. Sick to my stomach, again. Please don't let this be true, I thought.

I sat at a picnic table with Sam, near the catering tent. Graham had the markets under control and Sam had her volunteer assistant running things in her tent. Ken Lincoln had returned to the Plaza after the police officers had secured Jeff in the back of the police cruiser and contacted him with the news of our meeting. He and a couple of officers were interviewing the volunteers while another detective was interviewing Jeff, who had been moved to the security trailer for this purpose. Sam and I waited nervously to see if Jeff's last threat had been another red herring or the truth.

'So the little boy's OK?' Sam asked, while we both ate burgers fresh off the grill. It sure paid to have a best friend who was a cook. Whenever I had a problem and the urge to do some emotional eating, she was right there for me.

'Yeah. I went down to the cage to bring up another box of masks and he jumped up and scared the shit out of me,' I laughed. 'I'll certainly never be able to look at a clown the same way again.'

201

'Huh?'

'He was wearing one of the clown masks. I turned and all I saw were those red lips coming at me.'

'Oh, I can see how that might freak you out a bit.'

'Well, I let him keep the mask. He seemed to think the whole thing was kind of funny.'

'How the heck did he ever get down there?' Sam asked.

'He told me he had wanted a puppet but his mom wouldn't buy one for him. So he snuck away from his mom and followed one of the clowns downstairs and he got turned around when the clown went into the locked dressing-room area. I guess he just wandered around until he stumbled into one of the storage cages. He was in the back, trying to find the puppet he wanted and then he got locked in.'

'Pretty resourceful little kid.'

'More like spoiled brat,' I said. 'But I'm trying not to speak badly of him since he was missing and all that.'

'So why didn't they find him last night?' Sam said. 'I thought they searched the entire building.'

'He apparently fell asleep tucked in the back. He wrapped himself in a bunch of T-shirts to keep warm and then he never heard a thing until I went down there this morning.'

'Well, that's a happy ending,' Sam smiled. 'And as a mom, those really are the kind I like to hear.'

'Well, I'm hoping that's the end, period, and that in the next ten minutes Ken Lincoln is going to come over, tell me everything is OK, arrest Jeff for interfering with an investigation or something and then we'll all get back to normal.'

'Or what is passing for normal this week,' Sam reminded me.

'Yeah, I'll deal with all that next week, OK? One crisis at a time.'

'Well, here's your ending coming,' Sam said, looking over across the Plaza where Ken Lincoln was making his way towards us. 'Is it going to be happy or not?'

'That's not his happy face,' I sighed.

Ken sat down on the picnic bench beside me.

'Well?' I asked, not bothering to waste time with small talk.

'One of your volunteers seems to be missing. Janice Seifert?'

He turned to me. 'She was working in tent number one. Female, twenty-two years old, dark brown hair, green eyes.'

'Oh, her. I remember her from the first day. She was really great about getting everyone organized and getting things set up.'

'Well, she missed a couple of shifts here and nobody seemed to notice.'

'Ken, at least twenty percent of the volunteer shifts are missed during the festival. It just happens with volunteers at an event like this. They over-schedule them just like the airlines double-sell their seats, for that exact reason.'

'OK. We've got some officers at her house and her room-mate hasn't seen her either. But she sometimes stayed at a boyfriend's house, so we can't prove anything yet. We've got officers trying to track her down.'

'She's missing,' I said, sadness creeping over me again. 'He wanted to do something and this is what he did. He wouldn't pull the same gag twice, this time it's real.'

'Kate, we're tracking her down. She's probably just camping with her boyfriend or something. Jeff's a jerk but I don't think he's a killer.'

'Neither do I. But I think kidnapping would be OK in his mind. As long as something didn't go wrong, like he got arrested, and she's stuck somewhere now.'

'OK, well, we're going to keep interviewing her family and friends. I'll keep you posted, OK?'

'All right.'

Ken's cell phone rang and he turned away from me to answer it. Sam and I pretended not to eavesdrop while we finished our burgers. Ken hung up from his call and then turned back to me.

'We have a problem,' he said.

'What?' I asked.

'There's just been a dead body discovered in a dumpster behind City Hall.'

'That just makes it a nice well-rounded week, doesn't it?' I asked.

'Yeah, well Kate, this body had two things on it. It had a domino in its mouth and a festival nametag around its neck.'

203

Sam gasped and I swallowed hard. 'Is it the missing girl?' I asked.

'No, this is a man. Can you come over and see if you can identify the body?' he asked.

'I don't really know all the volunteers,' I started.

'That was more of a rhetorical question,' he explained, standing up and waiting for me to join him. 'I'd like to know if you know him or not. We'll stop and get Doug too. Between you two, you see a lot of the volunteers down here.'

I followed him across the Plaza, stopping momentarily to pick up Doug and then crossing the street. Ken led us through City Hall and out the back door. There was a uniformed officer waiting there to guide us around to the loading docks where the trash bin was located. There were two men in coveralls with Coroners Office printed on the back, who were pulling the body out of the dumpster and settling it into a body bag on the waiting gurney. Ken held us back until they were finished and then we walked over to the body. One of the attendants unzipped the bag down to about chest level. I took hold of Doug's arm and took a deep breath, trying to steel myself for the view. The body was dirty and a little puffy from the heat and exposure, and the smell was a little ripe, but not a lot worse than the overall smell of the garbage that surrounded us. The young man wore a bright orange security vest that was on backwards, and I could see some blood had seeped through at his stomach level, probably where there was some sort of incision to remove some sort of internal organ. I stared at the bloated face, trying to imagine it slimmer and with a bit more colour in it. Nothing seemed familiar to me. Doug studied it too, but his face didn't look quite as clueless as mine.

'I think his name is Danny,' Doug said. 'He was a volunteer for the security team. Last I saw him was a couple of nights ago. He did the late evening Plaza patrol, I think. I'd have to check the schedule to be sure.'

Ken nodded at the coroner's team and they zipped the bag up and loaded the body into the waiting van. 'I'll want to see those schedules.'

'I'll get them for you right away,' Doug promised.

'If that was the night that Janice went missing,' I said, 'I bet this guy got in the way and Jeff took care of him.'

'Kate, I told you, we found a game piece. This is one of the Bishop's victims.'

'But that could be Jeff. You said . . .'

Ken pulled us both away from the scene, heading back towards the entrance to City Hall.

'What did I tell you about keeping this quiet?' he asked me angrily. 'This is none of your concern.'

'I just think you should consider all the possibilities,' I argued. 'I think you should really look at Jeff . . .'

'We have, Kate, and Jeff isn't the Bishop,' he whispered. 'The DNA doesn't match.'

'What DNA?' I asked. 'You never said you had DNA from the Bishop.'

'Kate, please.'

'That's not possible,' I gasped. 'It has to match.'

'It is possible, Kate. What we've got here is two people doing two separate things and I really need you to not say a word about any of this.'

'You're wrong, Ken. I just have this feeling.'

'Kate, I have talked to you about this once already!' Ken said sharply. Much more sharply than he had ever spoken to me before.

Many words jumped into my mouth, things I wanted to say to him, things that I would have said if he were anybody else and not threatening to throw me in jail. I swallowed them all back and simply nodded. I nodded my agreement, my under-standing, my subservience to him, for the moment. He stared back at me, trying to determine if I really meant it or was just humouring him. Finally, his eyes softened a little bit and he looked up at Doug.

'I'll need this guy's volunteer information sheet too,' Ken said. 'It will have his emergency contact information on it.'

'I'll get that from the office for you.'

'Good. I'll be back over there in another twenty minutes or so.'

'Thanks, Ken,' I said, but only to be polite, not because I particularly liked him right now.

When we got back to the Plaza, Doug went to the security trailer to get the schedules Ken had wanted and I volunteered to go and get a copy of Danny's file. After all, I knew where the keys to the filing cabinet were, if no one else was there to help me. Luckily there was someone there, and I didn't have to continue my felonious behaviour. I brought a copy of the file back down to the trailer and poured a coffee for Doug and myself. We sat and waited for Ken to return; we mostly sat in silence.

Fortunately, we didn't have to wait too long. Ken opened the door and climbed up the stairs, sitting down heavily on the sofa.

'I have more bad news,' he said, without preamble.

'Don't tell me there's another body,' I asked.

'Not yet. But we found Janice Seifert's boyfriend and he hasn't seen her for a couple of days. So she's officially missing.'

'And nobody reported her missing?' I asked.

'Everyone thought she was with someone else. And you didn't notice she was missing either.'

'I told you, she was a volunteer and they come and they go. If someone calls and says let's go camping, they go camping and ignore their shifts. I mean they're not all like that but it happens and we don't really think anything of it. And what about Jeff?' I asked, not actually expecting an answer.

'Do you have the stuff I wanted?' Ken asked, ignoring my question.

Doug handed him the file folder and Ken pulled himself wearily up into a standing position. 'OK, well I'll talk to you guys if I need anything else. Or if there's any news.'

'We'll be here,' Doug said.

Ken let himself out and I finished my coffee.

'I've got to work,' I said. 'I can't just sit here and wait.'

'Me too,' Doug agreed.

'Wow, no arguments?'

'They have Jeff at the station, they're questioning him, I seriously doubt he'll manage to break free in the next six hours or so. I think you'll be safe.'

'Good.' I took the coffee cups to the sink and rinsed them out. 'Well, I'll be at the market tents if anyone needs me.'

'Keep your radio on,' he reminded me.

I checked on tents one and three and then joined Graham

in tent two. I checked my watch and was surprised to find it was only just noon. It felt like it should be midnight.

By two o'clock in the afternoon there were over ten thousand people at the festival site and, despite myself, I got wrapped up in the crowds and sales and forgot about my frustrations with Jeff and the police for a little while. The day flew by and whether the people had come downtown for the festival or because of the headlines, they spent their money and enjoyed themselves. It was well after our four o'clock closing time before we got the last tent closed up and it took us several hours to clean up the tent and pack everything back down into the storage lockers. I sent everyone home and dragged my tired butt over to an empty lawn chair at the security trailer. Sam was in her corner of the Plaza, still cleaning up, but the rest of the Plaza was finally clear. There were only a few scattered people closing up the tents and securing everything for the night. Everyone was headed home for an early night, for a change, because we had to be back here bright and early to tear everything down. The Plaza had to be cleared by noon for another opening for another show, as the old song almost goes. I noticed one of the festival market tents wasn't closed; the door flap was slapping around in the breeze. I didn't think I had the energy to make it across the Plaza again, but I didn't see anyone around who I could ask to go and take care of it for me. So I pushed myself out of my very comfortable chair and made my way to the far side of the Plaza. I jumped when I saw someone in the tent, but relaxed slightly when I recognized Sam's assistant from the catering tent.

'Can I help you with something?' I asked.

'I saw the tent was still open and I thought I'd secure it for you. You looked pretty tired there at the security trailer,' he said.

'Thanks, that was nice of you. But I'm sure Sam will be looking for you. There must be a ton of work to do in the catering tent.'

'This will only take a minute,' he said. 'And I'm sure Sam would appreciate that I was helping out her friend.'

'Well, I appreciate it too. But I've got it now. Thanks.'

He smiled at me and then turned to go.

'Hey,' I called. 'I don't think I caught your name.'

'Nope, I don't think you did either,' he laughed, as he hurried back to the catering tent.

I tied the tent flap down, making sure everything else was in place, and then I turned and headed back for the trailer. But as I passed the slowly draining reflecting pool, something caught my eye.

The filter and maintenance access was right beside the pool. And a red shoelace had floated through the filter as the pool was draining. I leaned over and tried to pull it out, but it was attached to something heavy. I bent over and pulled harder, but the shoelace was stuck on something. I crouched down further, leaning over the pool, trying to see if I could free it and gave it a good tug, or if I could see through the filter grate, to see what had made its way inside there.

'Oh my God,' I whispered, was that a shoe in there, attached to the shoelace?

I gave it another good tug and saw that it was a shoe, a shoe that was attached to a foot tucked way under, back behind the filter system, in the maintenance access area. I moved back and tried lifting up the grate, but it was too heavy for me. I stood up and looked around frantically, praying someone was close to me.

'Doug,' I screamed, recognizing the figure standing across the pool. He must have been watching me, trying to figure out what I was doing. And I must have sounded very convincing because he headed for me full out, straight across the reflecting pool.

'I think she's in here.' I waved at him when he was half-way across the pool. 'The missing girl.'

Doug ran faster than I thought was possible and together we pulled the grate off the sidewalk and slid it out of the way. He leaned down into the narrow opening and struggled to pull the lifeless body out. When he had a shoulder up, I grabbed the arm and helped him drag the girl up on to the sidewalk. She was ice cold and soaking wet. Her dark hair hung in soggy ringlets and her skin was pale as the winter snow. I grabbed her under the shoulders and pulled her out into the last of the evening sunshine on the sidewalk. I felt frantically for a pulse but couldn't find one. I noticed her clothes were on inside out and there was a playing card tucked into her waistband. I didn't stop to see if anything was missing as I frantically shook her and called her name.

'Can you do CPR?' Doug asked me.

'I got it,' I said, already tipping her head back and trying to make sure her airway was clear.

Sam had run over from the catering tent, hearing the commotion.

'Oh my God,' she gasped. 'Can I do anything?'

'Get anything we can warm her up with,' I ordered her. 'Towels, aprons, anything you have.'

She turned and raced to the tent, yelling instructions to her volunteers before she was even halfway there.

'Doug to Tommy, over,' he said into his radio while I blew air into the girl's lungs.

'Go for Tommy, over,' the radio answered.

'We found the missing girl, down by the reflecting pool. We need the fire and rescue and an ambulance, over.'

'We're on our way, over,' came the answer.

Doug dropped his radio and felt her neck for a pulse.

'Still nothing,' he shook his head.

'Help me,' I said, between breaths. Already I heard sirens coming towards us. The closest fire hall was three blocks away.

Sam was back, covering the poor girl in towels, a look of horror passing over her face as she felt how cold her skin really was.

'Kate?' she asked, the question hanging in the air.

I didn't stop. I couldn't stop. Doug starting pumping on the girl's chest, counting out beats as I continued to try to get some air into her lungs. One, two, three, four, five and then a breath, just like in class. Over and over, without thinking about anything else. Like about how cold she felt or how she couldn't die because it would be all my fault no matter what anyone said. People started to gather around us but I continued to concentrate on what I was doing. The crowd seemed to swirl around us as I felt a little dizzy from the exertion, but I still didn't stop. The Emergency Response truck arrived, accompanied by a fire truck, and soon the firefighters were running towards us, the captain already on his radio as he assessed the situation.

'I can take over for you,' a firefighter said, kneeling down beside me, but I didn't stop to answer, I just leaned over and forced another breath into her lungs.

Soon, there were more sirens in the air as an ambulance pulled up on to the scene. A firefighter waved the paramedics in, who raced up. One pulled out a stethoscope, pushing Doug aside, and shook his head. Then he ripped her shirt open, putting electrodes on her chest while I continued to breathe for her. Their machine jumped to life, but not with the normal kind of heartbeat you saw on TV. One of them took over the chest compressions for Doug. He stepped back around behind me.

'I'll take over ma'am,' one of the firefighters said to me.

'I got it,' I said, between breaths.

'Ma'am, I can take over now,' he insisted, holding an AMBU bag in his hand, while the paramedic struggled to get an IV started in her arm.

I ignored him and leaned back down to the girl.

'Kate, let them take over,' Doug said firmly, and I felt his hands on my shoulders.

'I'm OK,' I insisted.

'Kate, please,' he said, wrapping his arms around my chest and pulling me away from her.

'I can do this,' I insisted, trying to struggle and break free, even though I saw the firefighter move in and take over for me, putting the mask over her mouth and squeezing the air into her.

Doug continued to pull me back from the scene, his arms wrapped around my arms and chest, holding me securely despite my struggles. I saw Sam watching us, wanting to come and comfort me, but she looked hesitant to interrupt and then turned back and headed to her catering tent.

'They're taking care of her, Kate,' Doug tried to explain to me. 'We did everything we could.'

'Let me go!'

'If you don't calm down I'm going to handcuff you to that tree.'

'I am calm.'

'You're not. Now look over there! Do you see that they are taking care of her?' he asked me. 'We've done everything we can do. Now you have to let it go.'

I stopped kicking and looked back at the scene. There were police officers, firefighters, security staff, volunteers and paramedics everywhere. I don't know when they had all arrived, but they had it all under control. There was nothing more I could do. I felt my legs grow weak and Doug gently lowered me to the grass. He sat down behind me and moved his arms up to my shoulders and hugged me gently. We watched as they loaded the still unconscious girl on to a stretcher and wheeled her to the ambulance, still working frantically on her. The crowd slowly began to dissipate as the ambulance drove out of the Plaza. I jumped when the lights and sirens suddenly came to life and it raced off to the hospital.

'Did you notice her pants?' I asked.

'What do you mean?'

'Did you notice that her pants were on inside out?' I asked. 'I was right. I don't care what that DNA said. Jeff has to be the Bishop.'

'No, Kate, he's a lunatic but that's all.'

'I don't think you're right about that,' I whispered. 'That poor girl.'

'Kate, I have to go and check in with Tommy and Bruce,' Doug explained, as he pulled away from me. 'You stay here and I'll be back as soon as I can.'

'Don't worry about me, I'm fine.'

'Well stay here anyway, OK?' he asked.

'OK.'

I watched him walk across the Plaza toward his security team, who were talking with the festival producer. He joined them and they waited until the last of the crowd had finally cleared out, realizing there was nothing else to see, and then they disappeared into the security trailer. I reached down and pulled my sandals off, got up and headed for the reflecting pool. I tossed my sandals on to the sidewalk, sat down on the edge and slowly lowered my aching feet into the icy water. For a long time I just sat there, moving my feet back and forth and watching the waves ripple outwards to the centre of the pool.

I finally tired of this senseless reverie, pulled my cigarettes

211

out of my pocket and took one out. The packet of matches was empty. I tossed it into the water and searched my pockets for a light. I couldn't find one anywhere, which didn't really surprise me the way this day had been going. I felt someone come up behind me, lean over and hold a lighter out for me.

'Need a light, ma'am?'

'Thanks, Doug.'

He lit the flame and I cupped his hand, inhaling deeply.

'Thanks again,' I said half-heartedly.

'You don't sound so good, girl.'

'I'm OK.'

He sat down beside me, cross-legged, our thighs touching.

'You're lying,' he said.

'OK, I'm lying. I just don't feel like talking about it.'

'Everything's going to be all right, you know,' he promised me.

'I know. It just doesn't seem to matter right now. I'm just so tired, Doug.'

'It will be all right. Something like this is very draining emotionally. You should get yourself a good dinner, a couple of beers, and hit the sack for the next twelve hours or so.'

'I don't feel like going home. There's no one there,' I said, sounding much more pathetic than I had intended.

His phone rang and he reached around and grabbed it off his belt.

'Hello?' He listened for a few moments. 'I'll let them know. See you tomorrow.'

He hung up the phone and picked up his radio. 'This is Doug to all staff. We just got word from the hospital and the first report is that Janice Seifert is breathing on her own. Everyone have a good night, I'm signing off and I'll see you in the morning, over and out.'

He turned the radio off and put it back in his belt.

'Good news.' I smiled weakly.

'Kate, are you OK? I can drive you over to Sam's house if you want?' he offered.

I shook my head, not knowing what I was feeling or what I wanted.

Doug stood up beside me and held out his hand. 'OK then, come on and get up. You're coming with me.'

'I have a better idea,' I said, pulling my cigarettes out of my pocket and setting them on the sidewalk.

'What's that?' he asked.

'I'm going swimming,' I said as I stood up in the water, turned around and fell backward, just like the iced tea commercials. Luckily, there was still enough water left in the pool that it didn't hurt too badly.

'Kate, you're going to freeze, get out of there,' he said, but he was stifling a laugh. 'Besides, there's no lifeguard on duty, remember?'

'All right,' I said, pouting.

I stood up and moved to the edge and held out my hand for him to help me up.

'No way, I'm not falling for that one,' he laughed at me.

'What?'

'You pulling me in.'

'I would never do that,' I protested. 'I can go home and change but you're stuck here supervising for the night.'

'Really. You know, you almost sound like you mean it.'

'Quit being such a cynical cop and help me out,' I ordered him, waving my hand for him to take.

'OK, OK, I'll trust you,' he finally said, taking my hand. 'Even though I'm pretty sure I'll live to regret it.'

And he was right because I couldn't resist. I leaned back as hard as I could and I pulled him in.

'You are an evil person,' he said, pulling himself up out of the water and shaking his head.

He looked awfully good wet, I thought, as he waded over to the edge of the pool and climbed out. I followed him and held out my hand and let him pull me up this time. He started walking across the Plaza, pulling me behind him.

'Where are we going?' I asked, grabbing my sandals and hurrying to keep up with him.

'To the security trailer. I've got some beer in the fridge and towels in the bathroom.'

'I don't think I have the energy left to walk that far.'

He grabbed my hand and pulled me toward the trailer. 'I'll help you.'

We walked in silence across the Plaza. I saw Sam standing in her catering tent, staring after me, but I refused to make eye contact with her. I know she wanted to talk to me, to take me home to her house, but I couldn't deal with her right now. She was something else I would deal with tomorrow. At the trailer, he opened the door and pushed me up the steps. I stood in the middle of the floor dripping, while he went into the bathroom and brought out a couple of bath towels.

'I've got a sweatshirt you can put on if you want to change out of those wet things,' he said. 'We can hang them in the bathroom to drip dry.'

'That would be great, I'm getting a little cold now.'

He tossed me a sweatshirt and turned his back. I heard his jeans unzip and forced myself to turn away. It was much harder to do than it sounds. I slipped quickly out of my shorts and T-shirt and pulled the sweatshirt on over my head. I turned around and saw him smiling at me.

'I thought you were an honourable man,' I said, feeling myself blushing.

'Trust me, it's taking every bit of honour I have to stay standing right here.'

'Give me your things and I'll hang them up in the bathroom,' I said, noticing he had changed into a pair of shorts and forgotten to put a shirt on.

Doug handed me his jeans and shirt. I tried to wring everything out and then I hung them wherever I could find a spot in the bathroom to drip dry. I dropped on the couch while he pulled a couple of beers out of the fridge and opened them. He sat on the couch next to me and handed me a beer.

'Have you ever been through anything like this before?' I asked him.

'Yes.'

'Really?'

'A couple of times,' he said. 'I've found a couple of dead bodies, had a couple of missing kids over the years. Had one guy cut a couple of fingers off at one festival. A couple of people having heart attacks.'

'So, what, you get used to this kind of stuff?' I asked.

'Oh, God, no Kate, never. You just learn to not take it personally.'

'I wish.'

'Don't beat yourself up about this. It's not your fault that psycho reacted this way. Remember, you fired him, we threw him out, there were a lot of people involved here. You said Gus even fired him a while back and he never did anything to Gus, right?'

'He never had Gus's face on his pillowcase.'

'Yeah, I have to admit that was a first for me too,' Doug said. 'And that was kind of creepy.'

'My mind knows you're right about this . . .'

'But your heart . . .?' he asked.

'My heart is having problems with everything right now.'

'Well, you have to work on that. You can either let it eat you alive or you can realize that it would have happened no matter what you did.'

'You think?'

'I know from experience. I think I may have underestimated him to begin with. I think somebody wound as tightly as Jeff would have gone off at some point, no matter what.'

'Doug?'

'What? More beer?'

I turned and looked at him, staring into those blue eyes, not remembering exactly what I had wanted to say. I felt our thighs touching, the warmth of his leg against mine. The smile lines crinkling around his eyes as he waited for me to speak.

'What?' he asked, reaching down to take my hand.

I leaned over and kissed him. I gave it my all too, firm lips, inquisitive tongue, fingers running through his hair. Then I pulled away, not knowing what his reaction would be and suddenly feeling humiliated by my impromptu action. Until he reached over and brushed the hair off my face. His hand dropped down and traced the shape of my lips with his finger.

'You are so beautiful and I am very attracted to you. I would like this to continue very much,' he said.

'I'm sensing a but in there,' I said, feeling my heart sink into my stomach.

'I don't want you this way,' he said, smiling at me, so close we were almost touching. 'I want you to be with me because you really want to be, not because you're overwhelmed by all these emotions you don't know what to do with. Do you understand?'

215

I felt tears stinging in the corners of my eyes. 'I don't want to be alone tonight.'

'I won't leave you alone, I promise,' he said, pulling me closer to him and wrapping his arms around me. 'We'll laugh, we'll cry, we'll do whatever you want to do. Well, almost whatever you want to do. And then tomorrow, when you feel better, we can talk about other things.'

'Doug, you know you don't have to do this. I really should go home.'

He didn't loosen his grip on me.

'I know I don't have to do this, I want to,' he said. 'Come on; let's take advantage of this trailer. We've got beer, we'll order a pizza, we've got satellite TV, a stereo and we've got it all to ourselves for the night.'

'I shouldn't.'

'I get it,' he said. 'You only wanted me for my body?'

I couldn't help myself and laughed. 'Well, yes, but . . .'

'It feels better to laugh, doesn't it?'

'Yes.'

'Well maybe I don't want to be alone tonight either,' he said.

'Maybe I can help you with that,' I finally agreed, letting myself relax into his arms.

'Do you want to see what's on TV?' he asked.

'Any good movies on?' I asked.

'Let's find out.' He grabbed the remote and started flipping through the channels.

'Want another beer?' I asked, while he continued with the remote.

'Please,' he said, finally letting me go and handing me his empty can.

I put the empties in the sink and pulled two more out of the fridge.

'You've got goosebumps,' he said, staring at my legs as I walked back to the couch.

'I'm a little cold.'

'I've got a sleeping bag up top, do you want me to get it?' he said.

'I'll get it, I'm already up.'

I climbed on to the couch and opened the cupboard above

it. I stood on my tiptoes and reached in to pull the sleeping bag out.

'You're making this mighty hard on me,' he laughed, wrapping his arms around my legs to steady me.

'Just being here with you is making this very hard on me, Doug,' I said, dropping the sleeping bag on top of him and jumping off the couch. I sat down beside him and pulled the sleeping bag around me, like a blanket. Something fell out and I saw a small black object roll across the kitchen floor. 'I dropped something.'

Doug was up like a shot, chasing it as it rolled across the floor.

'What is it?' I asked, tucking my feet under me, afraid it might have six legs and a grudge for being disturbed.

He picked it up and tossed it over to me. I ducked and then it hit the windowsill and bounced off, landing on my lap.

'It's only a checker,' he said, noticing I was about to squeal.

I picked up the plastic game piece and handed it back to him.

'Why did you go chasing after it so quickly?' I asked.

'Because I thought it might be a cockroach or something at first and I didn't want you to scream.'

'Like I was about to do?'

'Yeah, something like that.'

'I'm sorry, I'm such a girl sometimes.'

He tossed the game piece back up into the cupboard and joined me on the couch.

'Don't apologize for that,' he said, one hand on my knee and the other searching for the remote control.

'So you're a big checker player?'

'We've got a few games around here. Sometimes the nights are long and boring. But cribbage is the game of choice this summer.'

'I'm more into the trivia,' I said. 'Especially with a smart partner.'

'I found a movie,' he said, pointing to the TV.

'Something good?' I asked.

He crawled under the sleeping bag, sitting very close and putting his arm around me again, pulling me towards him.

'It's a James Bond movie. I'm not sure which one,' he said. 'You're the trivia expert here.'

I looked up at the TV and watched for a minute. 'It's *Live and Let Die*. Roger Moore and Jane Seymour. Classic seventies-style James Bond.'

'I'm impressed.'

'Thank you. But that was an easy one. Next time you'll have to try a tougher movie, something a little more obscure.'

'Kate, should we talk about your boyfriend some time?'

'Do you know how many actors have played James Bond?' I asked.

'Kate, please.'

'What brought that subject up?' I asked.

'Well, he seems to be this big unknown, to me at least. Everyone kind of alludes to him and you can't seem to come straight out and deny him.'

'There is no boyfriend,' I said. 'We broke up. How's that?'

'I know I should say I'm sorry, but I'm not. As a matter of fact, I'm really hoping that's true.'

'I'd rather not talk about it. It's in the past. It's over. That's all you need to know.'

'Is that why you wanted to stay with me tonight?' he asked.

'No. I wanted to stay with you because I think I've fallen in lust with you this week.'

'You can't fall in love with someone in a week,' he laughed at me.

'There's a Freudian slip for you,' I laughed.

'What?'

'I said lust, not love.'

'Oh, my mistake.' He blushed.

'OK, honestly and seriously for a minute, I have to admit that I actually felt a serious attraction to you the moment I saw you.'

'Me too.'

'Was it because I had my shirt off?' I asked.

'That didn't hurt.'

He turned to kiss me but we were interrupted by a knock on the door.

'This is why I never bring girls to the security trailer,' he said. 'Not a lot of privacy.'

'So does that mean I'm special?'

'I'll be back in a minute.' He ignored my question as he got up and crossed over to the door. He opened it a crack to see who was there, and then opened it all the way, stepping through and closing it after him.

I heard them mumble outside for a few minutes and then he came back in, locking the door behind him.

'If you lock the door, how is your crew going to get in?'

'There's only one guy on tonight and I gave him the key to the festival office. He can get his coffee from there tonight and sit in my truck if it gets too cold.'

'You're going to destroy my reputation. He's going to tell everybody I was here with you.'

'Don't worry, I just told him you were really upset and needed to talk. Your reputation is safe.'

He made some microwave popcorn and cracked another couple of beers for us. He handed me the bag of popcorn and set the beer on the window ledge, then joined me back under the sleeping bag.

'Now, I have to warn you,' I said. 'I'm a James Bond fan, so if we're going to watch the movie, we have to actually watch the movie.'

'Well, I have to admit that I'm a bit of a neophyte, so if we're going to watch the movie, you might have to explain a few things to me.'

'I can do that,' I promised.

I tucked myself back under his arm, nibbled at the popcorn and we sat there, watching the movie. About halfway through it, I found my eyes start to grow heavy. I fell asleep long before James Bond got his man. Or his woman.

It was dangerous to be here, and that's what made it so much fun. He had been here all day and all night watching the drama unfold, watching the people and the emotional outbursts; had been part of it all. It was like a feeding ground for him, fear, loathing, sadness and hatred everywhere. And every time he walked by a police officer and smiled politely, he got the wonderful adrenalin rush in his gut, the one he craved more and more every day. He gave a little sigh at the thought of having to leave this beautiful scene that he had orchestrated,

219

but realized that if he wanted to finish this game tomorrow, he had to play it safe tonight. He crushed out his cigarette and stood up from the park bench. He walked slowly across the Plaza, savouring his every footstep. He stopped for a moment outside the security trailer, and rested his cheek against the cool window pane, knowing she was in there. He reached up and put a hand on the door handle, just about to squeeze it open, when he heard a noise further down the Plaza. He slowly released his grip and turned to go and investigate the disturbance. It was important that he made no mistakes tonight. He needed one more day to finish the game.

Sunday

I woke up with the sun in my eyes and looked around, trying to remember where I was. The curtains had opened a couple of inches and I automatically reached up and pulled them closed. I turned my head and saw Doug lying beside me and I couldn't help it, a smile broke out across my face. Now I remembered. I stretched out and ran my hands down my body. Sweatshirt and underwear were still in place. I had a vague memory of someone putting a pillow under my head and pulling a blanket up around my shoulders, but I didn't really remember much else from the night before. Doug must have sensed I was awake because he turned over and started nuzzling my neck.

'Good morning,' I whispered.

'Good morning,' he said between nuzzles, which were sending shivers up and down my spine.

'Before you get too carried away, I need to know what time is it?'

'Why?' he laughed. 'Do you have something better to do?'

'We both have a meeting at ten and I have to have to shower and change.'

He pulled his arm out from under the sleeping bag and looked at this watch.

'We're safe, it's only seven. OK to proceed with plan A?'

'If you don't, I'll kill you,' I said, more throatily than I had intended, as he kissed my neck and moved down to my collar-bone.

'Kate, I'm about to make one of the biggest mistakes of my life,' he said, lifting his head up and looking at me with those eyes. Those eyes that I had known were going to get me into trouble from the first time I saw them.

'What do you mean?' I asked.

'I'm about to change my mind.'

'I'm not following your train of thought,' I said, wishing he would stop talking.

He rolled over on his back, pulling me on top of him.

'Let me see if I can help you understand,' he said, as he kissed me.

'I think I'm beginning to follow,' I said as he pulled me into his arms. 'You better try again just to make sure I really understand.'

He kissed me again and I found myself hungry for him, the stubble on his face, the strength in his arms as they seemed to pull me impossibly close to him, even the stale smell of his cologne, and I felt my heart start to beat faster. For a moment, I wondered if I should really do this. But it was only a moment and then my hands were all over him, tracing the outline of his muscles, running through his hair, pulling him impossibly closer to me. I felt his hands slide up under my sweatshirt, massaging my back, tracing the pattern of my ribs. I couldn't stand the anticipation for one more second and I sat up and pulled off the shirt, falling back on top of him and warming to the feel of his hands finally finding my aching breasts. He kicked my sweatshirt out of the way, to the end of the bed, and then was suddenly on top of me again, lips starting at my neck again and moving lower and lower. My breath was coming in gasps and I was almost ashamed of myself. I looked up at him again and was suddenly confused – was it Cam's face staring back at me or Doug's? And for a moment again, I wondered what I was doing, but I pushed that thought aside as his warm breath caressed my stomach and his fingers played with the back of my knee.

Then there was a knock at the door.

'Ignore it,' I whispered in his ear, knowing that if this stopped it would never start again.

'I can't,' he said.

'Ignore it,' I said more insistently, my wandering hands trying to hold him in bed with me.

'I'll get it and get rid of them in a flash,' he promised, as he jumped out of bed and pulled his jeans on.

I was right and I was beginning to get the feeling that this was terribly, terribly wrong. Doug zipped his fly and I pulled the blankets up around my neck, trying to find where my sweatshirt had disappeared to. Doug reached out to flip the lock on the door, then he swung it open.

'Hi, I'm looking for Kate Carpenter. I was told she was down here last night and I'm wondering if you know where she went from here.'

I sat straight up in the bed when I heard that voice, pulling the covers tightly around me as I finally found my shirt.

'Cam?' His name leapt out of my throat before I could stop it. My stomach followed the sound, nausea overtaking me, with guilt following closely behind.

He took a step into the trailer, trying to follow the sound of my voice. He saw me trying to pull on my sweatshirt, and then eyed Doug, shirtless, his jeans zipped, but the belt and button hanging open. Cam looked at me, silence hanging in the air, the pain in his eyes overwhelming.

'I'm sorry, I didn't mean to bother you,' he said.

I couldn't stand to look at him for a moment longer and broke away from his stare. That look in his eyes broke my heart. I watched him as he turned and stormed across the Plaza toward his car. I finally got my sweatshirt on and bounded off the bed to the door.

'Cam,' I screamed across the empty Plaza.

I felt Doug's hand on my shoulder and I turned to see almost the same look in his eyes that I had just seen in Cam's. I shook his hand off my shoulder and stepped out on to the Plaza, feeling the cold brick on my bare feet, and I started to shiver. It felt like hardly enough penance for what I had just done to these two men.

'Come back into the trailer, you're freezing out there,' Doug said, taking my hand and pulling me back into the trailer.

'I'm so sorry,' I said to him. 'I didn't imagine anything like this would happen. I didn't think I'd ever see him again.'

'I know,' he said, pulling me to him and hugging me.

But I pulled away. 'I'm sorry, I've got to go home. He shouldn't have seen that or found out this way. I've just got to explain to him what's happened.'

'I understand,' he said, reluctantly letting me go. 'Your stuff is still damp, would you like to borrow a pair of my sweat-pants?' he asked, holding them out to me.

'Thanks, Doug, you're really being nice about this.'

'Call me sometime, OK?' he asked.

'I will,' I said, kissing him on the cheek.

'Do you want me to give you a ride?' he asked, as I made my way to the door.

'No, I'm good. The time it will take me to walk there will give me time to think about what I'm actually going to say to him.'

'Kate, are you going to be OK? He seemed pretty angry.'

'I'll be OK. I promise I'll call you.'

And then I ran down the street before he could say anything else. There was a cab on the corner, which I grabbed and took home. I should have walked. I paced the lobby for ten minutes, trying to sort out my thoughts. I took the elevator up to my floor and then paced the hallway. I stood at the door to the apartment, wondering if Cam was even inside, and as much as I knew I had to face him, I didn't think I was ready to do it now. I put my key in the door and turned the lock. The lights were on so he must be here. I locked the door behind me and dropped my stuff in the hallway, making my way slowly into the living room. Cam sat on the couch, watching TV. I walked over to the set and turned it off.

'When did you get back?' I asked.

'Last night.'

'How was the cruise?'

'Without you there, it was terrible. I guess you didn't miss me, though.'

'I missed you like crazy,' I said. 'That back there, that was nothing.'

'It didn't look like nothing to me, Katie.'

I crossed the living room and sat beside him. I took his hand but he pulled it away from me.

'I don't blame you for being angry. But I'm angry too. You walked out on me almost a week ago. I didn't expect to ever see you again.'

'You knew I'd be home when the cruise was over.'

'And how would I know that?' I asked.

'Because I love you,' he said.

'I didn't think you loved me when you left. I thought that was the end when you left. I spent all week being desperate, being emotional, crying all the time, not knowing if I'd ever see you again. And then there was a little boy missing and then one of the volunteers disappeared and this whole serial killer thing . . .'

'I heard about all those things,' he said. 'I thought you might have needed me, so I caught a flight home a couple of days early.'

'I did need you. It totally freaked me out how much I needed you. I didn't know what to do anymore. And you weren't there. Do you know how many stupid things I did this week?'

'So then it's all right? I'm just supposed to think it's my fault and apologize now?' he asked, disbelief in his voice.

'Fuck you.'

'No, fuck you. You are not going to make this my fault,' he said, storming into the kitchen and almost ripping the fridge door off the hinges, as he opened it up to find a beer.

I found my heart racing and my chest heaving as months of pain welled up inside me, trying to break free. I picked up an ashtray off the coffee table and threw it into the kitchen. He didn't see it coming and jumped when it hit the fridge door, causing a sizeable dent.

'Go to hell,' I screamed, losing control. 'This is all your fault.'

He closed the fridge door and stepped over the shattered ashtray on the floor.

'You could have killed me with that.'

'I wasn't trying to kill you, just cause you half the pain that you have caused me.'

'What in God's name have I done to cause you pain? Good Lord, Katie, I have done nothing but be patient and understanding and try and wait for you to be ready to commit to being a couple with me. What else can I possibly do to try and make you happy?'

'Happy? You've been trying to make me happy? More like what haven't you done?' I cried. 'You tricked me, Cam. You made me love you like I have never loved anyone else in my entire life. You insinuated your way into my life and made

225

me wonder how I ever lived without you. And then, when something happened, that's all I could think about, how could I get through this without you? What would I do if you left? I have never had to go through something like that before. You are a bastard. How dare you love me like that?'

I fell back on the couch, sobbing into my hands, when I felt the couch sink beside me as he sat down.

'I met someone on the cruise,' he whispered.

'I don't need to hear the details. Just leave.'

'I dined with her, I danced with her. She was very pretty.'

I felt my heart twisting, as if he were actually pulling it out of my chest with his bare hands.

'And I even tried to sleep with her. But all I could see was you.'

'Really?' I asked, not believing it could be true.

'I couldn't. At least not until I found out if there was still a you interested in having me around,' he said. 'You see, I seem to be all crazy in love with you too.'

'I was so lost without you. It scared me, Cam. A year ago I was just fine on my own.'

'Were you really? I thought I was fine too, until we met. And then I knew something had been missing all that time.'

'But if we're supposed to be such soul mates, why does it hurt so much?'

He wrapped his arms around me and pulled me close to him. 'I don't know.'

'I am so sorry for what you just saw. And for this week. And for the last six months. I swear I'll be exactly who you want me to be. I'll try really hard.'

'Katie, you may make me crazy, but that's the girl I fell in love with. I think we have to take each other as is. Mostly. There might be a few minor things we could talk about later.'

'Do I still have to learn to clean the house?' I took a stab at humour.

He rewarded me with a little laugh. 'Where does this leave us?'

'I don't know,' I sobbed. 'I want there to be an us.'

'I do too, Katie.'

'Can there still be an us?' I asked.

'I don't know. We both moved so fast this week.'

'So where do we go from here?' I asked.

'I guess I could stay with one of my friends,' he suggested.

'No, I can't go backward,' I said. 'If we're going to try to work this out, you have to stay here. I can't do it if you move out.'

'And what about your friend?' he asked.

My heart sank. 'How are we ever going to get back to where we were when you saw . . .? Cam, can you forgive me?'

'I don't think we can ever get back to where we were,' he said.

'Oh.'

'No, Katie, I didn't mean it that way. I meant we don't want to go back to where we were. I think we find a new place to start. We can't change the past,' he said. 'And I'm going to try to forgive and forget, Katie, if you can do the same for me. I'm not ready to lose you.'

I wrapped my arms around him and hugged him tightly, praying he meant what he said. And regretting everything I had done this week, just like Sam had said I would. Not knowing what else to do, I hugged him even tighter and began to cry.

It was hours before I could finally let go of Cam. I clung to him like a frightened child, afraid he would change his mind and leave again. Eventually I called the festival office and apologized for missing the meeting, blaming it on a family emergency. I showered and changed and managed to convince Cam I had to go do this. It didn't make it easier but I had to try and clean up some of the mess I had made. This time I did walk to the Plex, taking my time and trying to clear my head. I had a plastic bag with the sweatpants to return but beyond that, it was all kind of murky in my head. I hesitated at the end of the Plaza. Tents were coming down, boxes were being packed and the security trailer was already hitched up to the truck but Doug was nowhere in sight. I slowly made my way over and leaned against the truck, figuring I'd wait a few minutes and see if anyone was around. That got boring really quickly. I knocked on the trailer door and heard a muffled noise. I decided to take that as permission to enter and let

227

myself in. The trailer was darkened, with all the curtains closed, and Doug was lying on the top bunk, with his back turned to me. I set the bag with the sweatpants on the floor and stood there, hoping he might start this conversation.

'Hi there,' he said, not looking at me.

'Hi,' I said.

'Everything all right at home?'

'Yeah,' I lied and then changed my mind. 'Well not really.'

'Yeah.' His voice was muffled by the pillow, but I thought I detected a note of sadness.

'Doug, I'm really so sorry for what happened.'

'Don't be. It was my fault. I shouldn't have let it go so far. I knew you had a guy.'

'I swear to you I didn't. He left me, Doug. I didn't think I'd ever see him again. I would have never started anything if I thought he was coming back.'

'Yeah, well shit happens, doesn't it?'

'Sure seems to in my life right now.' I tried a joke but it didn't seem to work very well.

'What do you want?' he asked.

'I want you to know how sorry I am,' I said. 'You were there when I needed you and I didn't mean for this to happen to you. I want you to know that until I saw Cam at the trailer door this morning, I really thought it was over between us.'

'Do you feel better now?' he asked, in a tone of voice I didn't think he was capable of.

'Not really.'

'And what would make you feel better?'

'If you just said you understood.'

He was silent for a moment. I almost couldn't stand the tension, but I didn't turn away. I took it like the big screw-up that I was.

'I'll get over you, Kate. Don't worry about me,' he said, as he slowly turned around.

For a minute I felt dizzy. He held a gun in his hand and his face wasn't Doug's. He jumped off the bunk and came over to me. I started to back up until I was up against the wall and he was right up against me. He brought the gun up and rubbed the barrel down the side of my cheek. I felt my throat tighten and my breath came out in shallow little gasps.

'I'm sorry, did I startle you?' he whispered in my ear.

'What do you want?' I whispered, my voice overcome by my fear.

'Wrong question,' he said. 'Want to try again?'

'What do you want me to ask?' I said, trying to focus on anything but the barrel of the gun lying against my cheek.

'I thought you might start with *who are you*,' he suggested.

'I know who you are,' I said. 'You were Sam's assistant at the catering tent. The one she was fighting with all the time. We've talked several times this week.'

'See, I always thought that what a man does should not be associated with who he is,' he said. 'But maybe that's a little too philosophical for our present situation.'

'OK, then, who are you?' I asked.

'I'm the one that did all the dirty work for Jeff. I can't believe that you really thought he had the balls to kill someone? But then again, you've never seen his balls. That's what made him so very angry, you know. He just wanted to be with you. Naked and sweaty and fucking you for days, that was his big dream. I'm not sure what he saw in you, though, I find you a little on the whiny side myself.'

'How do you know Jeff?' I felt a tremor in my voice, as the cold barrel of the gun traced the outline of my lips.

'Now there's the twenty-five thousand dollar question. Am I some sort of psycho that found him on the streets and hooked up with him? Did we meet in jail? Maybe I'm his evil twin?'

'He's taller than you,' I said, before I could stop myself.

'You're right. We're not twins. But he is my brother. He's just the stupid spineless one and I'm the one with a brilliant mind who's not afraid to do what needs to be done. I guess you could say I'm the evil one. But then since he's not really good, I suppose that's not really an appropriate comparative, is it?'

'I'm sorry for your brother. I'm sorry he's in jail. I could talk to the police. Maybe we could get the charges dropped.'

'Oh, that's so funny,' he laughed. 'You think I'm stupid.'

'No . . .'

'You think this is about Jeff? Honey, I really couldn't care less if he rots in jail for the rest of his life. He was fun when he was free, I mean I got to come down to the festival and meet you and try and help him get a date. But I've been doing this for years and years all by myself. I'll be just fine while he does his time.'

'What do you mean?' I asked, feeling I did know what he meant.

'Oh, I don't like to brag.'

'No, tell me.'

'I brought you a present,' he said, reaching into his pocket and pulling something out. He held his open hand right under my nose, where I couldn't help but see it. There was a little plastic noose in the palm. 'Let's see, was it Colonel Mustard in the library with a rope?'

'Clue?' I asked.

'A game player. See we already have so much in common.'

'You're the Bishop?' I asked. 'You killed all those people?'

'Well, it's a game,' he said. 'They didn't have to die. If they had played smart, they might have won. And now it's our turn to play, you and I.'

'People will be looking for me,' I said.

'Really? Good. It makes it more exciting. Tell me who's going to be looking for you?'

'If I'm not back right away my boyfriend will be here. He's very overprotective.'

'Well, that's very exciting. The boyfriend. Who else?'

'I'm serious,' I said. 'And Doug will be back here any minute.'

'Oh, I do hope so. I was kind of counting on that. I thought you two would be really fun to play with together. Now, if we got your boyfriend here too, that could be very interesting. Do you have any more men in your life we should contact?' he said, laughing at me. 'You do seem to get around with the guys, don't you?'

'Look, if you just let me go now, I won't say anything to anyone. You can just disappear and nobody will ever know about you.'

'See, now that's not really worthy of you. Not even my brother would believe that one,' he shook his head. 'So disappointing. All right, I'd just like to get some loose ends tied up before any of those people who are looking for you get here.'

230

'What do you mean?' I asked.

'Do you really want to know?' he asked. 'It might just make it worse for you.'

I felt tears well in my eyes and tried to blink them back.

'Please,' I begged, not even knowing what I was begging for.

'Oh all right. But this is going to hurt you more than it's going to hurt me,' he laughed, and he brought the gun down hard on the back of my head. 'Checkmate.'

I felt nauseated and I was incredibly uncomfortable. I tried to move to a more comfortable position but something was holding me tightly and movement just sent waves of nausea coursing through my body. I tried to open my eyes and all I saw were a rainbow of colours swimming around the room. I blinked a few more times and tried to bring my hands up to rub my eyes, but they wouldn't move. I blinked a few more times and finally saw the trailer come into focus around me. My hands were on the table, bound with tape, and someone else's hand rested on top of them, holding them down. I realized I was sitting on something, that's why I was uncomfortable. I turned my head and saw him, and realized I was sitting on his lap, protecting him from anyone that might come through the door.

'It just took you the longest time to wake up.' He smiled at me. 'I guess I don't know my own strength.'

'What have you done?' I asked him, my voice sounding funny inside my pounding head, my words not really making sense in my mind.

'I was so afraid that someone would get here before you woke up. That would have spoiled everything.'

I tried to move sideways, hoping to slip off his lap, but a hand came around my waist and held me tight.

'Where do you think you're going?' he asked.

'Nowhere. What are we doing here?' I asked, my pain making me braver than I generally was.

'Waiting for that.' He smiled as the door handle turned and the door opened.

'Kate?' Doug asked, stepping up into the trailer, unsure of what awaited him. 'What's going on here?'

231

'I'm sorry,' I sobbed.

'Oh, she is very sorry,' he said, leaning his head from behind me, so Doug could see him. 'I heard the whole sorry apology. It was quite touching, actually. I'm sure you would have been moved and forgiven her anything. But, unfortunately for you, in the end she dumped you.'

'Get out of my trailer,' Doug said, stepping up. I wasn't sure whether he was talking to me or the killer.

Suddenly I felt something cold at my throat, and it was sharp. I'm guessing there was some sort of ugly knife there, ready to decapitate or eviscerate or any of those other terrible things that it had been used for in the past.

'Step back there, GI Joe,' the Bishop said, pulling the knife harder against my throat.

'Just calm down,' Doug said, his security persona taking over, as he tried to control the situation. 'Kate, what's going on here?'

'Tell him,' he whispered into my ear.

'Doug, this is Jeff's brother. I'm sorry I don't know his real name, but apparently he is also called the Bishop. I came by to talk to you and he was in the trailer.'

'Is this about Jeff?' Doug said. 'I'm sure we can try and do something to help him.'

'You know, I'm getting a little tired of all this Jeff stuff. I really don't give much of a fuck about my brother. Frankly, I don't really give much of a fuck about any one of you. This is about *me*. Jeff was supposed to get Kate home, because I wanted to play with her for a while. And he didn't. So I decided to come and get her myself. You know what they say, if you want something done right, do it yourself.' He grabbed a handful of my hair and pulled my head back so I was looking up into his eyes. 'Frankly, you're a little older than I thought you would be.'

'Don't hurt her,' Doug said, calmly but firmly.

'Oh, but that's exactly what I'm going to do.' He smiled. 'However, we do have a slight problem. I can't do anything fun here. One little scream and all sorts of people will come running. So what I need you to do is to drive the truck out of here to some place more secluded. Some place where we can all get to know one another.'

232

'I can't do that, man,' Doug said.

The knife moved slowly down my throat, down my chest and to the top of my blouse. I held my breath as it slid under my blouse, and I gasped as he ripped it up quickly, tearing the first button off.

'Sure you can,' he said. 'You can drive us right out of here. Because every time you say no or you argue with me, she loses something. At first it will be buttons and clothing and things like that. But eventually, we'll run out of clothes and have to start doing fingers and toes and other things.'

Doug stared at him, his breathing harsh, but he held himself back.

'Don't you just love this game?' the Bishop laughed.

'Where do you want me to drive to?'

'Why don't we go out into the country? Let's find a nice field where there aren't any houses too close. It should be dark in a few hours and we'll have some nice private time together,' he said, as he pushed a piece of paper across the table towards Doug. 'I've drawn you a nice little map.'

Doug took the paper, turned around and put his hand on the doorknob.

'Don't do it, Doug,' I begged him.

The knife suddenly came down on the table, a hair's breadth from my tied hands. He just looked at me and smiled as a tear escaped my eye.

'He'll kill us, Doug,' I whispered.

'Yes I will. But this way, you get another hour or so. Maybe you can come up with a plan to foil my brilliant scheme.'

Doug opened the door and my heart sank.

'And I'll be watching everything you do,' the Bishop called, continuing his instructions to Doug. He shoved me roughly aside and ripped open the curtains. 'Starting with watching you walk to the front of the truck and get in without talking to anyone.'

Doug didn't say a word as he climbed down the steps and closed the door behind him. I heard him secure the steps. I pulled myself back up into a sitting position and watched through the crack in the window, as Doug did as he was told and walked to the front of the truck, where he opened the door, started the truck and we pulled out of the Plaza. We

233

were going to die.

'Makes you want to cry, doesn't it?' he asked, smiling at me, reading my mind.

If my throat hadn't been totally dry from sheer terror, I would have spit in his face, knife or no knife.

The truck pulled out of the Plaza and the Bishop positioned himself in the back, behind the table. He watched Doug intently through the back window of the truck, eyes averting occasionally to the sides, making sure no one was following us. I sat there, bound hands and feet, not having a clue how to even begin to get out of this. There was only one thing I knew how to do.

'Do you have a name?' I asked him.

'Of course I do.'

Remember, he liked games, I reminded myself.

'Look, I can't sit here quietly while you drive me to my death. I want to talk.'

'Think you're going to convince me that you're a wonderful person and I shouldn't kill you?'

'Well, if it's a game, I should at least get to try and play, shouldn't I?' It was amazing how suddenly having nothing to lose was freeing me from my fear.

'OK. I'll give you that point. You can call me Jack.'

'Is that your real name?'

'If we're playing a game, you can't expect me to give you the answers, can you?'

'OK, I'll give you that point.'

'Good.'

'So, Jack, if you were to cut me loose, I could make a pot of coffee.'

'So you could toss it into my face and escape. Nope, I saw that on a TV movie once.'

'No, not that. Although the thought did cross my mind, I must admit. But when I tried to work it through I realized it would never work. I just really, really need a coffee right now. I'll get it going and then you can tie me back up and you can pour the hot coffee.'

He sat and looked at me, trying to decide if I meant what I said. Then he pulled the knife out of the table, where it had been stuck since narrowly missing my hand.

'You are interesting,' he said. 'I can't quite figure you out yet. Most women are begging for their lives right about now.'

'Do you want me to beg?' I asked.

'Oh, you will beg in time.' He smiled. And then the knife came down again, but it missed my hand again and just attacked the duct tape that was securing me. 'You can make the coffee. I'm dying to see what you're going to try and do.'

He released my hands and feet. I pulled the tape off, along with most of the hair on my arm, and rubbed my wrists, trying to get some circulation back. He pulled the gun out of his waistband and held it at table level.

'Remember, you come too close with anything I even think is dangerous and I will end this all right now.'

'Yeah, I got that part,' I said, standing up and plugging in the coffee pot. I filled it with water from the fridge and put in an extra scoop of coffee, thinking I would need all the caffeine I could get right now, and once it was dripping I sat back down at the table, offering my hands to be taped back up again.

'If you promise to be good I won't tie you back up again,' he offered.

'Right, and if I promised to be good, you'd believe me?' I asked.

He pulled the duct tape off the window ledge and taped one of my hands to the leg of the table. 'At least this way you can still drink your coffee.'

'So, you're really Jeff's brother?' I asked.

'Yes.' He got up and stood in front of the counter, swaying slightly as the truck moved through traffic. 'Mugs?'

'Cupboard on your right,' I said, pointing with my free hand.

'Do you take anything?' he asked.

'Just black, thanks.'

He poured a cup for me and set it on the table in front of me. He sat back down, but I noticed he was a little further away from me than he had been.

'I just thought Jeff was crazy. I thought he was talking to himself all the time.'

'I know. It was fun. Hiding on the other side of the tent, always being just slightly out of your range of vision.'

235

'How did you manage to pull it off?'

'Well, firstly, I am very good at what I do. But I've been at the festival all week long, watching you, watching everyone. I even watched the clowns. Clowns are very interesting, you know. People don't realize there's really a person under the mask. All they see is the red lips, big wig and star on their cheek. And kids are even easier to deal with when you're a nice friendly clown with some balloon animals. I got this little boy to follow me down into the basement. It's funny that when you're at an outdoor festival dressed as a clown, no one actually questions what you're doing there. Not the staff, not the volunteers, not even the security people.'

'You were a clown?'

'Yep. Several times. You even gave me hell once for smoking when I was in costume. Sam was really mad at me that day because I just disappeared on her. Do you know what was really funny? When I bought a burger from her while I was dressed as a clown, she never even knew it was me.'

'Oh my God.'

'And even when I was stuck in deep-fat-fryer hell, it was so easy to get her to talk about you. She was actually pretty pissed at you this week. Thought you were really making some bad decisions.'

'Fuck you.'

'Yep, I got to keep a nice close eye on what you were doing the whole time. And I got to keep giving Jeff all sorts of hints as to where you were and what you were up to. I was even at the orientation meeting, the one where you rushed in late. I've had my eye on you, Kate. Ever since Jeff started telling me about you.'

'I guess I should be honoured.'

'You should be. I don't usually spend this much time on anyone. Normally, you can just go to the nearest shopping mall and pick up a willing victim without any problems at all.'

'So why'd you work so hard on me?' I asked.

'Well, it was Jeff's birthday last month and I guess I kind of promised him.'

'Anything for your brother?'

'Well, anything for my brother as long as it suits me.'

I noticed we were in the suburbs now, and the houses were starting to thin. Another twenty minutes at most and we would be out in the country. I slugged back my coffee, trying to force my brain to work faster.

'Getting nervous?' he asked.

I hated that smile that always crept up when he was feeling self-satisfied. I was going to take great pleasure in wiping it off his face if I ever figured out how to do that.

'A little.'

'I have something that can help you with that, you know,' he said, opening up his jean jacket and pulling a case out from the inside pocket. He opened it up and there was a syringe inside filled with clear fluid.

'It's tempting but no thanks,' I said, afraid he might not give me a choice.

'You sure?' he asked. 'It'll just make everything nice and mellow.'

'If I'm going to play this game with you, I think it would be much more fun if I had my wits about me, don't you?'

'I'm only thinking about you, Kate,' he said, still smiling.

'I'm sure you are.'

We left the city behind as the sun began to set, and soon there were nothing but fields surrounding us. I think we were on the old Simons Valley Road but I hadn't been paying a lot of attention to where we had been going. Either way, it didn't really matter. It was just the three of us now. And one of us was an armed killer. Unfortunately, I thought the odds were on his side. Doug turned off the road on to an overgrown driveway that led into a field and pulled to a stop by a deserted old barn. The door to the truck opened and Doug walked back to the trailer. Part of me wished he would just run, there was no need for both of us to die here. But he didn't. He opened the door, pulled down the steps and climbed up, stopping just inside the door.

'What now?' Doug asked.

Jack had picked up the gun and was pointing it at Doug. He slid out of the banquette, grabbing his knife and syringe, and shimmied past Doug, standing beside the stove. 'Have a seat.'

Doug slipped into the banquette and scurried around close

to me. Jack came closer to me and cut me free from the table.

'Tape him up,' Jack instructed me.

I grabbed the tape from the ledge and looked at Doug, hoping he had a plan and would share it with me soon.

'Doug?' I asked, getting nothing from him.

'Do what he says,' Doug told me.

'He's just going to kill us,' I cried. 'He's going to torture us and let us die slowly and in fear. At least now, if I don't do this, it would be quick.'

'She's probably right, you know,' Jack laughed. 'Shouldn't you try something heroic right now? I mean, you are the big brave man, right?'

'Let her go,' Doug said. 'Do whatever you want to me but let her go.'

'No, let him go,' I said. 'This all started with me and Jeff and it has nothing to do with Doug.'

'Shut up, Kate,' Doug hissed at me and then turned back to the Bishop. 'I mean it. Do what you want to me, I won't fight you, but let her out of here first.'

'Doug, you get out,' I insisted. 'I couldn't live with myself if anything happened to you. Same deal as for him, I won't fight you or anything.'

'But I like it when people fight me,' he pretended to whine. 'Now, commence with the tying up there please.'

'Kate, can you just stop being selfish and self-serving for one minute here. I'm trying to save your life,' Doug said.

'Well, what do you think I'm trying to do? Do you think I really want to be here alone with this psycho? I'm being gallant.'

'You're being stupid is what you're being. Look, I'm trained for this and I want you to just shut up and let me make a deal for you.'

'Don't you dare tell me to shut up,' I hissed back at him.

'Well it's about time someone told you to shut up,' he answered. 'You're a freaking little spoiled bitch just wandering around and doing anything you want to anyone you want.'

'How dare you!'

'OK, that's enough from you two lovebirds,' Jack interrupted us. 'I asked you to tie him up and I asked nicely. Please don't make me ask again.'

'You tie me up before I make a deal with him and I'll kill you myself,' Doug threatened me.

'I said that's enough,' Jack said, his voice louder.

'Fuck you!' I screamed at Doug, ignoring the killer standing behind me. 'I'll do whatever I think is best to get us out of here. Who the hell are you to tell me what to do?'

'I'm someone who actually knows what I'm doing and isn't just meddling in something that isn't really any of my business.'

'I'm the one that he's been threatening for the last hour. I would say this is my business.'

'OK, the fun is over,' Jack said, his voice full of tension. 'Tie him the fuck up or I'll shoot him.'

I was furious and turned angrily to him, lost in the moment. 'Quit fucking interrupting me. I am trying to make a point here.'

I hadn't really meant to deal with Jack in that manner, but it just came out. I had to work on my temper. If I had a future to work on it that is. Jack slowly pulled the gun up to my eye level and pointed it at me, pulling the trigger back slowly. I had never fired a gun or even held a gun, but I knew that when they did that in movies, bad things always happened.

'That's it, Kate. You've pissed me off. You lose!'

And then there was a blast. It was loud, ear-splitting and nothing like I ever expected it to be. I had heard a gun go off before, and I had even felt a bullet go close enough to tear a small hole in my skin. That had hurt like crazy. I wasn't looking forward to what this was going to feel like. Time stood still, as I held my breath and waited for the impact, my eyes never leaving Jack's eyes. I wanted him to see that he really hadn't scared me after all. And then the strangest thing happened. Jack fell to his knees. And then I noticed the blood staining his shirt and that his breathing had suddenly become ragged. Jack fell the rest of the way to the floor, landing hard on the tiles, the gun slipping from his grip. I looked up and out the front of the trailer, where the curtains now wafted in the breeze that was blowing through the shattered glass of the window.

'You two OK?'

'Ken?' I asked.

'Hi Kate, you OK?'

'I think so,' I said, looking down and surprised still that there was no blood seeping down the front of my shirt.

'Doug?' Ken asked.

'I'm good,' Doug said, pulling himself from out behind the table and kicking the gun from Jack's reach.

'Ken, what are you doing here?' I asked.

My mind was not able to wrap itself around his appearance here in the country. I looked down and saw Jack lay unmoving on the floor and he was not breathing. His blood stained the floor and counters. From the amount of blood on the floor, I suspected we were safe.

'I had a walkie-talkie on the front seat of the truck,' Doug said. 'As soon as we started driving I got Ken on the line and told him where I was headed. He beat me out here.'

'Barely,' Ken said.

'For a minute there I didn't think you had made it.'

'And you couldn't have shared this with me?' I asked.

'Kate, what was he supposed to say?' Ken asked me.

'Those darned serial killers don't give much warning,' Doug said. He reached out for my hand and pulled me towards the door. 'Come on, let's get out of here.'

I seemed to have fallen on to the sofa at some point, and as I stood up, my legs felt very wobbly, but I managed to step over Jack and let Doug help me down. As soon as he let go, I found myself sitting down in the grass of the field but I was happy with that, the less distance to fall when I finally fainted, which I was pretty sure was coming next.

'Half the police force should be out here in about another minute or so,' Ken told me. 'Then we'll get you back home. We can do statements tomorrow.'

'Does anyone have a cigarette?' I asked.

Doug pulled one out and handed it to me, along with a lighter. After I fumbled with the lighter three or four times, he took it from my hand and lit the cigarette for me.

'I'm fine,' I said, more to reassure myself than anything else.

'I'm just going to go to my car and call in,' Ken said.

Doug sat down on the grass beside me and lit a cigarette of his own.

'So, you really going to dump me?' he asked. 'Or was that

240

part of his game?'

'You really want to discuss this now?' I asked, hoping he was kidding.

'I really don't want to discuss it period,' he admitted. 'I was actually thinking of driving out to Vancouver for the summer. I've got a couple of good opportunities there.'

'Vancouver is nice,' I said.

'But you're not going to beg me not to go?'

'I'm sorry.'

'Yeah. Me too.'

It was hours later and pitch dark. I hadn't bothered to turn on the lights because I didn't really want to face myself right now. I had run out of tears but not emotions. I was saddened and ashamed by my actions this week and freaked out by my near death experience. The police had driven me back into town, and I had made them drop me off at the theatre, so I could pick up some stuff, I had said. In reality, I just needed to be alone for a while. I was sat there in the dark wishing I had ice cream or a big bottle of red wine, when there was a quiet knock on my door. At first I thought I was hearing things and then it happened again.

'Go away,' answered the petulant child inside me.

'If you don't let me in I'll just use my key.'

I got up and opened the door.

'How'd you know I was here?' I asked.

'It's you, Katie, where else would you be but at your theatre?'

'Yeah, I guess you're right.'

He reached up and wiped some smeared mascara from under my eyes.

'What are you doing here, Cam?' I asked.

'Ken called me to ask how you were doing. And he told me everything.'

'Oh God, now you're pissed at me, aren't you?'

'What?'

'Well, I got all involved with a serial killer and stuff and I put myself in danger and you keep telling me to keep my nose out of things but I never listen to you and now you're pissed off at me.'

'No, I'm not.'

'You're not?'

'Ken told me about the whole week. And he told me that you didn't try to get involved in anything this time, that trouble just kept finding you.'

'Then he didn't tell you everything,' I admitted.

'What do you mean?'

'I did something really stupid. I broke into Jeff's apartment trying to see if I could find out where he had taken that little boy.'

'You what?'

'It was stupid. I wasn't thinking straight. They were going to arrest me for interfering with a police investigation.'

'Well that's not the first time,' he laughed.

'No, I mean really and seriously. I almost screwed up the entire case and ruined the evidence.'

'So why are you telling me this when Ken decided to keep your secret for you?' Cam asked.

'Because I shouldn't keep anything from you. I don't want us to have any lies or anything between us ever again.'

'So you're going to tell me everything?' he asked.

'Yes, I am.'

'I don't know if I'm ready for that.'

'Don't tease me when I'm trying to be as wonderful as you are. This doesn't just come naturally to me, you know.'

'I know,' he laughed.

'So, why are you here, Cam?'

'I came to take you home.'

'Are you sure you want me there?'

He held out his hand to me. I hesitated a moment and then grasped his hand. Hanging on very tightly.

'Where's your backpack?' he asked.

'There.' I pointed. He picked it up and slung it on his shoulder.

'All right, let's go see what kind of mess you made of my kitchen this week.' He smiled at me.

'Oh God,' I said.

'What?'

'Man, if you think you're mad now,' I laughed. 'You're really going to be pissed off when you see the fridge!'

'Well, I know there's a nice new dent on the outside.'

'You haven't seen what's living inside it yet though.'

'Oh, Katie, it's only been a week. How bad could it be?'

'Well Cam, you know how some people have a green thumb? I don't do well with plants but I seem to do well with left-overs myself.'

He draped his arm around my shoulder and gave me a squeeze.

'I guess it's a good thing the building is going condo and we have to move, huh?'

'It'll be easier than cleaning.'

He laughed, as I closed my office door and made sure it was locked up. And then I started crying. Again. He pulled me back into his protective embrace and we walked off into the sunset. Or, since it was just my life and not a Hollywood movie, down the hall to the fire escape.

I got up early the next morning, surprised to find Cam still sleeping, and put the coffee pot on. I opened the front door to bring in the newspaper, but when I read the headline *Local Woman Beats Bishop at His Own Game*, I closed the door and left the newspaper in the hallway and raced back up the stairs into my warm bed. It was nice to be where I finally knew I belonged.

Summer

It had been a long hard three weeks. I had nightmares every night for the first week about the Bishop. I had nightmares every night the second week about Cam leaving again. But this week I had managed to sleep a bit more and dream a bit less and I was beginning to feel like life was returning to normal again. Cam and I had done lots of talking. We had set a few ground rules for our relationship and defined what we were and what we both wanted. I felt very grown up because I actually felt comfortable in talking about our future together. Most of the time. I had even started to talk about the possibility of having a family. Someday.

And I was back at the theatre, in my comfortable office, with my comfortable staff, and a few new bodies, ready to start a summer of rental events and sun tanning. We had a bunch of extra bookings and I wasn't even going to get as much time off as I had thought. I guess crime does pay, at least in making people want to book your theatre for their events.

Graham and I had finished going through the schedules last week and we needed three new ushers to get through the summer. I was pretty sure I could keep them going through the next season as well. Not all my regulars were coming back. Graham had pulled a bunch of resumés from the job fair and called them in for a second interview. We called it that but I was pretty sure I was just going to hire these people. Graham had already interviewed them and assured me they were great. Even though he was a hugely hormonal nineteen-year-old, I knew he took the theatre business seriously and would only have appropriate candidates here today. He was in the main lobby, bringing the first one up. I took the opportunity to fill my coffee and then sat at my desk and organized my questionnaire.

244

'Kate, this is Izumi Ivanovich. Izumi, this is Kate Carpenter, the house manager.'

She leaned over the desk and shook my hand. 'Pleasure to meet you.'

'Please, have a seat.' I smiled at her. 'Can we get you a coffee or anything?' I offered.

'No, I'm fine, really.'

'I don't mean to be rude, but you have an interesting name,' I said.

'Thank you. My mom is from Japan and my dad is from the Ukraine, so I'm a bit of a multicultural mix-up.'

'Wow, how did they ever meet?'

'In Banff. They both went there to work and ski one winter and they ended up being a waitress and bartender at the same restaurant. They met and fell in love and applied for landed immigrant status in Canada. Next thing you know, they own a restaurant and a nice house in Canmore and I'm explaining my name to everyone.'

'I'm sorry,' I apologized. 'That was rude of me.'

'It's OK, my best friend Katerina Nguyen and I are used to it,' she laughed.

'So, did Graham go over the hours and that with you?'

'He did. It's perfect for me. I'm taking some summer classes at the University.'

'Good, well we're happy with your experience with the public so we'd like to offer you the job if you're still interested.'

'I sure am.'

'Great. I'm going to send you back down to the lobby with these forms and then I'll give you a copy of your schedule when you're done.'

'Fine, thank you very much for this opportunity,' she said, taking the pen I offered her and our standard pile of paperwork.

'Well, you won't get rich but you will have fun,' I promised her.

Graham was coming down the hall with a young lady and a young man. I gave him a quizzical look as they came into the office but waited for him to explain.

'Kate, this is Krista,' Graham said. 'And this is her interpreter John.'

245

'Hello, Krista.' I smiled at her, still wondering why she needed an interpreter.

And then John's hands started moving and I began to understand.

'I am very pleased to meet you, too,' John said, interpreting the signs that Krista had responded with. She reached out to shake my hand.

'Please, have a seat,' I said, pointing at the chairs.

'You seem a little shocked,' Krista said, though it was the interpreter's voice I heard.

'Honestly, I am a little. You're deaf?' I felt stupid at the obvious question.

'Yes.' She smiled at me. 'I'm deaf.'

'And you don't think that might be a problem working in a theatre?' I asked. 'I mean I can't pay both you and your interpreter.'

She laughed, a joyous sound unencumbered by a trace of self-consciousness, swinging her long red hair over her shoulders.

'I only brought John today to make the interview easier.'

'So do you normally read lips then?' I asked.

'No, I don't. It's not like in the movies. There aren't many people that actually do that. And the people that do read lips well are people who have had some hearing and language. I was born deaf. I use sign language or I write notes.'

'Oh,' I said, thinking I was probably wasting my time here but not sure how to tell her.

'I have very neat handwriting,' she said, waiting to see my reaction.

I saw the humour dancing in her eyes and then laughed out loud.

'Krista, you are a lovely and charming young lady but I don't know if you would be able to do the job effectively.'

'I've been here several times and watched your ushers,' she signed. 'I didn't see anything that I couldn't handle.'

'I make an announcement for the ushers to close the doors. You wouldn't be able to hear that.'

'No, but I would see all the other doors close. One of the ushers told me that's what she looks for, because when she's inside the theatre she can't hear your announcement either.'

246

'What about if a patron is causing a disturbance or using a cell phone during the play.'

'My eyes work pretty well, that's the kind of stuff you usually see in a dark theatre.'

'A fire alarm. What if the fire alarm rings?'

'Those things are so jarring that you can actually feel them vibrate in the floors and walls. And again, I see the other ushers opening the doors and rushing people out and I would do the same thing.'

'What about if a patron asks you a question?'

'I did say I have very neat handwriting, didn't I?'

'Krista, I have to be honest with you,' I said, though not wanting to disappoint her efforts. 'I just don't know if this would work or not.'

'I'm willing to make you a deal,' she offered.

'What's that?'

'I'll work for free for a week. That will give you a chance to see if I can do it just like all the other ushers. If you are satisfied, you can hire me full time after that week.'

I thought about it for a minute. I guess I didn't really have anything to lose and it would give her a chance to bow out gracefully if things didn't work out.

'OK, I'll try it,' I agreed.

'Great.' She smiled. 'But there's one more thing.'

'What?'

'If you hire me, you have to pay me for that first week I worked for free. Otherwise you would be taking advantage of me.'

I laughed at her again. 'You're pretty gutsy, you know?'

'Yeah, well I generally have to work a little harder to get treated normally,' she said. 'I hope it doesn't offend you.'

'It reminds me of me,' I said. 'So, if you want to be treated like everyone else, you need to take all these forms down to the lobby and fill them out. When you're done, we'll give you a copy of your schedule.'

'Thank you,' she signed, and that was one sign I didn't need interpreted.

Two hours later we had three new ushers, with all their paperwork and a basic orientation with them done, ready for their first shift in a couple of weeks at the Jann Arden concert. I was just putting some things away and tidying up my desk. Graham sat in the window, watching the street for his girlfriend, who was picking him up.

'Cam's here,' he told me.

'Already?' I asked. 'He's early.'

'And he's not alone,' Graham said.

'Who's with him?' I asked, leaning over Graham to try and see out the window.

'I can't tell but there is definitely someone in the back seat of his car.'

'Well, I better get going. Will you finish cleaning up here?'

'Sure. See you next week.'

I grabbed my pack and raced down the fire escape, my quick short cut to the street. Cam was leaning against his car, waiting for me. I kissed him on the cheek, in deference to whoever was waiting inside.

'Did you have a good day, sweetie?' he asked.

'Not bad,' I said. 'I got the staff hired that I needed and my office cleaned up. That's pretty much what I set out to do. How about you?'

'I had a good day.'

'Good.' I wondered why he wasn't hurrying to introduce whoever was sitting in the back seat.

'There's someone I want you to meet,' he said, opening the back door.

A man in an impeccable pinstriped suit with a crimson tie and starched white shirt climbed out of the back of Cam's car. I had my pleased-to-meet-you smile on my face until I saw the pin on his lapel.

'Kate, this is Mr Jones,' Cam said.

'No, I am not doing this,' I said.

Cam opened the passenger side door and held my arm firmly.

'Katie, get in the car.'

'No, Cam, you said we'd talk about this. You said I wouldn't have to do this until I was ready.'

'Katie, get in the car right now.'

I looked fearfully at Mr Jones and climbed in. Cam didn't wait for me to change my mind and he got in the driver's side, while Mr Jones got in the front seat beside me, preventing any sort of escape.

'It's going to be all right, Ms Carpenter,' he said, smiling at me. I felt my heart racing as Cam pulled the car out into the traffic.